The story, based on a work by the highly praised novelist Alexander Baron, follows the bitter-sweet, sometimes cruel, but fascinating love stories, between the women of Europe and the soldiers they meet. Since the armies have moved from country to country with each change in the fortunes of war, it follows that the relationships between the troops and their girls can never be permanent. The ironies of the affaires, the tragedies in the lives of the main characters, who are the luckless victims of world conflict, build up as the novel progresses, creating a powerful impression of the empty fate of a conquering hero.

THE VICTORS

MILTON SHULMAN

Based on *The Human Kind*
by ALEXANDER BARON

A PANTHER BOOK

THE VICTORS

A Panther Book

First published in Great Britain
in Panther Books October 1963

This book is based on *The Human Kind* by Alexander Baron, which was first published in Great Britain by Jonathan Cape Ltd 1953

*Printed in Great Britain by Cox and Wyman Ltd.,
London, Reading and Fakenham, and published
by Hamilton & Co. (Stafford), Ltd.,*
108 *Brompton Road, London, S.W.*3

THE VICTORS

ONE

ON a fine summer night in the year 1942, two soldiers stood on sentry duty outside a stores depot in an English seaport. The soldiers, like the stores in the depot, were American. Their names were Theodore Trower and Frank Chase. Both were young men, in their early twenties.

Their uniforms were neat and new, as was to be expected in a regiment that had only landed at Liverpool eight weeks before. With the butts of their rifles placed correctly at their shoes, both men stood formally in the "at ease" position.

Their drill-book postures, their stillness, a touch of self-conscious vanity in the lift of their chins, were not strictly necessary at this moment, for an air raid was at its height. The entrance of a dugout shelter was close to them, and the young men's orders clearly stated that they could take shelter when bombers were overhead.

The bombers were, without doubt, overhead now. The dark vault of sky, so empty to the eyes except for the red wink of bursting shells, echoed with the savage, uneven roar of Heinkel engines. Within the immense night calm the distant whistle and whisper of falling bombs became the most ordinary of noises. The thud of explosions smote from every direction and from time to time all other sounds were engulfed by the clifflike fall, prolonged and awe-inspiring, of some large building.

The houses that faced the sentries were thrown into relief by the glow of distant fires, sometimes faint, sometimes waxing into a bright, enormous glare. Anti-aircraft batteries ripped and slammed. One group of guns, dug in a few streets away, shook the night with a deafening outburst each time the bombers passed overhead.

The reason why the two young Americans did not take shelter was simple. Frank Chase did not move because Ted Trower did not move. And Private Trower stood firmly at his post in order to match Private Chase who, a few yards away, might have been some brave military statue.

Private Trower had been taught by fiction (for he was a reader of the kind of novels that his high-school teachers had called good) that he would have to suppress fear when he first heard the roar of the guns. Well, here he was, with the whole orchestra of bomb and artillery muffling his ears for the first time in his life, and he was undeniably enjoying the experience.

Perhaps it was a release after the dull, fatiguing months at Fort Riley and those strange, other-worldly days among the crap-shooting crowds on the troopship. Perhaps he felt at last in presence of the drama of war; for it had been a terrible anti-climax, after writing the first letter to his parents from the European Theatre of Operations (name reeking of battle smoke) to find himself in an England of innumerable, uneventful streets and shabbily-dressed people who simply did not notice one more G.I. on the pavement; not at all the embattled, blazing fortress of the Quentin Reynolds broadcasts that had enthralled him back in '40. Perhaps, simply, being young, he knew nothing about death. To stand under fire at last was for him both a relief and a test to be honourably faced.

He had followed the war for two years the way his friends followed the baseball scores. In the cinema of his mind he had identified passionately with the heroic actors, first the British, later the Russians. In any quarters Trower's bunk could always be located; pinned close by on the wall was a map of the Russian front with red- and green-headed pins marking the battle lines.

Just now in the cinema of his mind the hero was neither British nor Russian, but at last in truth himself. He was simultaneously composing a letter to his father about tonight's epic (omitting to mention that the depot he guarded with such valour was filled mainly with boots and woollen underwear) and seeing on the screen his father in the family drug-store, reading it aloud to the kids hunched over their banana-splits. Home—Phoenix, Arizona—was more immediate to him as he dreamed than his surroundings.

The shrilling of ambulance bells aroused him. He glanced at his companion. Chase was eyeing him with a small, ironic grin, telling him that his heroics were seen through. Trower mouthed back, "Nuts". He felt very good, very close to the other man, sharing something big.

The rumbling had died away. In the silence a faint distant engine-beat muttered. Within seconds it grew louder, a threatening rise and fall of sound that was met by the thud of distant batteries, then by the outburst of nearer guns. A new wave of bombers was coming in from the sea. The war of guns and engines filled the sky again. The engines were overhead now, shouting, beating, beating down through the frenzy of noise. Trower was hypnotized; neither exultant nor frightened; simply hypnotized by the shouting engines of his enemies directly overhead.

Out of the tumult his instincts plucked one noise, a whistle, more shrill and more prolonged than the others, a projectile of sound coming straight at him, a crescendo, screaming. In a common animal impulse the two men hurled themselves for the dugout entrance.

Trower did not feel himself hit the floor, nor Chase's body colliding with him. He huddled against the sandbags. A terrible white light filled his eyes. The dugout rocked and an immense detonation pressed down upon him. Amid the ringing, remote echoes that filled his eardrums he heard the crack and tinkle of blasted windows. He opened his eyes. Dust was settling around him like a thinning fog.

There was no more pride in Trower, no dreams in his head. Like a child, he was aware only of bodily discomfiture, the rapid, sickening beat of his heart, a sickness rising into his throat and strange dislodgements in his bowels.

Chase lay beside him, hands clamped to his ears. Chase moved his hands away, looked up at him. Trower was able to look back at him, sane again. They grinned foolishly, and peered out into the red night. Now that the dreadful whistle, aimed at them, had ended, the din meant nothing to them.

Trower heard a stranger's voice. It took him a second to realize that it belonged to Chase.

"And you volunteered!"

He heard himself answering, humble, self-excusing, "It was the day after Pearl Harbour."

"Hero!"

Himself, lamely, "Well, we have to teach those bastar[illegible]."

He broke off. Silence for a moment.

Chase's voice again, "Boy, I fell right on top of you." Chase laughed, "Why couldn't you have been a dame?"

Trower said, "Right now I could use a woman," with all the heartiness of (it was his secret) a virgin. Chase often talked about his women. Ted Trower envied him.

From their shelter they watched the roadway. Neither

of them moved. Trower could speak again, but he could not move. He had tasted fear for the first time; he was weak and he cowered in his hole.

Down the street, on the opposite pavement, a solitary figure came into sight. The steady step, the slow, deliberate approach fascinated Ted Trower. At his side Chase was staring, too. Somewhere beyond buildings a bomb fell, and a great white glare suffused the sky. On the opposite pavement, in the waning glare, they could see the solitary walker in the night: an English policeman, patrolling his precinct.

He wore a steel helmet, but otherwise he might have been whiling away a weary spell of duty on a peaceful summer night. He was an ageing man, bulky round the waist, with the face of a mild ox: an ordinary bobby, never to be promoted. He walked with the slow, heavy, everlasting step of all English policemen.

Trower looked at Chase. Chase looked at Trower, then nodded. In silence the two young men picked up their rifles, clambered out of the shelter and took up their posts at the gate.

They heard a fire-engine race by. The guns were thudding farther away now. The policeman trod towards them. As he came abreast of them, across the road, he saw them, and he waved at them. They waved back, and when he had turned the corner they grinned at each other.

Everything was going on. Bombs reverberated. Great buildings crashed into rubble. Fires burned against the night. But the firm tread of life could not be halted, and the sentries stood at their posts.

TWO

ALLIES INVADE SICILY!

July 10, 1943

Coliseum News brings the world to your doorstep . . . In the greatest Allied offensive to date, U.S., British and Canadian forces land on Sicily, stepping-stone to Italy, itself!

General Montgomery's famous Eighth Army, striking from the east, overcomes heavy Axis resistance, and sweeps onward.

The American landings, begun in darkness, continue till dawn, on the south Sicilian coast near Gela. The great combined operation has come to a climax. Fighting in this area was bitter before the Americans finally broke through to swing far to the north and west, driving not only heart-sick Italians but crack German troops before them.

General Patton, accompanied by his famous pearl-handled .45 goes over the side of his ship to take personal command of repulsing Axis counter-attacks.

The invasion [illegible] *to a successful start!*

Town after town, boasting allegiance to Il Duce, Benito Mussolini, falls to the invaders.

Under Eisenhower and Alexander, with the valiant Canadians and the indomitable British Eighth Army as comrades in invasion, U.S. troops have met their most crucial test in this war, and have scored their greatest success!

Rompers

CHORUS GIRLS TELL IT TO THE MARINES

These famous precision dancers from Radio City's Music Hall pay a visit to the Marine Corps base at Quantico . . .
These lovely ladies, with an esprit de corps all their own, get a personally conducted tour around the obstacle course.
The Marines show them the ropes, and the girls show a thing or two in return!
The obstacle course is no obstacle to them, as one can see by their smiling faces—and the motto of these long-stemmed roses seems to be: come on in, fellers, it's great to be a Marine!

Special

FRONT LINE FIGHTING IN SICILY

Combat cameramen capture typical battle action in Sicily! These official pictures show what happened when an American infantry squad, detailed to reconnoitre a supposedly abandoned village, find it held by German rear-guard detachments. Pinned down at first by machine-gun and mortar nests, but there are still the snipers to contend with.

In this brief but deadly engagement, the final score: one American dead against twelve enemy killed and two captured!

After the battle, rest for the weary. Here are the men who are fighting for us in Sicily: Sergeant Joseph R. Craig, Scranton, Pennsylvania; Private Albert Greenberg, Chicago; Private Walter Knofke, Denver; Private George Baker, New York City; Corporal Frank Chase, Los Angeles; Private Theodore Trower, Phoenix, Arizona; Private Robert Grogan, Joplin, Missouri . . . And their prisoners, two not so masterful members of the master race!

Their conquering days are over. A study in contrasts, the vanquished—and the victors!

The Victors

THE platoon straddled the hot, white Sicilian road like two moving black lines of ants. Each man cast beside him a shadow as gnarled and twisted as the trees that looked down on this bare valley. Ahead lay the scooped-out hills, faint blue in the sunglare. At the foot of the hills a town nestled, a tantalizing cluster of white dolls' houses.

Sergeant Joseph Craig was not taken in by the illusion. He had walked a lot of miles through Africa and Sicily, seen a lot of towns and buried a lot of dead.

He paused on the slope to look down at his squad, assessing the degree of their fatigue from their silence, the hunch of their shoulders under shirts splotched black with sweat, and their lethargic, monotonous step. He had no illusions about the village, but professionally—he looked a professional—he judged that he would find there the shade, rest and water that his men needed.

He moved into the lead again. Professionally, he checked how his newer men were doing. He never hoped for anything from replacements, only to have reasonable, ordinary guys who did their jobs and kept putting one foot in front of the other till they were hit. Baker, now, the New Yorker—there was a nice, ordinary guy. He was polite and quiet and never complained. Give the squad ten and he was squatting there with a pad on his knee, writing home to his wife. Grogan, Greenberg, Trower and the others—he still had to wipe their noses and their arses for them occasionally, but those of them who lived long enough would learn. Chase was the smartest of the bunch. He'd made corporal and he'd be a good one if he stopped being too sure of himself.

Corporal Chase, trudging along, looking at the sergeant's back, did not look self-assured at the moment. He was as tired as any man. His face was drained empty. His eyes looked outward, trained in a few weeks by the lash of bullets always to watch; but his thoughts looked inward, going over what had happened last night.

They had been stuck in that slit trench for forty-eight hours, himself, Baker and O'Toole. Across the broad, bare plain that faced them was the enemy, invisible but deadly to any man who tried to move forward.

O'Toole had dysentery. He sat huddled at one end of the trench with his eyes shut, his head lolling on one side, breathing heavily. He was too weak to crawl to a latrine when his spasms came; with the snipers active, the risk was too great. He kept a biscuit tin beside him and from time to time either Baker or Chase would empty it for him. His trousers were soaked with blood and slime. The tin made the pocket of close, overheated air smell terrible. It attracted flies in buzzing, black swarms that had to be brushed off every scrap of food they tried to eat.

Baker had been kidding Chase about his stripes. He'd got them only a few days before when Corporal Schwab had stepped on a land mine. The talk had made O'Toole open his eyes and Chase helped him drink some water from his canteen.

For no reason at all, they were suddenly arguing about jazz. O'Toole, who had played a saxophone in small bands in the Middle West, was becoming animated about Bix Beiderbeck and Cab Calloway. Chase was disagreeing just to be argumentative. In the distance, the artillery had mysteriously stopped firing. It had seemed a long time since there had been any sound of war.

"I'll tell you what," O'Toole had been saying. "I got plans when I get back to the States. I'm gonna have my own band when I get back," and lifting his right hand he began to wave an imaginary baton and hum the Wabash Blues. The tune and his imagination seemed to animate him. Too quickly for either of the others to restrain him, he straightened up to conduct his imaginary New Orleans band.

For a moment as he beat time gaily, his head topped the parapet. He was saying, "When I get back I'm gonna . . . ."

Those were his last words. The bullet hit him between the eyes. His face was unspoilt and surprised but his brains went all over Chase's boots.

Private (First Class) Trower, marching in the long, scattered file, also watched the bobbing shoulders of the sergeant up ahead.

Far down the ribbon of road a truck appeared to have run on to the verge. Around it was a small swarm of human activity. The sergeant, one hand cupped to shield his eyes, was also squinting at it.

Trower trudged in an unobservant daze; unobservant because he had still not yet learned all the lessons of survival, and also because, more deeply than he understood, he trusted that stocky, helmeted protector who walked up ahead, Sergeant Craig.

Not so long ago by the calendar (long, long ago in his mind) he and Chase had arrived in Tunisia as replacements. The sergeant had paused in front of Trower during the first parade, peered into his face and walked on without comment; and Trower had been struck with childish dismay.

The compact, battered face of the sergeant, dried like a prune, and his eyes, impassive yet bitter, had hinted to Trower of some strange awful world of experience of which he knew nothing, and the dismissive flick of the sergeant's glance had humiliated him, rejected him, made him feel a boy. He had tried hard in battle training, too hard it seemed, he had been too transparently eager, for one day the sergeant had grunted at him, "Whaddya think this is, stupid idiot, a football game?"

That was all way behind now. Sergeant and private were part of a single entity now, the squad, whose men lolloped along the roadsides as if tied together on a long, slack, invisible rope. Between then and now were the landings (seasickness, heat, the reek of oil, the slow wallow of the boat, time crawling, then the thump-down of the ramps, blinding sunlight, and himself lurching through warm water on to a white glare of beach, weak, sick and not caring, tasting the first of many anti-climaxes) and the repeated mystery of battle.

It was a new world, unreal as a dream; a succession of broken dreams, good dreams and bad dreams; on the move all the time yet not feeling that he was going anywhere; unaware of himself as an active doer, only feeling that things were being done to him. His memory was a muddle of blinding sunlight, mosquitoes, thirst, parching white dust; days that were quiet and drowsy and nights that were fearsomely alive, riven by the noise, the racking fear (each week he discovered, between new spurts of courage, new depths of fear) and the firework flashes of war. A boy from Phoenix, Arizona, had found his adventure, and unaccountably it was other irreconcilable things, boredom and nightmares.

As they approached the town, Sergeant Craig realized that there was not one truck in front of him but two. The second was on its side, tilted into a crater near the side of the road. The upright truck was half-filled with bulky canvas sacks. Judging by their bumpy contours, they could be sacks of potatoes.

But Craig knew that this was not a truckload of vegetables. The earnest work party, diligently and silently going about their task at the truck's rear, was something he had seen before.

This was a burial squad stuffing the bodies of some half-dozen corpses into individual sacks and carrying the sacks to the truck. The torn-up road and the smashed vehicle plainly indicated an exploded landmine. Some of the disposal squad wore gas masks, others made do with handkerchiefs tied across their noses and mouths. The sick-sweet ambrosia of death hung heavy in the air.

Craig, with a wave of his hand, signalled the squad over to the farther edge of the road. Silently, they continued their slow, resigned march. Most marched by careless, a few stared interestedly, a few others averted their eyes.

Trower was fascinated by a dead soldier at the opposite side of the truck. He had not yet been put in his sack. The legs of the corpse lay sprawled in an ungainly Y-shape. And a stiff left arm, by some accident, was extended rigidly upwards and pointing to the sky. Trower found himself wondering how so stiff and awkward a corpse could be stuffed into the sacks. His thought was as detached as if he sought the answer to a crossword clue.

None of the men noticed the figure of Christ almost opposite the burial squad. It was an elaborate iron crucifix with a realistic figure of Jesus, complete with stigmata, nailed to it. The shrine had only recently been decked with flowers. The men had seen a lot of these crosses along the roads of Sicily. They had stopped noticing them.

When they reached the town that had looked so white and inviting from a distance, the familiar mirage gave way to the familiar reality. The houses gaped open to the sky, the gutters were heaped with refuse, the cobblestones had been squeezed out of the road by blast, the squares were disfigured by splintered timber and mounds of rubble. The crackle of flames, the remote growl of far-away artillery, and the crunch of the squad's boots were the only sounds to be heard in this broken place.

The sun was now directly overhead. The open doors and smashed windows framed patches of cool blackness. The town seemed deserted. But an occasional scurry of sound in the debris—perhaps a cat, perhaps human footsteps—kept Craig alert through his weariness.

When they had reached a deserted street in the middle of the town, Craig raised his right arm and brought the men to a halt. He studied them as they stood before him plastered in white dust and sweat.

"All right," he said, "fall out."

As they began to shuffle wearily to the nearest shade, he halted them again.

"Hold it!" he said, raising his voice just enough to give it a note of authority. "I'm giving you ten minutes, and I don't want anybody getting lost. I don't want any looting and I don't want anybody going inside any houses. They're full of booby traps, and I'm not hanging around to scrape any stupid idiot off a wall. Is that clear?" He paused to see if he had been understood. Only blank and tired eyes greeted his words.

"Okay. Fall out," he said.

Like magnetized iron filings, they polarized to the shady areas of the street.

"Anybody need water," called out Craig. "Give me your canteens."

Greenberg and Chase handed over their canteens, and then silently moved over to the others who were already slumped with their backs against the stuccoed walls of the houses lining the the street. Craig looked over at Chase who had just put a cigarette in his mouth but seemed to be having difficulty summoning up enough energy to get a match to light it. The look was meant to convey to Chase that, as corporal, he was in charge while Craig was away. Chase gave no indication that he had got the message.

"Keep an eye on 'em," said Craig, making sure Chase understood his responsibilities.

"All right," said Chase, wearily.

Craig, with the extra canteens slung over his shoulder, moved up the street in search of water and turned at the first corner. This street was as deserted as the others. The walls of the large buildings were covered with big slogans, boldly painted.

"Believe, Obey, Fight."

"To Have Many Enemies Is to Have Much Honour."

"Die Valorously For The Fascist Empire."

The outsides of the buildings were Fascist but inside them there was no Fascism. Each front door opened straight into a living room, and they were all the same; a big double bed, religious pictures on the walls, stiffly posed photographs of wedding groups and black-bordered portraits of dead parents, and everywhere, spilled on every floor, heaps of letters.

Craig wondered about those letters. He had seen them now in country after country, hoards of letters spilled, it seemed, by every retreating soldier, every fleeing civilian. They were curious mounds of despair marking the trail of war across Africa and Europe.

At the head of the street, Craig discovered what he'd been looking for. It was a fountain in the centre of a small, dusty square in front of an old church. The water streamed from the mouth of a lion's head carved in stone.

The church, with its wide flight of steps sweeping upwards towards a heavy, carved door, ruled over the square.

Craig removed his helmet and allowed the delicious wetness to pour over the back of his head and trickle down his face. Refreshed, he gathered some water into his cupped hands and drank. Then he started to fill the canteens.

Suddenly a sting of instinct warned him that he was not alone; and instinct swivelled him round with rifle muzzle raised.

Facing him on the church steps stood an old woman in black, with a dark wrinkled face and wispy white hair. She stood there bent and silent, staring at him with a terrible intensity. Her hands were clasped in an attitude of prayer. She opened her toothless mouth and pointed into it. She did not speak but whimpered like an animal.

Craig put down his gun and took some biscuits out of his K-ration. Before he had had time to motion to her to come for them, she had hobbled towards him in a rapid scuttle, snatched the biscuits from his hand and scurried back to the church steps. Her face screwed up with some secret pain, she began to gnaw at the food with her toothless gums. Craig watched her for a moment and then turned back to filling his canteens. As he walked down the street to return to the squad, he gave a last look over his shoulder at the small black form alone on the wide steps.

When Craig returned to the squad's halting-place he found the street deserted. A bunch of stupid, undisciplined bastards, he thought. The minute his back was turned they buggered off like a gang of schoolkids. All he was trying to do was keep them from getting their fool heads blown off and they obviously didn't care a nickel for his advice.

The first place he looked into was a barber's shop. Asleep in the old-fashioned barber's chair was Knofke, a short man who was known as the platoon clown. Amiable and easy-going, he had a line of quick, comic patter for almost every occasion. His arms folded over his stomach, he was lying back in the chair with a beatific smile on his face. His feet were propped on a chair in front of him and his rifle rested on his lap.

Craig, with a look of resigned contempt, kicked the chair away from under Knofke's feet. The little man jerked into a bolt upright position, blinking fear and astonishment. Instinctively, he jerked up his rifle.

"Get out!" shouted Craig, picking up Knofke's pack from a table and thrusting it at him. "Where are the rest of 'em?"

Knofke, still recovering from his nap, stumbled to the door holding his helmet, pack and rifle in an unsteady array.

"I don't know, sarge," he said. "I think they're next door."

Craig pushed Knofke into the street.

"Stay right here," he said, his voice gritty with irritation. "Don't move!"

He could hear the sound of men's voices coming from a store nearby. Craig moved towards the noise. A humble little clothing shop that could be found in the back streets of any town anywhere, its window frames had been jerked awry with blast and the jagged teeth of glass still showed round the edges.

Parting the beaded curtain that formed the door, Craig could see three of his squad ransacking the shelves sparsely filled with men's haberdashery.

One man, Nicholson, was sitting on the counter wearing a panama hat and rifling some boxes in his lap. Another, Greenberg, had a bow-tie round his neck and was stuffing socks into his haversack. Marini, the third, was standing in front of a cracked mirror, admiring himself in a grey homburg.

Craig watched them for a few moments in silence.

"I thought I said no looting," he said finally, and they turned towards him with the stunned look of guilty schoolboys.

"Stupid idiots!" Craig shouted. "Where's the rest of you?"

The men shrugged their shoulders and with embarrassed haste tried to rid themselves of their loot. Craig tossed Greenberg his water bottle with a contemptuous gesture.

"Right! Get outside!" he ordered. "Get moving! You know you could get shot for this? Out! Out! Come on!"

Replacing their helmets and picking up their rifles, they sheepishly filed out of the store.

Next door Craig found the rest of his men. They were in a toyshop, a tiny, rather sad, toyshop with only a few simple toys of wood and tin and coloured paper on its shelves. It contained no sleeping, long-lashed dolls, no exciting models of tanks and guns and aeroplanes, no intricate mechanical sets or beautifully packaged puzzle games. It was the kind of place that belonged in a story book, with a little old man behind the counter and Pinocchio pressing his nose against the window pane.

A couple of men had found a packet of coloured streamers and were flinging them at each other, the flimsy coils of pink and yellow and blue writhing through the gloom of the shop and settling on their heads and shoulders. Baker was on his knees winding up a clockwork toy he had found, a little acrobat on a horizontal bar. The acrobat wore a peaked cap, a striped jersey and tights. A fierce black moustache was painted across his face. When Baker wound him up he would spring stiffly over and over the bar until the spring ran down. Baker's face was innocent with delight as he watched the antics of the toy.

Corporal Chase was in a far corner of the room wearing a paper hat and strumming away on a toy guitar, Grogan was seated beside him on the floor, also wearing a paper hat, and tapping with his fingers on some toy drums. They were singing, badly, "Dinah, Won't You Blow Your Horn", and trying to harmonize.

Trower, kneeling by the counter, had a concentrated look on his face as he tried to make a music box, shaped like a grand piano, work.

Craig, with the men from the clothing store bunched close behind him, watched the scene in the toyshop with fascinated revulsion.

"All right, children," he finally shouted, and turning towards Chase with a disgusted look, he added, "Leave you in charge, you stupid idiot."

Chase caught the canteen Craig flung at him, and said nothing.

"All right, everybody out!"

And just as they started to leave the shop, Trower, still on his knees, managed to get the music-box going. From it came a childish, romantic, sweet tune. The notes were clear, soft and fragile with the tinkling quality of a tiny dulcimer. On top of the toy piano, two dolls in evening clothes began a jerky, mechanical waltz in tune with the music.

The penetrating sweet sound caused them all to pause. They listened as the little box tinkled over and over again its frail music. They watched solemnly the impeccably dressed tin dancers repeating over and over again their stiff, unvarying routine.

Unconsciously, Craig took a couple of steps towards Trower and the music-box. Emboldened, the others one by one followed suit. Soon they were all gathered round it, squatting or standing silently, and listening. In some way, this faint music was hurting and healing these filthy, sweat-sodden men as they leaned on their rifles, lost in sombre fascination. The music box tinkled on.

It was Craig who was the first to pull himself together, shake the tune out of his head and look at his watch.

"Let's go," he said quietly.

For an instant, the men looked at him vacantly as if they had been tugged out of some seductive dream. Then slowly they began to follow him out.

For weeks after, when they were bivouacked in scented lemon groves, or huddled in fox holes under the hammering heat, or groaning with dysentery, or lying in the darkness while the earth trembled with gunfire; while the misery and degradation of war ate more and more deeply into them, one or another of the squad would whistle to himself a vague and half-remembered fragment of music. It was the tune, childish and heart-breaking, that the music-box had played.

THREE

COLISEUM NEWS FLASH

FOOD RIOTS IN ITALY

Hard times in Naples, where retreating Germans wrecked water and electric facilities after attempting to starve the city's people into submission. First task of the new Allied Military Government is to feed the population of Naples. But these pictures of people fighting for food show that it's a long time since anyone here has seen white bread. Matters get a little out of hand. Trouble makers, claiming to be resistance fighters, cause confusion, but are soon dispersed—and orderly distribution goes forward.

* * *

Ladies, please!

MAULING MAIDENS

The W.W.A.—Women's Wrestling Association—is about to set political Washington on its ear. The old wrestling racket has a familiar ring—it's square in shape—but these girls go into action with all the fury of a couple of customers at a sale of the last pair of nylons in the country. Ladies, please! There are gentlemen present! Again, and as always, just what the customers ordered. Ha, ha, ha, ha, ha!

The Victors

CHASE said, "What have we got to guard this place for?"

"Go ask the captain," Sergeant Craig answered. "He gives the orders. You got it clear? I'm leaving you with the squad. Two hours. Mount sentries, No one enters the place. Repeat, no one. That's the captain's orders. Couple hours, I'll be back with a relief for you."

The building might have been a monastery. It had massive stone walls with small barred windows high up that gave no clue as to what was inside. Big iron gates opened into a long, shady arcade supported by massive stone pillars. Vaulted arches and an ancient, iron-studded door to the interior added to the cloister effect.

"O.K., sarge."

Craig had turned away when Chase called, "Is it all right if we go inside? It's pretty hot in this sun."

"Sicily was hot. You call this hot?"

"They shipped us across to Italy, some Italian guy in Dog Company said it wouldn't be so hot. It's just as hot to me."

"Africa, Sicily, Italy, what's the difference?" The engines of the trucks were starting up. Craig added, "The orders are, nobody goes inside."

"O.K."

The sergeant swung himself up into the cab of a truck. The convoy moved off in a din of engines, along the steep road in the Italian hills that led to the company's bivouac area.

As the truck got under way, Craig leaned out of the open window at his side for a last look at Chase and the men he had left behind. The seven of them were still lolling against the building's wall trying to take advantage of the thin strip of shade created by the tiled roof overhanging the wall by several inches. Chase, he could see, had taken off his helmet and was lighting a cigarette.

Craig felt a twinge of doubt. He was still not sure about Chase, although in battle the new corporal had justified his sergeant's recommendation.

Craig understood men who believed in the war, he understood men who merely accepted it as a misfortune of nature, and he understood men who resented it. But Frank Chase did none of these things. He merely, except when he was in battle, ignored it.

He was quiet, yet he had a self-confidence that could not be cracked. He had the kind of arrogance that goes with a friendly relaxed manner. It was hard to speak to him without getting angry at the sceptical assessment in his eyes. The war was for suckers. Discipline was for suckers. Chase made a minimal, mocking submission to the demands of both, disclaiming all responsibility. He would pass on orders in a voice that made them sound ridiculous; and with a grimace of disclaimer. Still, he saw that they were carried out, since this made life easier for himself. It also made life easier for Sergeant Craig, and as he considered Chase to have more brains and character than anybody else in the squad, he dismissed his doubts.

The company camp was in a field of parched brown grass behind a dry-stone wall. A deserted peasant cottage had been taken over as HQ and a gap knocked in the wall to admit vehicles. Not far from the cottage, camouflage netting had been put up to form a small transport park.

There was a quiet air of disciplined disorder about the place. Trucks were being unloaded, gasoline tins, blankets, crates of cans—the clutter of war—were being carried back and forth with ant-like routine, ugly piles of things marred the serene indifference of this olive grove.

Craig's job was to find a location where the men would be protected from air observation. Leaping from the cab of the truck as it turned in through the gap in the wall, Craig soon had the rest of the platoon at work hacking pits in the hillside under some trees. He was surprised, when he looked at his watch, that it was already time for him to return to the men he had left on guard in the village.

A truck loaded with soldiers started to pull out of the transport area. Craig raced towards it. A dog followed him, yapping. The driver, seeing Craig in his mirror, stopped with the engine running. Craig climbed up into the cab and joined the two men already there. Beside the driver was the sergeant in charge of the relief guard. Nothing was said until the truck got under way.

"Pretty soft for your guys," said the other sergeant, not resentfully but just to make conversation. "Coming and going by truck. I can remember when we used to march 'em two miles just to get breakfast."

"Yeah? Well I don't see your guys walking."

The bumpy road, the dust and the almost suicidal confidence with which the whistling driver took the bends kept further conversation to a minimum.

As soon as he saw the massive, grey building again, Craig's misgivings returned in a rush. It looked ominously deserted.

"Where's your sentries, Craig?" jeered the other sergeant, as the truck pulled up outside the heavy, prison-like gates.

Craig was out of the cab before it had stopped. He hurried through the gates, along the arcade.

"Little Bo-Peep has lost her sheep," called out the other sergeant. Craig was in no mood to answer back.

At the end of the pillar-lined corridor, Craig turned right and faced the iron-studded doors of the main building. He pushed the doors open impatiently and entered into the inky blackness of the interior. With the dazzle of sunlight behind him, Craig had to stop to allow his eyes to get accustomed to the blinding darkness.

He could see that he was standing at the head of a stone staircase that ran steeply down against the front wall, with no rail on its outer side. A damp coolness rose up at him. An unfamiliar smell hung in the air, cold and cloying, a mixture of leaf-mould and cheap scent. From the deeper darkness at the foot of the stairs, Craig could hear the sound of smothered voices, bursts of song and the occasional crash of glass.

Grimly, he started to walk down the stone steps. He knew he was in a winery before he actually saw the big barrels stacked in the middle of the floor, and the racks along the walls cradling masses of dusty bottles.

Half-way down the stairs Craig could see all he needed to see.

The sound, which had been muffled up above, reverberated with deafening sharpness as it bounced back and forth against the cavernous walls. Rummaging among the wine racks were a couple of men. They lifted out bottles, smashed their necks off and poured the red liquid down their open mouths at arms' length.

Knofke and Nicholson were tossing bottles at each other like Indian clubs, unperturbed by the splinters of glass that burst about them each time one of them missed a catch. Even Trower was lying under the barrels with a sleepy and serene smile. Grogan and Greenberg were busily taking out bottles from the racks and packing them into boxes that they carried.

Chase was sitting in a corner of the huge room with his back against racks of cobwebbed bottles. Beside him sputtered a small candle. An empty bottle lay at his feet. He was eating biscuits from a tin in his lap, and one hand gripped a newly-opened bottle. His face wore a benign air of disinterest.

For a moment Craig could do nothing but watch with frantic disbelief the sight in front of him. Then he ran down the remaining stairs and strode towards Chase. With his hands on his hips, he stared down at Chase. Chase looked up at him vaguely and innocently.

"Are you crazy?" Craig finally cried in a hoarse whisper. "Are you crazy? How could you let this happen?"

Chase blinked his eyes and stared back at Craig as if contemplating some profound philosophical thought. It took him some time to answer.

"It seemed like a good idea at the time," said Chase, mouthing each word as if it required some special effort.

Craig's face was distorted with fury.

"You're through!" he shouted at Chase. "Finally, definitely through. You're going to be on K.P. till the day you die."

Chase nodded in solemn agreement.

"I guess so," he replied, offering Craig the bottle in his hand. "Drink?"

Craig grabbed the bottle out of Chase's hand and sent it flying across the cellar.

"All right," he shouted, turning on the others, "the party's over." No one budged. "The party's over, I said. Do you hear me? On the double!"

The drinking, the talking and the shouting went on unabated. Craig dashed over to where Grogan and Greenberg were still piling up bottles in their respective boxes. Greenberg, coming out from behind one of the racks, waved a bottle-filled hand at Craig.

"Hiya, Sarge," he said, swaying uncertainly.

"Come on. Upstairs!" snapped Craig. Nothing happened.

Craig pulled the box of bottles out of Grogan's hand

and put it on the floor. "All of you, come on. On the double."

Grogan, a huge lumbering fellow known as Moose in the squad, stared with listless eyes at the furious sergeant. He went on taking bottles out of the racks. As he was about to put another bottle into the box, Craig grabbed his arm and tried to wrest the bottle away. Grogan pushed him impatiently away.

Craig, blind with fury, drew back his right arm and hit Grogan hard below the chin. The Moose toppled over on his back amidst a shower of breaking bottles.

The echoing din brought a sobering silence to the cellar. Craig grabbed Grogan by the collars of his tunic and with one muscular tug pulled the half-conscious man to his feet.

"You can report me for that, if you want to," he snarled. And then turning to the others, "Anyone else get funny, and I'll do it again."

The noise of the overturned racks and smashed glass and Craig's frenzy had their effect.

"Now, all of you, get moving!" he shouted, shoving Grogan who, large, hulking and semi-conscious, stumbled and half-crawled his way up the stairs.

Craig was all over the cellar now, chasing, cursing, pushing and hauling his men towards the square of daylight at the top of the stairs.

"F... off."

"Ah, Sarge!"

"Washa matter? Who ya shovin'!"

"Lemme go, ya son-of-a-bitch!"

The protests ranged from injured cries to physical resistance, but the men were cowed by Craig's fury. To Craig this display of drunken indiscipline was a personal insult. The men sensed their sergeant's personal involvement in their conduct. Although their minds were clouded with the effect of the grappa they'd been drinking, they dimly recognized the fact that they had let Craig down. Slowly and limply, they began to pull themselves together and make their way out of the cellar.

Chase, too, realized that as a corporal he should be doing something to help his sergeant. Staggering to his feet, he was trying to lift some of the men who were scattered about the floor as if a shell had burst among them. He managed, after much effort, to raise Trower out from under the huge wine barrel where he had been lying prostrate.

"Turn them spigots off!" Craig shouted to Chase.

"Yes, Sergeant," Chase answered meekly and started to grope his way around the cellar.

Like an angry sheepdog Craig finally drove the men out of the cellar. Some staggered up the stairs in twos, supporting each other in drunken comradeship. One man crawled up on all fours. Trower, half-way up the stairs, fell over the side and had to be helped up again. They were now all full of boozy good-will. In thick-tongued, heavy voices they tried to display their affection for Craig. Grogan, full of maudlin repentance, kept impeding him by clinging to him and moaning, thick tongued, "I'm sorry, Sergeant. I'm awful sorry."

Chase had the gift of sobering quickly.

"With all they've drunk on empty stomachs, they'll get sunstroke out there," he said to Craig.

"You should have thought of that before," said Craig harshly.

Outside the building the sergeant and corporal of the relieving squad watched this parade of dead-drunk soldiers with silent derision. Grogan, a huge, swaying hulk, was still putting his arms round Craig and mumbling, "Gee, I'm sorry, Sergeant, I'm awful sorry."

The private soldiers of the relief guard were not as restrained as their non-coms. They howled with laughter as the burning sun made its impact on men who had spent two hours guzzling wine in the cool dampness of the winery. Like axed trees, Chase's men started to topple.

Some became violently sick. Another on his knees beside his supine comrade tried to revive him and then burst into tears. The sicker, the more humiliating, the more pitiful the men looked, the more comic they appeared to the relieving squad.

"Well, now I've seen everything..." said the sergeant of the new guard.

"Don't laugh too soon," Craig muttered sourly. "Just give me a hand, thanks."

Most of Craig's men were now propped, like so many wax dummies, in a neat row along one side of the building. Those who had begun to recover staggered towards the rear of the truck waiting to take them to the company camp. With some assistance, they managed to clamber into the truck where they flopped exhausted like hooked fish. But some had to be carried to the vehicle and dumped inside like logs.

"Well, there you are, Craig," announced the relieving sergeant when the job was done. "Fine a body of men as I've ever seen."

He was rather pleased with his ironic joke until he looked around to find his own men.

"Hey! Where've mine gone?" he asked, realizing at the same moment that they, too, had disappeared into the wine cellar.

Craig pointed at the open door of the winery.

"I told you not to laugh too soon," he said. "So long!"

At the door of the cab Craig became aware of Chase following him. Chase looked subdued and very sheepish.

"Oh, no," said Craig, as the corporal reached up to climb into the cab. "In the back, in the back. I don't want to look at you."

"I understand," Chase said humbly, and walked to the rear of the truck.

For almost a half-hour the truck bounced and lurched along the torn, rutted road. The men in the back, unsheltered from the sun's glare, were squirming in a heap like worms in a fisherman's pot. With each sway of the truck they rolled and thumped from one side of the floor to the other, grabbing, threshing and kicking at each other, moaning, crying out, protesting, quarrelling, and from time to time hauling themselves up the side-boards, to hang over and be sick like landlubbers at sea.

Chase, leaning against the back of the cab, thoughtfully watched his pitiful squad. Then slowly he began to pick at the stitches of his corporal's stripes.

When the truck reached the Company bivouac, it had to slow down to make the turn through the gap in the wall. Some fatigue men near Company HQ were the first to recognize the contents of the truck.

"Hey, look!" shouted the first sentry they passed. "The meat wagon!"

The fatigue men quickly took up the joke with cries of "Bring out your dead!...Where're the undertakers?... Any tombstones at the PX?"

Craig sat in the cab listening bitterly. The truck stopped almost directly in front of the Company HQ.

"Hey, don't stop here," said Craig to the driver urgently. "Keep going. Keep going. Cut across the field and get under those trees."

"Air-raid discipline," said the driver virtuously, "Mustn't make wheel-tracks, Sarge."

"Yeah, I know," said Craig unable to suppress the note of bitterness in his voice. "Why didn't you pull right up in front of the door? Then no one would have missed us."

Craig sat hopelessly in the driver's cab. The field ahead looked vast and empty as the Sahara, between the truck and a sheltering olive grove just a hundred or so yards away. And now, close by, the Company Commander had come out of headquarters and waited, tall and impassive.

"I worked hard for these stripes, too," Craig muttered half to himself and half to the driver. "I was up for staff."

"That's the way it goes," the driver said. "Do your best and then some jerk comes along and louses it up for you."

Craig seemed crushed by the unfairness of it all. He sat there waiting for the end of his career.

Then, from behind him, he heard a thumping and a shuffling. He turned round. Trower had risen from among the heaped bodies, like a corpse from a common grave, and was lowering himself over the back of the truck. Chase was already out of the truck helping him. When Trower reached the ground he stood there for a few seconds, clinging to the truck for support. Then he straightened up and began to follow Chase who was already walking stiffly away.

As Chase passed the front of the truck, he grinned at Craig and in a corpse's whisper said, "Faith, Sarge! Have a little faith!"

Craig, still in the cab, watched spellbound. One by one the men crawled to the tailboard, heaved themselves over, steadied themselves, and began to stalk across the field behind Chase and Trower.

One, two, three—Craig could hardly believe what he saw. These men were performing a miracle. As the lowest form of military life, the despised infantry, they had nothing to lose. This was for him.

They were all on their feet now, strung across the field in a wobbling single file, walking past the Captain one by one, all of them silent, all of them looking straight to the front, all walking with the stiff, uneasy stride of clock-work toys. They might have been so many zombies out of a film as they made their way towards the olive grove.

And as Chase, at the head of the precarious file, passed

the Company Commander, he lifted his right arm in a fine, sweeping gesture. The Captain calmly returned the salute.

One by one they reached the olive grove. As soon as they were in amongst the trees they pitched to the ground. The Captain watched them imperturbably as they disappeared into the shadows of the grove.

Craig, who had been watching the Captain, swung himself out of the cab and moved after his men. As he passed the Company Commander, he heard the officer call "Sergeant!"

Craig walked back to the Captain.

"Yes, sir?" he said, ready for the worst.

"Looks like you worked those men pretty hard today," said the Captain, with an admonitory shake of his head.

"Yes, sir."

"Well, there's no sense in being a slave driver."

"No, sir."

"I mean, no point in working them into the ground, is there?"

"No, sir."

"They look like a pretty good bunch to me. Huh?"

"Yes, sir."

"And this is a rest area. I think you can afford to take it easy with them now and then."

"Yes, sir."

"They're going back into combat pretty soon."

"Yes, sir."

"And...er...well that's it."

"Yes, sir."

Craig, stunned and unbelieving, saluted, turned on his heels and continued on his way to the olive grove. Chase was sitting comfortably against a tree. He was the only one of the squad still awake. The rest were sleeping under the trees.

Craig looked down at Chase who returned his gaze with a quizzical, almost injured, air.

"Thanks," said Craig. "But you're still getting busted. You ain't safe."

"I know," replied Chase equably. "I guess I'm just not the type."

Digging into the pocket of his blouse, Chase pulled out his corporal's stripes and handed them to Craig.

"But why did you let them get drunk?" said Craig.

"I don't know."

The frankness of the answer silenced Craig.

"I ought to wake 'em up and get them dug in," said Craig after a moment, indicating the sleeping men.

"Plenty of time, Sarge," said Chase, recovering his assurance now that he was no longer burdened by a corporal's responsibility. "Let 'em sleep it off. They deserve it."

Before Craig could reply, Chase had pulled a wine bottle out from under his blouse and offered it to the Sergeant, "Here's your share. You deserve it, too."

Craig looked at Chase. There was a long pause. Craig took the bottle, pulled out its cork and drank half of it without stopping for breath. Wiping the neck of the bottle, he handed it back to Chase. Chase, refusing the bottle, indicated his canteen.

"I'm all right," he said with just a shadow of a grin. "I got a very nice dry white wine here. That's all yours."

Craig watched Chase take a long swig from his wine-filled canteen.

"I can't make you out, fellow," he said. "I could have sworn you had leadership qualities. You could have made sergeant in another six months. But you got no sense of responsibility. You just don't give a damn. Why? Why?"

Chase shrugged his shoulders.

"I don't know," he said. "But don't let it worry you, Sergeant."

He drank. The Sergeant drank. They lay down and made themselves comfortable. Soon they were asleep among their sleeping men.

* * *

The Allied advance had been stalled somewhere up the boot of Italy. For six weeks the Division had been in reserve with nothing to do but rest, wait and prepare for the next move. The Company had taken over a barracks which had previously been occupied by German troops. The signs of their past presence and their hasty departure were evident on the walls. A large swastika had been only partially removed and painted slogans in German had not been entirely covered over by G.I. pin-ups in various states of undress. A photograph of Hitler had been converted into a serviceable dart-board. The moustache was the recognized bull's eye.

It was early evening. The sun had dropped like a luminous orange into the horizon leaving the sky tinged with its glow. It was still hot but it seemed cool with the sun's disappearance. Outside the barracks, on the parade ground, a noisy baseball game was being played.

The patter of friendly abuse and encouragement from both players and spectators drifted in through the open windows punctuated by the periodic smack of ball against bat.

Most of the men in the barracks were occupied in the desultory business of passing time. One was reading a paper, another was rather painfully writing a letter and another merely lay on his bunk watching.

But some were preparing to visit the local village that had been their sole escape from army life for the past few weeks. Craig, on the edge of his bunk, was methodically polishing his boots with a concentrated frown on his face. He worked the brush with such speedy and expert jabs that at times the tattoo on his right forearm seemed to be moving.

Chase and Trower, having just finished shaving, were still in their underwear and about to dress. Chase, whistling to himself, was obviously in high spirits. The thought of girls always made him euphoric. He had a sweet, regular dish in the village. And she made love in a ferocious, biting Latin way that flattered his virility. The bruises on his neck and shoulders were mementos of their nights together. He was rather proud of them.

A few bunks away Chase noted George Baker buckling his belt and getting ready to leave. Baker, a man in his early 'thirties, never had much to say for himself. He was frightened of words and used them as sparingly as possible. The brooding quality of his dark, square face suggested a mind weighing up the right and wrong of all he saw.

"Tonight the night, Baker?" said Chase. There was a suspicious innocence in the tone of the question. So innocent that it was obvious it had been asked before. Baker ignored it. His face merely took on a grimmer sullenness.

"Leave him alone," said Craig, without looking up from his intense shoe-polishing.

Chase chuckled. Baker was a jerk. All that effort to make an Italian dame and he hadn't laid her yet. Chase noted the mound of provisions on Baker's bunk.

"You know what, Baker?" said Chase, pulling up his trousers and buttoning his fly. "You're too nice to her. Cut down on the groceries just once, and you will suddenly become attractive..."

Craig looked up from his shoes.

"Talk, talk, talk," he said. "Why don't you shut up, you stupid idiot?"

"I'm only trying to help," Chase said.

There was no reply. Craig picked up his other shoe and began to work on it. Trower, who had finished dressing and had been listening to these exchanges with amused neutrality, began tearing out a picture of a Russian girl soldier from his copy of the Stars and Stripes. He pinned the svelte figure with grenades dangling round her middle over his bunk alongside rotogravure photographs of Churchill and Roosevelt.

In silence Baker fixed on his cartridge belt and started to leave the barracks with a muttered "So long."

Chase waited until Baker had almost reached the door. "You forgot the cornbeef and chocolate, George," he called out after him in a voice heavy with virtuous solicitude.

Baker stopped awkwardly, returned to his bunk and picked up the cans and parcels. He said nothing as he went out. Chase's face split into a cheerful grin. Craig, having finished his boots, relaxed on his bunk with a dog-eared paperback of a Zane Grey Western. Trower lit a cigarette and continued to wait patiently for Chase.

"It's not normal, you know," said Chase to no one in particular.

"Listen", said Craig, looking over the top of his paperback, "if she don't want to be like the rest of them, that's her business, and it's his business." His voice rose sharply. "But it ain't yours."

"If he keeps on sitting on that front step of hers," Chase continued undeterred by Craig's disapproval, "he's going to develop a square behind."

"So what?" Craig's patience was dribbling away. "You're not in charge of behinds around here. Or are you?"

Chase chuckled.

"Funny though, when you think of it." he said. "This little town, I mean. First all the husbands and boy friends go into the army, and then the Germans come in and take over the women. Then we kick the Germans out, and we move in, and we take over. Don't you think that's funny?"

Craig ignored him.

"Well, if she's such a nice girl," Chase said, determined to provoke some response out of Craig, "and her husband's been away three years, where'd she get that six-month-old bambino, hey?"

Craig lost his temper.

"From a drunken Kraut in a dark alley," he said, "who also gave her a broken arm. Now blow, will you? Go have a nice kaffee-klatsch with that phoney blonde of yours. She'll tell you all about the Germans. She should know."

Chase, carefully combing his hair, took no offence.

"That's what I said," he replied. "Place is like a barnyard."

"You ought to know," said Craig, sinking back on to the bunk. "You're the head rooster."

"Really?" Chase said, flattered. He looked over at Trower and winked. "Hey, Sergeant, tell me, were you really a burglar before the war?"

"What?" The question was so unexpected, Craig could summon up only a startled ejaculation in reply. Trower laughed.

"Is it true you served a stretch in Joliet?" Chase went on innocently.

"Get out of here," shouted Craig. He pointed to Trower, "And take the Russian-lover with you."

"I never said a word," said Trower, startled to find himself being attacked. "Anyway, all I ever said about Russians was I'd like to meet some Russian G.I.'s someday. Is that a crime?"

"No, that's no crime," said Craig. "I'd like to meet some Russian sergeants and find out how they handle stupid idiots like I got."

Chase, putting on his helmet at a jaunty angle, looked at his sergeant and sadly shook his head.

"You don't like me any more."

"I never did," said Craig, deliberately humping himself over his paperback.

"Liar," said Chase, signalling Trower to leave with him. They went out, snickering. Craig's lips moved silently, slowly as he concentrated on the paperback.

The barracks were not far from the centre of the village. Baker, as he walked, hardly heard the hubbub of noise that from dawn to dusk filled the streets. He was heavy with resentment at the kidding he had taken from Chase. The resentment was at himself for taking it.

He was a mild man. He was not afraid of other men. It simply seemed unnatural to fight them. Yet, every time he ignored an insult and went on his peaceful way, he felt a heavy regret at being one of the mild men of this world.

He had married when he was twenty-one. Before the war, he had paid his taxes, done his job efficiently in the home loan office, the sort of man who is esteemed by the boss but only slowly promoted, and had gone home with relief each evening to his wife. His real life began when he shut his front door on the rest of the species and smiled at Kay and the kid. In the wilderness of New York, these two were his private world, and though he frowned over the newspapers he had no impulse to face any involvement outside the shelter of his own home.

Then a war, a far-off quarrel of remote people, one of the things he had frowned over in the newspapers, in a moment reached out and lifted him across four thousand miles, from his own warm small world into another.

He did not complain. Within his own little world he was aware and glad of being an American. Parting from his home was an ache that never diminished; but he accepted the price of being a citizen. A mild man, he fortified himself, like millions of other mild men, to become staunch and trustworthy in battle.

The village was alive and noisy in the cool of the evening. Almost every doorstep had its gossiping little group of women and old men—there were only old men. Shrill children played on the cobbles.

Other Americans were going into the village. Two G.I'.s in front of him stopped before a house and whistled. Almost before the whistle had died away, two girls in pathetic dresses and elaborate hair styles bounded from the house and greeted them. Linking arms, they went off chattering.

As the rivulet of men flooded into the street, most of them carrying small bundles of food, they were picked up by female partners. It was like the stream of men in a factory town coming home from work. Some disappeared into a near-by tavern; others vanished into houses, closing the doors or drawing together the stringed curtains behind them.

A stout Mess Sergeant, loaded down with tinned goods, was greeted with raucous acclaim by a gleefully shouting brood of ragged children. Alerted by the shouts and laughter, a plump, slatternly but beaming woman came to the door to smile a genuine welcome. Surrounded by the kids like a warship by tugs—the same kind of kids and good-natured wife would probably have surrounded him back in the States—he was pulled smiling into the house.

George Baker saw Maria just where he had expected to see her. She was sitting on her doorstep with her six-month-old baby in her arms. She watched this fraternization with an expression that might have been contempt on her dark, mobile face. Yet some tension in her posture hinted that she, too, was waiting. Though she must have been aware of Baker's approach, she made no sign of recognition until he reached her.

"Buona sera, Maria."

"Buona sera, Giorgio," the girl said without smiling.

Baker sat down beside her on the doorstep. Baker was careful not to sit too close to her and a discreet distance separated them. He watched her in silence for a moment. Maria hugged the beshawled baby to her breast, as if sheltering behind it from the man. She tried not to look at him. Baker remembered the tins of food he had brought. Casually, almost surreptitiously, he put the tins down on the step near her. Maria noticed the gesture and was determined not to ignore it.

"Grazie," she said. "Lei è molto gentile."

"It's nothing," said Baker.

Ever since they had first met in a local grocery store where he had gone to get some matches, there had been this tension between them. They had continued to see each other after their first meeting but they had kept apart, out of loyalty to their own ties, out of respect for each other and because of a vague, unexpressed disgust with the orgy of promiscuous love-making going on around them.

Their evenings together had been spent outside her house, talking. Recovering from the heat of the day, they had eaten almonds and laughed at silly jokes they had managed to exchange in a hybrid patois of simple English and Italian. Whenever their conversation lagged, they became aware of the strain between them and then they would fall silent, exchanging fierce, hasty glances, quickly averted, and quickly break into small-talk again.

Baker tried to avoid looking at the expanse of thigh above her knee that had been exposed by the movements of the infant against her tight, short dress.

Around them children played and old people contemplated the vanishing evening. The girl and Baker said nothing. Once or twice they looked at each other, but their glances never met. They both watched with negative curiosity a G.I. advancing towards one of the houses. A young woman rose from her doorstep and ran eagerly to greet him. He accepted her shrill welcome nonchalantly and gave her a patronizing hug. Smacking her bottom playfully, he guided her into the house. Baker was keenly conscious of the difference between his own situation and that of the dominant G.I.

"Siggy and Lucia are getting along fine," he said, breaking the silence between them.

"Lucia is whore," said Maria flatly in a tone that encouraged no contradiction.

Baker wasn't prepared to argue the point. Changing the subject, he turned his attention to the plump baby in Maria's arms. Gently, he touched its fine dark hair.

"Pretty," he said.

"She is good."

"Yes."

It seemed all there was to say. In silence Baker continued to play with the baby's hair.

Maria, too, as if recognizing that the baby formed a physical link between them, drew away slightly. Deliberately, as a rebuff, she asked the next question.

"Giorgio, you think my husband, he's still alive?"

The cutting edge of the words flicked through Baker like a rapier. He flushed guiltily and took his hand away from the baby. Yet he could not bear to hurt her. Reassuringly, he lied.

"I think there's a pretty good chance. We took a lot of prisoners in Africa."

"But so long, no letter. Nothing."

"Doesn't prove anything."

For a moment Maria said nothing. Then she sprung her trap.

"You get letter today, Giorgio?"

The remark impaled Baker with its directness.

"Yes," he replied, startled.

"How is wife?"

"All right. She's okay."

"And children?"

"You know we just have the boy."

"Ah, yes. He play the baseball."

"Maria!" Baker was desperate.

"You love wife very much, yes?" The girl was determined to hurt both of them with her tattoo of questions.

"Yes," said Baker.

"Yes. You love wife. I love husband."

"All right. Please..." his eyes pleaded with her.

"Yes. Whole world full of love," the girl laughed bitterly. "In peace not so much love. Only in war. You love wife, you love me. I love husband, I love you."

It was the first time Baker had heard her use the words. From despair his emotions were suddenly kindled into expectant hope. He moved towards her tenderly. She shrugged off his advances almost impatiently.

"No, listen," she said. She had obviously prepared this speech and was determined to say it. "You are good man. I know you want help me. You are husband without wife, I am wife without husband. But we are not animal. Everybody can be animal, but we are not animal. You understand? I cannot be, you cannot be. So I think better you don't come back no more. I think this very much..."

"Please..." Baker tried to speak.

"No." She blazed with a determination that was near hysteria. "You go away now and don't come back. Go find woman. You need sleep with woman. Please. Go! Go!"

Baker was helpless. He could see in her eyes no compassion. Slowly, only his eyes pleading, he rose. Maria stared firmly away from his gaze. Seeing the food he had brought her, she seized it and extended it to him.

"You take!" It was the gesture she knew would finally

humiliate him and end it all. The baby, startled by the raised voices, began to cry.

"Oh, for God's sake!" Baker was shaking with rage and frustration.

"Yes, you take!" continued the girl, mercilessly. "Thank you, but take, and go!"

Baker knew there was nothing more to be said. He took the tins she was holding out to him.

At that moment they were suddenly conscious of a difference in the texture of the noise around them. Instead of the hubbub and chatter of talk and domestic clatter, they heard a confusion of shrill screams, the panicky clacking of wooden sandals on the pavement and hurried slamming of doors.

An old woman rushed past with averted face, screaming. "Gl'Indiani! Malocchio!" she cried and vanished into the next door house.

They looked away to the end of the street and there, swaying in the middle of the suddenly emptied roadway, was an Indian soldier, a Sikh. He wore British battle dress and a khaki turban.

Baker had heard of this unreasoning fear that the local population felt for the Sikhs. He had never seen it himself but some of the men in the Company had told him about it. It was not the colour of their skin that stimulated this panic. American negroes had been accepted by the locals without any feeling of race consciousness. Indeed, the women loved them, not out of a hunger for the physical love-making of which they had been deprived with the disappearance of their men, but simply because these buoyant, uninhibited black men were the gayest, sometimes the finest-looking and the most unfortunate of all the poor devils in uniform whom the war had cast up amongst them.

It was the very opposite with the Indians. Although they, too, were fine-looking men with classically handsome features who bore themselves well and generally behaved with meticulous and mature courtesy, the Southern Italians and Sicilians instinctively feared them.

Perhaps some ancient superstition was at work, some ancestral Mediterranean fear of the men from the East. Whatever it was, it was a fact that a couple of Sikh soldiers had only to come walking, quiet, dignified and absorbed in their own conversation, along a street, and civilians would give them a wide and fearful berth, while women crossed themselves and snatched their children indoors.

The Indian, obviously drunk, came lurching down the street as doors banged shut and the street emptied. Baker and Maria realized that they were alone, watched by many pairs of eyes from the black, barred windows.

Maria, clutching her baby to her, moved to escape into her house. Baker grabbed her arm.

"What's the matter?" he asked, surprised at her panic.

"They are devil," cried Maria, trying to break away from his restraining arm. "They have bad eye. He make baby sick. Malocchio."

"Don't be silly. There is no evil eye. There's no such thing."

The Indian was now not far from them. He halted and looked about him in a vague, drunken bewilderment. He crossed to a closed door and began to bang on it with his clenched fists, crying out in a language neither the girl nor Baker could understand. There was something terrifying about these strange sounds in the silence. The baby began to cry again.

Maria tried again to push past Baker and move into the house.

"Please let me put baby inside. He hurt baby." Her eyes were fixed with hypnotic fear on the Indian.

"No he won't. They're nice fellows. Just like anybody else. He's just had a little too much to drink. That's all."

"Giorgio. . .please!"

"No. I won't let you run like the rest of them. There's nothing to be afraid of."

Baker's reassuring words meant nothing to the girl. She was too frightened to recognize, as he did how lost and lonely the lithe, dark-skinned man along the street looked, as he thumped imploringly on a closed door.

The Indian saw the couple and came towards them. The girl looked up at Baker, silently begging him to let her go. Holding her arm he could feel how violently she was quivering. She could have torn herself from his grasp, but it was his will that kept her where she was; it was her animal acceptance of his will, a first implicit recognition of shared fates.

The Indian halted in front of them and Maria pressed her baby close to her, trying to cover the child's face from the baleful eye she feared.

"Hullo, Johnny. Having a good time?" said Baker. His voice was casual and friendly.

The Indian uttered a high-pitched laugh of delight and repeated, like a pleased child, "Hallo, Johnny." He was young and slender. Even his fierce beard could not hide the fact that he was hardly more than a boy.

Baker smiled. "Too much wine, eh?" He mimed drinking, then whirled his forefinger round. "Like this, eh? In here." He tapped his head.

The Indian beamed and nodded his head rapidly. "No good, no good." He clasped his head on his hands and closed his eyes, gently swaying.

"Are you dizzy?" Baker's voice was still casual.

"Yess, yess. Yess, yess. Vairy dizzy, vairy dizzy." The Indian shook his head in violent, but sad, agreement. The baby began to cry again and the Indian leaned towards it. Maria stood rigid with terror with her eyes upon the face of Baker.

"Little baby," said the Indian. "Poor baby cries. I have babies—three." He held up three fingers.

"How old are they?" asked Baker.

The Indian paused, as if the act of memory was difficult.

"Four," he said, holding up one hand. "Six...nine." He used the fingers of both hands to indicate the figures. "I had another...she died."

Baker could see that Maria listened with downcast eyes to the reedy sing-song of the Indian's voice.

"Your lady let me hold the baby?" said the Indian, looking at Baker.

Maria tensed as if trying to run away again.

"Let him hold it," Baker said to Maria. The girl shrank away in an agony of indecision.

"He won't hurt her," said Baker. "You always let me hold her and he knows how better than me. You heard him—he's got three of his own. Let him have her. Don't be afraid."

Maria hesitated, every instinct in her fighting against his suggestion. Then, not daring to disobey him, she handed the baby carefully to Baker. She clutched her hands together as if regretting what she had done.

"Here!" Baker handed the baby to the Indian, who at once began to chick and chuckle with delight, rocking the little girl skilfully in his arms. He hummed a tune, a strangely high-pitched and broken tune, and dandled the baby happily. The baby stopped crying and began to smile.

"Ek! Ek!" cried the Indian. "Look, she is smiling. She smiles at me!"

Baker looked at the girl. Her face was filled with relief.

"She likes you," said Baker to the Indian. "All right, give her back now."

The Indian obediently handed the child back to the soldier who put it gently into Maria's arms.

"Thank you very much," said the Indian. "Very nice baby." He held out his hand to Baker and solemnly shook hands. "I got to go now. Back to barracks. To sleep. Chirr'yo."

"Cheerio," said Baker.

"Chirr'yo," repeated the Indian. He took Maria's free left hand, kissed it, then touched the baby's head gently, almost as if in benediction. "Pretty baby. God bless baby."

"Cheerio," said Maria.

They watched him in silence as he walked, still a little uncertainly, down the deserted street. Baker was the first to speak.

"You're a good girl. That was a kind thing you did when you let him hold the baby."

Maria did not reply immediately, then she said, "You are good man. You have good heart. I put baby sleep now. You wait, please."

Baker sat down again on the doorstep and lit a cigarette.

The street was filling up with the sound of chairs being brought outdoors again and the shouts of children kicking a ball. The tension was gone as if it had never been. Baker wound up the mechanical bear he had brought for Maria's baby and watched its stiff arm movements without really seeing them. He was resigned to his failure with her, sad, his desire still present but softened by affection.

He became aware of Maria framed in the doorway again. She looked different. She had done nothing to herself except pull a comb swiftly through her hair. Yet there was now about her an air of radiant defeat that stirred and mystified him.

Startled Baker stood up. They faced each other. No word was spoken between them. After a moment Maria took hold of the identity discs that were hanging around

Baker's neck, outside his shirt. She turned them over, studying them, then put them back inside his shirt, and slowly buttoned the top two buttons. Then, taking his hand, she drew him into the house.

Through some parted curtains, she led him into her bedroom. With her back against a wall, she waited for him. Above her head was a framed picture of a wedding couple. Baker did not see it as he softly kissed her cheek and her neck. Slowly her arm tightened round his neck with a fierce possessiveness as she drew his lips to hers and surrendered completely.

* * *

Not many days later, the Company moved out. The narrow street was filled with villagers, waving, cheering or weeping, as the men marched in straggling, resolute files, down the winding slope towards the trucks which waited to take them back to battle.

Maria, arms folded, watched the men, many of whose faces she now knew, pass her door and out of her life.

There was Craig and Chase and Trower and Grogan and Baker. She knew Baker's eyes were searching for hers as he marched by. She saw his face, torn with helpless longing, looking back at her over his shoulder. She could see his lips moving in a message that was drowned by the cheers and the marching feet.

She continued to watch the tail-end of the retreating file of men as it quickly turned a corner and passed out of view. All the time her body remained frozen and immobile in the doorway. Her eyes were dead.

She could hear the trucks starting up around the corner and the boisterous shouts of women and men as the Company clambered into the waiting vehicles. She could still see some of the girls frantically waving their good-byes at the bottom of the street. She longed to see

Baker once more, even from a distance, even to hurt herself dreadfully.

But she could not bring herself to join the others. She was too proud. And it was too painful. And it was too hopeless. At last the sound of trucks on the move reached her. Some of the women and children had already started to trudge back along the hot, dusty road. Her pride could restrain her no longer. She darted frantically from her doorway into the road. But already the last of the trucks was an indistinguishable retreating blur in the distance. She watched the billowing cloud of dust raised by the moving convoy until it was nothing but a drifting haze on the horizon. Then, with her arms still folded and her shoulders heavy with despair, she walked back into her house and closed the door behind her.

* * *

The body lay stiff and anonymous in the rubble. The colour of the uniform could have been grey or olive green. The blast had stripped it of its nationality. And the dark, with only a thin sliver of moon to help, conspired against identification.

At the top of some steps which flanked the rubble, behind a fragment of wall, shadows twitched with a tentative furtiveness. The moving shadows materialized into the head of a small boy. There was a gaunt, thin structure to the face that told of hunger and malnutrition. But the eyes, bright, hard and predatory, belied the look of hollow despair. They were eyes of survival and determination and cunning. The boy was about fourteen years old.

The eyes fixed familiarly on the corpse. Then back and forth they darted as they reacted instinctively to the possibilities of danger.

Suddenly the boy slipped from behind the broken wall

and slithered expertly down the steps. His hands, firm with the patina of experience, searched under the dead soldier's blouse. Out came a wallet and a small tin box. With quick gestures the wallet was stripped of its contents. Some paper money and some photographs. A woman smiling, not pretty, not ugly. A family portrait of a man, woman and small boy. The photographs were swiftly flung aside as the boy eagerly opened the tin box. It contained cigarettes. A glint of satisfaction flickered across his face.

Above the corpse and boy, two more figures appeared. Another boy and a girl, both ragged and equally wolfish, stared down at him. Instinctively, the first boy hid the cigarette tin under his shirt. The second boy, a grim, set look diffusing his face, launched himself down at him. They fought fiercely, silently and urgently.

Soon the first boy was on top. His small fists rained with concentrated energy on the boy's face beneath him. The second boy began to whimper and show that he had had enough. Behind the wall above, the girl was watching with a silent but neutral intensity.

The first boy, now victorious, rose and retrieved the box of cigarettes. Meaningfully, he slipped them under his shirt. They were his. The spoils of the victor.

He picked up the wallet which had fallen beside the corpse. With the studied skill of a card sharp, he flipped the money out of the wallet and split it three ways. The second boy's share he tossed to him and he waved the girl down to get hers. The money tucked away in pockets and blouse, the three children turned upon the corpse and began to strip it, quickly and efficiently.

* * *

Trower—Corporal Trower—felt good about the stripes on his arm. They must, he was sure, be conspicuous to everyone in the street, though nobody see to notice them.

He had, in a sense, inherited these stripes, from Fra Chase. When Chase had been busted after the riot in th winery, Trower had been picked to take his place. There was no ill-feeling on the part of the loser and no compunction on the part of the gainer. Chase didn't care one way or the other about promotion. Ted Trower did.

Other advantages apart, it was a good thing to write home about. He could imagine his old man bragging about it at the next meeting of the local Masonic Lodge.

Trower headed for a bar he liked, in the warren of slums behind the unit's latest quarters. In the few months since Sicily he had acquired an older and more solid air. He felt more mature. On a three days pass to Salerno (now a rear area) he had slept with an English nurse.

Her name was Molly. She was a cheerful, pleasant soul, and something of a prize for a G.I. English nurses, making the most of the shortage of women from home, almost invariably insisted on officers. Molly was a good-natured and sensual person to whom the body and personality of her companion were more important than his rank, and she had taken charge of the tall, dark, masculine young American as briskly as if he were a patient in her ward.

All the same, she had been a giggler, and of a banality that irritated Ted, who valued serious things like life and books and whatnot, and felt a certain loneliness at the lack of anyone he could confide his real thoughts in. Still, like all those healthy, normal but uninitiated young men rising twenty in years each of whom does not dream that he is only one among many, Ted had felt slightly ashamed of his incomplete experience; and that, thank goodness, was over.

So now he felt a bit older, a bit more assured within,

accordingly relieved; yet dampened by the triviality .he experience.

He was not out woman-hunting today. No longer .riven by the desperation of the young, he was content to wait. Not for the love of his life—he was too tough and realistic a young man to expect this along the desolate roads of war—but for the appearance of some woman with whom he could at least share a few good, unsordid moments; even perhaps find a little in common besides the body.

All he wanted, then, as he pushed in through the beaded curtains of the bar, was to come across one of his comrades as footloose and unadventurous as himself, and to enjoy a friendly drink.

The small Italian tavern was crowded with troops. The air was hung with blue cigarette smoke and pungent with a vermouthy smell. A few men sat at tables. The rest packed round the bar in an uproar while a middle-aged barmaid, too ugly to be anything but safe, was trying to cope with a clamour of orders.

At the bar, Trower looked round for someone he knew, and saw Knofke—one of the squad. He tapped the short man on the left shoulder and when he turned to his left, Trower tapped him again on his right shoulder. An old schoolboy trick.

When Knofke finally faced Trower with an amiable, querulous look, Trower with mock modesty pointed to the fresh corporal's stripes on his sleeves. Knofke feigned disinterest.

"Do I know you?" he said.

"Oh, no. I guess you don't know me," said Trower. "I'm just a clean-cut American corporal away from home."

"Well, I'm an American, too," said Knofke, entering into the act.

"You're an American? Well, what in the world are you

doing here?" Trower held out his arm and they shook hands again. "What part of Texas are you from?"

"Brooklyn."

"Brooklyn? Just a minute, son. You must be shooting me a line. That ain't in Texas."

"Why sure it is. Brooklyn, Texas."

"Are you sure you ain't a German spy? You're too little to be from Texas, sonny." Trower grabbed the man's shoulder with mock ferocity. "Speak to me spy. Talk American."

"Hamburger sandwich. Malted milk. Hot dogs. Apple pie à la mode with ice cream," Knofke said without hesitation.

"And don't you ever forget fried chicken! Well, ain't that wonderful. I'd like to buy you a drink, sir. What would you like to drink?"

"Beer," said Knofke, slapping the bar vigorously with one hand.

"Doua beer, cheri...waitress...ma'am," said Trower, successfully managing to catch the eye of the busy barmaid. "These Italians sure are wonderful," he continued, wrapping his arm affectionately around the little man's shoulder. "What are you doing here?"

The badinage was interrupted by the entry through the beaded curtain of four American soldiers. Their appearance was not noticed till the largest of the four, square-jawed and built like a wrestler, called out in a loud voice, "Coon hunting night. Any niggers in here?"

The hubbub petered away. Everyone looked at the four men.

The few remaining bits of conversation in the place trickled to a complete silence. Everyone's eyes swivelled from the speaker to two Negroes in American uniform sitting at one of the tables.

"Ah, a couple of real pretty ones, too," called out the big soldier, spotting his prey. The Negroes stopped talking, looked up and recognized their danger. They rose slowly from their chairs.

With a quick gesture and an expectant grin on his face, the white soldier signalled two of his companions into action. The fourth soldier, flicking open a knife he had drawn from his pocket, waved it menacingly at anyone in the room who might have felt compelled to take an interest in the uneven fight. No one showed any inclination to interfere.

A quick smash to the face of one of the Negroes sent him sprawling unconscious across an upturned table. The other was desperately trying to make a fight of it. But his flailing arms were soon caught and held by two of the men while a third proceeded to punch him methodically in the stomach. The Negro's mouth opened wide with agony as each blow shook his helpless body. His eyes rolled with painful incomprehension. His body soon hung limp and unconscious between the two men. They let him slump to the floor and the big soldier was about to kick the Negro's face when someone at the beaded curtain shouted, "M.P.'s."

The four soldiers, obviously familiar with this kind of situation, slithered out of the tavern with astonishing speed. They were followed in a concerted and undignified rush by every uniformed man in the place. No one wanted to be around to answer questions. Trower and Knofke joined the others in the stampede to get out. But at the door Trower suddenly realized he had left his cap behind on the bar.

He darted back and picked it up and was about to dash out again when he noticed that one of the Negroes had recovered consciousness and was painfully trying to get to his feet. It was the Negro who had been so brutally punched in the stomach. Instinctively, he hesitated and then rushed over to the battered man to help him up. But just as he was starting to pick up the struggling

Negro, Trower could see through the beaded curtain the familiar helmets and armbands of the military police. In panic, he ducked behind the bar counter, where he crouched trying to keep out of sight.

The barmaid's legs were so close to him that his shoulders almost touched them. She had been watching him all the time as he had tried to help the beaten Negro but now gave no indication that she knew he was crouched at her feet. Trower could see the ragged hem of her cheap dress, the holes in her black stockings and the scuffed, battered flat-heeled shoes. He tried hard not to breathe.

Four M.P.'s entered the tavern and surveyed the empty room with its tell-tale marks of hasty panic—the upturned chairs, the half-empty beer mugs, the cigarettes still glowing in ash-trays. The stolid, enigmatic looks on their faces indicated that they were not at all surprised by what they saw.

Three of the M.P.'s advanced on the prostrate Negroes and quickly and professionally picked them up and dragged them out. The other one, taking a pad and pencil out of his breast-pocket, went up to the counter to speak to the barmaid who was impassively watching this strange ritual.

"What happened?" he asked.

She shrugged her shoulders. "I don't know. They fight."

"Do you know any of them? Any damage?" The M.P. spoke deliberately so that the Italian woman might have a better chance of understanding him.

"Only business."

The M.P. jotted down a few words in his book and then put it back into his pocket.

"If this happens again we'll have to mark you off-limits," he said, without betraying any hint of either criticism or annoyance. "Sorry."

The barmaid said nothing. The M.P. followed his

companions out and the only sound to be heard in the tavern was the cheerful and robust singing voice of a girl on the radio.

> "*Let's remember Pearl Harbour*
> *As we go to meet the foe.*
> *Let's remember Pearl Harbour*
> *As we did the Alamo.*"

The barmaid waited until the M.P.'s were safely away. Then she tapped Trower on the head. He had been squeezing himself into as insignificant a human ball as possible while the barmaid spoke with the M.P. When he got to his feet he was sincerely grateful to the woman for having protected him. She might easily have been in trouble herself had the M.P.'s discovered Trower lurking behind the bar.

"Grazie mille," said Trower, summoning up his few words of Italian.

As he reached the farside of the counter on his way out, the barmaid put out her hand to stop him.

"Hey, why they fight?" she asked with a look of honest bewilderment on her face. "You same peoples, yes? Americani, Camerati. Why you fight?"

Trower was at a loss for words.

"I really don't know," he finally said feeling very inadequate. Putting on his cap, he waved to the woman and pausing at the curtain to give a quick look to his right and left to see that all was clear, he went out.

The radio was still blaring out its patriotic message.

> "*We will always remember*
> *How they died for liberty*
> *Let's remember Pearl Harbour*
> *And go on to victory.*"

The barmaid stood watching the beaded curtain as it

continued to rustle following Trower's exit. After a moment she shrugged her shoulders, came out from behind the counter and walked across the room to turn off the radio. Then she began to pick up the chairs and tables and restore the tavern to some kind of order.

FOUR

COLISEUM NEWS SPECIAL

INVASION!

On the sixth of June, 1944, the great secret is divulged. D-Day. Aboard a British warship with Admiral Ramsey, General Eisenhower keeps his finger on the pulse of battle by personal observation, and is joined by General Montgomery for consultations on the progress of our landings.

This is it, they're on the beach, plunging waist deep into the sea. These pictures take you right in among the men who are putting Dunkirk into reverse, planting themselves on the first bit of French soil to be won back after four years. The Tommies, the G.I. Joes, and Johnnie Canucks press on with "Now let's get at them."

And to the people of France there comes the voice of the Supreme Commander, General Eisenhower:—

"This landing is but the opening phase of the campaign in Western Europe. Great battles lie ahead. I call upon all who want freedom to stand with us now. Keep your faith staunch. Our arms are resolute. Together we shall achieve Victory."

The Victors

THEY were in France, and their road led to the enemy's heart. The regiment had come a long way round to this final consummation—Africa, Sicily, Italy, and Utah Beach.

The Company that wound in file of two out of a steep-banked Normandy lane towards a ruined village was the same by designation as a year before, but most of the faces were new. Wooden crosses, clustered in many places on two continents, bore many of the old names. Other men had been transferred, or shipped home with wounds, illness or battle fatigue.

Craig still trudged ahead of his squad stooping and tireless, with Corporal Trower behind him. The squad had come through well. Grogan and Chase were still there, Knofke and Greenberg. The rest were replacements. George Baker had been caught by a mortar burst on D plus 7.

The sides of the road were lined with wrecked, abandoned and still burning vehicles. The buildings had either crumbled like old cake or had been sliced open as if by some gigantic chopper to reveal the incongruous sight of staircases with nowhere to go or papered walls with neither roofs nor floors to support. The close-cropped hedges of the bocage country were unkempt and the fields were scarred with shell-holes and the rubbish of passing troops. Beyond the deserted village pillars of black smoke spoiled the blue summer sky. The murmur of high, invisible aircraft and the growl of distant artillery never stopped.

The originals in the squad had seen it all many times before. Only the landscape changed but the litter, destruction and stench were monotonously the same. They passed a clutter of traffic control signs, a smashed truck and a bombed-out church. They kept clear of the roadside, where uncleared mines were marked by a barrier of dirty white tapes and by danger-warning boards.

They rounded a bend in the road and came face to face with a tank. It was parked outside a house and filled the street from wall to wall. The door of the house was open. They stared up at the tank like urchins; a massive beast of steel crouching between its tracks, looking down at them along its depressed gun barrel.

The tank was unattended, but from within the house could be heard men's voices shouting, the shuffle of boots and a heavy bumping noise. Craig contemplated with a frown the seemingly abandoned Sherman tank with the name *Daisy May IV* painted in white on its turret. Along its sleek, steel flank had been painted, very neatly, a list of places and dates that proudly proclaimed the fighting record of the *Daisy May's* crew. *Dunkirk 1940*, *El Alamein 1942*, *Salerno 1943*, *Ponte Norte*—the British army could boast of no finer battle scars. And now, scrawled in cruder printing, was the lettering *Caen 1944*.

At that moment the tank's crew emerged from the doorway of the house, carrying between them an upright piano. The village had been deserted by its inhabitants. Passing troops had stripped these houses of everything movable; everything, apparently, but this aged piano; and now that, too, was going to war.

The four men, wearing black berets and tank overalls, staggered into the road, each stooping beneath the weight of his corner of the piano. They were shouting the usual confusion of advice to each other in a bedlam of Cockney, Welsh and Yorkshire accents. "Your end up a bit!" "Round to the right!" "Easy on, Charlie!"

Backing out of the door carrying his share of the piano, the tank sergeant spotted Craig and his men. "Won't be a minute, mate," he grunted, gesturing with his thumb towards the tank. There was a discordant jangle of strings as they put the piano down beside the tank and paused for breath after their exertions.

The sergeant, a tall, dour-looking man with close-cropped hair, took off his beret and stuffed it under the epaulette of his overalls. Mopping his brow, he surveyed with quiet satisfaction the old piano with its elaborate stand for sheet music and its ornate legs supporting the keyboard.

"Come in very handy this will," he said, half to Craig and half to himself. "The lad 'ere," he indicated the youngest of the crew "plays it like a bloody Paderewski." He paused for another deep breath. "Pick it up," he said to his men, stooping himself to the task of lifting the piano onto the tank.

Craig, a faint, bemused smile creasing his tough face, nodded.

"Enjoy yourself," he said, and casting a glance towards Grogan, the biggest man in his squad, he added, "Give him a hand, Moose."

Grogan, handing his rifle to Trower, leaped onto the Sherman and in a few moments of tugging and heaving the the piano stood upright on the tank's sloping deck.

Craig shouted, "Enjoy yourself." The British sergeant raised two fingers in derisive reply.

Craig gave an arm signal and the Americans shook out again into file, plodding towards the front line.

Behind them, working swiftly and expertly, the English tankmen settled the piano on some sandbags and lashed it to the side of the turret exactly opposite its menacing 75 mm. gun.

From inside the house came a small wooden stool which they also secured with ropes on top of the tank and facing the piano. The young, bright-faced Englishman sat down on the stool, faced the keyboard, stretched out his fingers and with whole-hearted relish began to bang out "*Bless 'em All.*" The sergeant and the other two men of the crew clambered down through the turret and into the bowels of the tank. The engines started, the tracks began to roll and the Sherman moved away along the road like an earth-ship, alongside the seemingly unending line of infantrymen marching stolidly to war.

In a few minutes the *Daisy May* had caught up with Craig's squad. The boy was still hammering away at "Bless 'em All". Competing with the noise of the engines could be heard from the turret the bellowing, singing voices of the tankmen inside. The tank, its engines still throbbing, paused beside Craig. The sergeant, wearing headphones and smoking a pipe, was poised authoritatively in the open turret. He nodded significantly at Craig. Craig got the message.

"All right, guys," he shouted. "A lift."

In an instant the squad had scrambled aboard—all ten of them. Not for a moment had the boy stopped pounding out his rollicking tune. The *Daisy May*, carrying its mixed cargo of Britons and Americans, continued its unruffled, swaying progress to the front. The men, grinning and waving at the foot-slogging troops they passed, raucously took up the song.

F... 'em all, f... 'em all,
The long and the short and the tall.
F... all the sergeants and W.O. Ones,
F... all the corporals and their bastard sons.

'Cos we're saying good-bye to them all,
As back to their billets they crawl.
You'll get no promotion this side of the ocean,
So cheer up my lads, f... 'em all.

Not till they got to the firing-line did they stop singing.

* * *

It's like knocking off clay pigeons in a shooting gallery, thought Craig as he studied the pillbox through his binoculars. He was lying on his stomach on a high ridge commanding an uninterrupted view of the saddle of ground beneath. The pillbox had been sited to command the junction of two roads running below it but the Americans had outflanked it on this even higher ground.

The aspirin-like mound of cement looked pathetically vulnerable in its isolation at the foot of the ridge. Through his field-glasses Craig had spotted the shimmer of light and shade at the bunker's slits that proved it was still occupied. The divisional advance had probably been too quick for these Germans to abandon this sitting-duck of a target.

Strung out along the ridge, the squad kept out of sight and waited for orders. Craig knew it was only a question of time before the Germans would try to get out of the pillbox. Once he got them in the open and away from the bunker, they'd probably give up when they realized the hopelessness of their position. He'd have to detach a couple of men to take them back to the Company P.W. point. There were probably six or seven Krauts in there.

Cautiously lifting his binoculars so that the sunlight would not convey a warning gleam to the pillbox, Craig was delighted to see that the bunker's steel door was slowly opening. For just a moment he caught a glimpse of a German steel helmet peering out and then it disappeared into the square of inner blackness. The steel door remained open.

Putting his binoculars down, Craig signalled to Chase and Grogan who were on either side of him. They raised their rifles to their shoulders and as they did so the rest of the squad followed suit. Peering expectantly along their rifle barrels, the men waited.

They had not long to wait. Out of the bunker's doorway they could see the tiny figure of a German soldier stealthily emerging. He was followed by two others. All three held their rifles at the ready and moved away from the pillbox in an apprehensive crouch. Craig held them fixed in his binoculars. There were others inside the bunker who would come out if they felt it safe. Once he had them strung out in the open country...

Just then a rifle shot came from the ridge. It raised a tiny spray of dust at the foot of the leading German. In an instant the three men had scuttled back into the pillbox slamming the steel door behind them.

Craig was furious.

"Stupid idiot!" he shouted to the men on his right where the shot had come from. "Who fired that shot?"

There was a moment's guilty silence as the men looked at each other. The combat veterans in the squad glared at the fresh replacements. It was Riggs at the far end of the line. He raised his right hand and sheepishly pulled his helmet down over his head to indicate his chagrin. He had been fumbling for a cigarette and accidentally squeezed the trigger.

Before Craig could reply or investigate, he was diverted by the sound of approaching footsteps. Striding out from the clump of trees on the wooded slope behind him came a group of soldiers wearing British battledress. The shoulder-flash *France* on their sleeves revealed who they were and the striped braid on their leader's epaulettes told Craig he was a Lieutenant of the Free French Forces.

Crawling away from the ridge for a few yards, Craig got up and went forward to meet the Lieutenant. Behind the officer and still emerging from the clump of trees were a number of Free French, including a stocky sergeant carrying a light machine-gun. The Lieutenant signalled his men to stay where they were as he moved towards Craig.

"We heard a shot. Do you have any problems, Sergeant?" The question was asked in a friendly tone and with hardly a trace of a French accent.

Craig pointed over the ridge towards the pillbox.

"We almost had them out, sir, but some stupid idiot fired and scared them back in."

The Lieutenant studied the ground in front of him. Craig could now see his face clearly. He was undoubtedly handsome. Or, at least, he had been. His left eye was covered by a black eye-patch and his fine, regular features were distorted by a thick scar that ran in a jagged weal from his hair-line right down his left cheek almost to his chin. The scar was relatively new.

"I think we can help you," the Lieutenant said, taking the binoculars Craig had offered him.

With his Sergeant he crawled to the edge of the ridge and joined the squad still waiting there. Settled there, the two Frenchmen trained their field-glasses on the pillbox. Just as they did so, the steel door slowly opened and they could see a helmeted German emerging carrying a white flag. Behind him, with their hands up, came five more Germans.

The Lieutenant lowered his glasses and irritation was written on his scarred face.

"Merde!" he swore, snatching the light machine-gun from his Sergeant. Sitting bolt upright, he fired from the hip in short, sharp bursts at the unarmed Germans below. His aim was accurate. The German with the flag was hit and dropped almost instantly. The others, bewildered, hesitated for a moment and then scrambled back into the shelter of the pillbox. Just before the door could be shut, the last German was riddled with bullets and toppled over backwards outside the bunker with his arms flung wide in a stiff, arched fall.

Impassively, the Lieutenant continued to fire at the pillbox. When the magazine was empty, he fitted a new one on to the machine-gun with the swift, expert movements of a battle veteran. Craig, puzzled, watched the Frenchman in silence as he continued to spray the door and slits of the pillbox with bullets. The white flag appeared again, waving frantically through one of the slits. It was greeted with a burst of bullets and was quickly withdrawn.

A few moments later the Germans, blindly trying to reply to this implacable attacker who would not recognize a surrender, fired a few harmless shots in reply.

A quick smile flitted across the Lieutenant's face. He lowered his gun and stopped firing.

"Ah, good!" he said. "Now they're resisting."

Politely, with almost old-world courtesy, he turned to Craig.

"I tell you what, Sergeant," he said. "Just move your men back and let them rest for a while. We will take over now, if you permit."

Craig never argued about an order to rest his men. He took the binoculars and led his squad away from the edge of the ridge. They grouped themselves in two rows on a small hillock behind the Lieutenant, relaxed, lit cigarettes and settled back to watch the show.

The French Sergeant, bending low, ran to his platoon waiting near the woods, gave them some rapid instructions and returned to the Lieutenant with two more men. Meanwhile the Lieutenant, now lying on his stomach, continued his intermittent firing at the pillbox. He paused for a few moments to take out a tin box of cigars, light one and then holding it in his left hand continued to fire the machine-gun with his right. The two soldiers who had come back with the Sergeant took up positions beside their officer and joined in with their rifles in peppering the bunker with bullets.

This covering fire from the ridge kept the Germans in the pillbox away from the slits. The reason became clear when another party of Frenchmen began to work their way downhill.

The Americans were exchanging speculations about all this; except for Sergeant Craig who was silent and deeply, professionally interested. He noted the equipment that the French storming party (as they seemed to be) carried, and drew certain conclusions. He had a half-hatched guess as to what they were up to, but he could not see the reason for it. He noted particularly their superb eye for terrain as they moved downhill, almost always in dead ground shielded by some contour from the enemy, and only occasionally making a short exposed dash to a new position under cover of the Lieutenant's harassing fire from the ridge. Good soldiers, these.

They were on level ground now, five of them, and Craig was now sure of their purpose; for they wormed up to the blind spots of the pillbox and began to grub under the walls. They were planting the satchels and he knew what the satchels contained. He had worked with engineers before.

Ignorant of these intruders crouched under their blind flank walls the occupants of the pillbox cautiously pushed the white flag out again. Again it was met with a burst of fire from the ridge.

It vanished. A few pathetic rifle shots spattered from the slits. The engineers lay almost beneath the slits and worked on like busy gardeners.

The assault engineers raced back up the hill. Two of them carried a revolving wooden coil which unrolled a trail of wire behind them. The wire ran from the top of the ridge down to the pillbox. The French Sergeant quickly attached the wire to some knobs on the plunger box which he had beside him. He lifted the box and carried it to the Lieutenant who was still smoking and firing with disdainful relish.

The Lieutenant raced his fingers over the plunger box, checking knobs and wires. There was silence. As a lone shot cracked from the bunker he pressed down the plunger.

The explosion thudded against the summer quiet as the pillbox rose into the air, cracking before their eyes into flying masonry, and disintegrated. The site was hidden by a cloud of smoke that rolled up the hill, slowed and thinned away.

Craig and his squad had watched the whole affair in silent fascination. Craig looked up. The Lieutenant was strolling towards him.

"There you are, Sergeant," said the Frenchman, as pleasantly as if he were inviting him to sit down to dinner. "You can have your men go down and check up, if you like, but I hardly think it will be necessary. Good hunting, eh?"

He started to move away and then stopped a few yards off as if struck by an afterthought. Perhaps it was the blank look in Craig's face that made him pause. His eyes stared steadily into Craig's. His voice grew flatter and harsher.

"Oh, and if you feel you have to make a report about this, my name is Cohn...So long."

Swinging his machine-gun onto his right shoulder, the Lieutenant strode away down the road that ran along the top of the ridge. The sappers, carrying their ammunition boxes, coils and plunger boxes, followed him in two ragged columns. Craig, his hands on his hips, watched them go in silence. So did the squad.

* * *

It was one more halt outside one more Norman town. When the orders came down the line the men sank down at the roadside and sprawled, not caring. They no longer had any curiosity, either about an order to halt or an order to move. They just obeyed in apathy. They were in that state where a week is too far back to remember. They never had any consciousness of place, for wherever they trudged, they always seemed to be in the same field or the same broken town; always dog-tired.

After a while more orders came, and groups of men moved into the surrounding fields and orchards. They put down their gear and began to dig. Trenching tools rose and fell in a resigned apathetic rhythm.

Joe Craig, now, by that relentless instrument of seniority, the death of others, raised to Staff-Sergeant, had his own orders. He steered a jeep cautiously into a town which had suffered the misfortune of being a German strongpoint. Allied bombers had come. The Wehrmacht had left. All that Craig could see were heaps of rubble spilled into the roadway and remnants of walls rising at the roadsides like broken teeth.

Craig was looking for a house with No. 48 as its address. He didn't know the name of the street. Nor did it matter since there were no street signs nor, indeed, streets. The Company was resting in a near-by orchard and would be taking over the town in a day or two. Staff-Sergeant Craig had been told to reconnoitre the place for a suitable field headquarters. Someone had said that No. 48 was the only house still standing.

It wasn't difficult to find. It stood strangely intact, surrounded on every side by jagged brick shells ripped open to the sky. Lace curtains were even billowing out through the open, unshuttered windows. The curtains seemed an indecent reminder of civilized life.

The house was built in the solid, respectable style of the comfortable French bourgeois. Its sombre façade was lightened by the symmetrical grace of its windows. It was surrounded by a high stone wall out of which the bombs had clouted a gap.

Craig, after checking the number 48 on one of the brick posts against the slip of paper in his hand, drove his jeep through the gap into a small garden. There was a short, curving driveway in front of the house and standing askew, several yards away from the driveway and almost touching the wall of the house, was a sleek, red European sports car. It had obviously been lifted there by bomb blast.

He climbed the short flight of steps to the door. Expertly, his fingertips brushed around the perimeter of the door for wires leading to booby traps. Satisfied, he tried the handle of the door and found it locked. With the butt of his rifle, he smashed at the lock. It refused to give way. He put his right shoulder hard against the door and it flew open.

Blinded for a moment by the gloom of the interior, Craig paused at the door, his eyes focused in the new light, and he saw that a woman was watching him from the other end of the hall. She stood in a doorway. He sensed that cellar stairs were behind her. She was clutching a pink blanket which she had wrapped around herself so that it covered her from her shoulders to her toes. She was blonde, not young, dishevelled, dirty and plainly terrified.

"Excuse me," said Craig, framed in an oblong of sunlight. With his rifle held across his chest, his unshaven face and uniform thick with the dust of the road, and the straps of his helmet hanging loose on either side of his face, he realized how he must look to her. He wanted to reassure her.

"Parlez-vous anglais?" he asked, speaking almost all the French he knew.

"Yes, I do," said the woman. "Can I help you?"

She spoke quietly, but even Craig could recognize the cultivation in her voice and accent. He was relieved that he would not have to cope with the situation in gestures and pidgin English.

"Yes, ma'am," he said, with a mixture of authority and deference. "We're coming in tomorrow or the day after, and we might want to use your house for field headquarters. I'm supposed to check it."

The woman moved out of the doorway and began mechanically to tidy up the room. She brushed some broken glass off an elegant, antique chest of drawers. It was obvious that she had been under some tremendous nervous pressure and that she was only holding herself together by a great exercise of will.

"Oh, I see," she said. Her voice was vague and automatic. "Yes, of course. I'm afraid it's not in very good condition."

"Neither is anything else around here," said Craig, moving into the centre of the hall.

The woman continued her somnambulistic tour of the room. She straightened a gracefully-carved wooden ornament on the wall, picked up a vase and then, dropping the blanket, sat wearily down on a handsome chair covered in maroon needle-point.

"Soldiers in the house. . ." Her words tailed off.

"You'll get paid. Sooner or later anyway." Craig was trying to be as polite and comforting as he knew.

"Yes, I understand," the woman murmured.

Now that he had grown accustomed to the light, Craig could see that beneath her grime and anxiety she had a beautifully-boned, sensitive face with eyes whose depths stirred. Her blonde hair, hanging in unkempt strands, was obviously used to meticulous care. There was a masculine fullness about her nose and lips that gave compelling strength and character to her face. She was in her early thirties.

She fumbled with the buttons of her grey, well-cut stylish suit, now soiled and wrinkled. Craig was impressed by her, respectful of her, without being physically interested in her. For one thing, most men in or just out of battle are sexually numbed. For another he preferred brunettes. Blondes made him nervous, particularly ritzy blondes.

"You speak good English," he said.

"Thank you," she replied, lifelessly. Folding her arms, she got up from her chair. "I'll show you the house."

Craig followed her into the living-room. It was a warm, pleasant room reflecting the culture and sophisticated tastes of those who had lived in it. It contained a piano, shelves of beautifully bound books, period furniture, and oil paintings and gouaches that ranged in style from minor Impressionists to surrealists. Now dust and fallen plaster covered everything like some greyish scurf. Some of the books and paintings were stacked in the centre of the room as if ready for packing. Broken glass littered the carpet.

Standing just inside the doorway, Craig had already summed up the room's military potentialities.

"Adjutant's office," he muttered.

The woman wandered about the room as if she were uncertain that it was still really there. She straightened pictures on the wall and sorted out some objets d'art on the mantelpiece in a dazed, almost instinctive, manner.

Craig was dully exhausted, and the style of the room was strange to him, but he was touched by the woman's motions, and he felt an intruder. He said, "Must be pretty nice when it's all fixed up."

"My husband and I used to come here whenever Paris got too much for us," she said, almost to herself, as she studied a small painting lying on the piano. "And in the summers, of course. It's lovely here in the summer."

She wandered, still in her dream-like way, to the centre

of the room and knelt down to look at the stacked paintings.

"What are you doing here now?" asked Craig. "No one's supposed to be here now. This town was supposed to be evacuated a week ago."

"When we heard there would be fighting here, I thought I might have time to get some paintings and some personal things that were very precious to us. I suppose it was stupid of me. I came too late and I couldn't get away in time."

She spoke in a flat, unemotional voice, almost drained of feeling. She got up from the pictures on the floor and went over to the book shelves where she began leafing through a book. Everything she looked at or touched was merely a way of passing time, of restoring her mental equilibrium, of re-assuring herself that her nightmare was over.

"You were here all during the bombing?" said Craig, a note of incredulity in the question.

"Yes."

"Alone?"

"Yes."

"Weren't you scared?"

"Yes. I was petrified." She paused, remembering it all. "I've never been so frightened in all my life. Last night was the worst of all..." Then she broke off, pulling herself together, and determined to erase the memory. "But you want to see the rest of the house." She moved towards the living-room door.

"Yes, ma'am," said Craig, about to follow her. His eye caught again one of the paintings on the wall. It was a stark vision of a lighthouse by Chirico, gaunt and forbidding. He stared at it, trying to understand.

"You came back to get stuff like this?" he said.

She looked back over her shoulder.

"Yes," she said, flatly.

She waited for him in the hall.

"Our officers are nice fellows," said Craig consolingly, "I mean they'll be careful. I mean, there's some of them that are stupid idiots, but these ones are okay."

"I really don't care," she said, in that vague, disembodied way. "I shall never return here anyway." She motioned with her left hand towards another door. "That's the dining-room...but I imagine your first concern is the sleeping accommodations. This way, please."

He followed her up the stairs. He noticed how poised and gracefully her body moved even though she was in such an exhausted and neurotic state. He tried to keep his eyes off her shapely legs which looked provocative in spite of the badly-laddered stockings.

"Where were you during the bombing?" he asked, as they climbed the stairs.

"In the cellar."

"Oh, you've got a cellar. That's good. We can stick your furniture down there." Craig was determined she should know they would be careful with her things. "Were you down there all the time?"

"Yes, all the time."

"Did you have any food?"

"At first. I was too greedy to make it last and I finished everything yesterday."

They had now climbed three flights of stairs and were at the top of the house.

"That was the cold," said Craig. "Cold always makes you hungry. You must have been freezing down there."

The woman stopped at the top of the stairs to catch her breath. She must have been very weak. The climb had tired her out. She went on talking.

"Yes, it was terribly cold. I had one blanket but it wasn't enough, and I was too frightened to go out for another one. But the worst of it was the rats..." There was genuine awe in her voice. "It's odd, I never dreamed there were rats in this house...It's very odd."

She pushed open a bedroom door and gestured him in. The patina of dust and plaster could not disguise the tasteful femininity of the room—the rose-coloured, flowered wallpaper, the elegant dressing-table with its mirror miraculously intact, the delicate bedside lamps with pink shades.

"My room," said the woman, passing through it into the adjoining bathroom.

"What?" said Craig, just coming through the door.

"My bedroom," she repeated.

Craig took a quick look at the room and studied its dimensions.

"Captain's room," he said.

Craig was visibly impressed by the bathroom's modern plumbing. It even had a bidet, he noted. Useful for washing the Captain's socks.

The woman was now in the next room. The bathroom linked the two rooms.

"My husband's room," she said, as Craig entered.

Again the taste was impeccable. Shelves of books, etchings, a couple of small pieces of sculpture, a collection of pipes—as masculine as her room was feminine.

"We'll put two Lieutenants in here," said Craig. "Got any more rooms?"

The woman had sat down on the bed.

"There's a small servant's room and a bathroom at the back of the kitchen," she said. "Perhaps I could stay there until it's safe to leave."

"That's all the rooms you've got?"

"I'm afraid that's all," she said, getting up from the bed and straightening up some objects on the desk. "We have no guest room. Philippe and I never wanted to share the house with anyone when we came here."

She moved towards the wardrobe to shut its open door.

The mention of her husband's name suddenly annoyed Craig.

"Where is your husband now?" he asked. "Why didn't he come instead of you."

"He was shot three months ago." The words were so emotionless she might have been commenting on the weather. "He...Philippe..." She lost her way in the sentence.

"Actually this is the first time I've been here since they took him away."

Craig realized he had provoked her into a painful memory. He was embarrassed. In the silence, his stomach rumbled loudly. He put his hand over it.

"I must be hungry," he said, apologetically. "I haven't eaten since six this morning. You must be starving, too. I've got some stuff in the jeep. Would you like to cook it?"

For a moment the woman lost her air of resigned inertia. Her eyes reflected her hunger.

"Thank you," she said. "I should be most grateful. Could we do it now, do you suppose?"

"Sure," said Craig.

The woman moved quickly to the door. The spur of food had given her some extra strength. She stopped, realizing that she might have been impolite.

"I'm sure you're dying to bathe, but the water went off the first day."

The thought of a bath brought a rare grin to Craig's unshaven face.

"Lady," he said, "it's been so long since I had a bath, I'd probably drown in a bath-tub. But I've got plenty of water out there in the jeep to cook with anyway."

He'd hardly finished speaking when he noticed a glazed look come into her eyes and her body began to waver and grow limp. He caught her just as she started to fall. His support steadied her. She freed herself from his awkward grasp and straightened up, shaking her head slightly.

"I'm sorry," she said. "I got dizzy for a moment."

"You're just about knocked out. Can you make it?"

"Oh, yes." She seemed to have recovered. "Yes, I can make it. Thank you."

Slowly, she descended the stairs to the kitchen while he went out to the jeep for their rations.

The woman talked as Craig ate. They were in the large, cool kitchen finishing off the meal. They had used some of the precious water for washing their faces and the woman's strong, bold beauty, now that her long hair was brushed back from her forehead, was strikingly evident. Craig concentrated on his food, spooning it into his mouth with voracious relish and swilling it down with loud gulps of wine. The dame could certainly cook, was the dominant thought that crossed his mind. She had done wonders with the canned meat. It showed what could be done with Army chow if the cooks could only cook.

He knew she was talking to him. He could hear snatches of her conversation but he preferred to concentrate on the food and the wine. He was too tired to keep track of her processes of thought and he had long ago mentally dismissed her as a "highbrow dame." He said nothing.

The food and drink, the cigarettes Craig had given her, the company of another human being and the cessation of the bombing, had unravelled her. Her mind, as numbed and cramped as her body by the nightmare confinement in the cellar, was stretching itself and coming back to life. In the damp darkness of her underground cave, with the giant tread of bombardment trampling upon her senses, she had dreamed herself away into an abstract, lyrical world. Now she was freeing those thoughts from the constricting prison of her mind. She was unconscious of the fact that her audience was neither listening nor caring. The words came in spasms with the over-eagerness of someone talking to a priest or a psychiatrist.

"And the bombs kept falling and the planes never stopped and the big guns roared and roared and I was sure the house would collapse around me and bury me and I would never be found except as a corpse." She smoked, resting her chin on her long, thin hand, and stared into space as if it were some deep, unfathomable well.

"And at first I thought I would lose my mind, and I think I would have but I forced myself to think and remember every line of poetry I ever knew and loved. I'm sure it saved my sanity. I know now that the body is nothing but the mind is everything. I remember, just when it seemed it would never end I kept thinking of that line... the universe is nothing but a flaw in the Purity of Non-Being..."

She picked up Craig's lighter from the table to re-light the cigarette which had gone out between her fingers. She kept talking all the while.

"Do you know the writing of Paul Valéry?" she asked. "In translation, I mean, of course. To my mind he's our greatest modern poet. Do you know *Le Cimetière Marin*? It's always been a favourite of mine."

She paused to think of the words.

> "*Ce toit tranquille où marchent les colombes.*
> *Entre les pins palpités, entre les tombes...*"

Craig was mopping up the remnants of the food on his plate with the help of an Army biscuit. The woman's chatter meant nothing to him. He put his cup clumsily on to his saucer and the clatter disturbed her flow of words. She suddenly became aware that she was talking to herself in the presence of an uninterested head bent, munching, over a plate.

"I'm sorry," she said, turning her eyes towards him.

"I've been chattering like an idiot. You must think me odd."

Craig swallowed the last drains of his coffee.

"Well, you've been under a strain," he said.

A gentle belch, which he could not control, erupted from him.

"Excuse me," he said, "My stomach's been ruined in the Army."

The woman studied him across the table. Her eyes were brooding.

"In the last days of Rome," she murmured, "the Goths were brought in to save the Empire from the German tribes... Thank you for liberating us."

"You're welcome," said Craig. He reached for his wine glass and found it empty.

"Could I have a little more wine, please?" he said.

"Oh yes, of course. I'm sorry." She got up from the table and returned in a few moments with a fresh bottle.

Craig was stretching himself, enjoying the sensual pleasure that the ache of fatigue affords when it flows through a relaxed body. His mouth was open in a wide yawn.

"You're tired," said the woman. "Must you return tonight?"

"I don't know. I guess not." While he was drawing the cork from the bottle, Craig considered the situation. Headquarters didn't expect him to report back about the house until morning. He could do as he liked until then. The prospect of sleeping in a decent bed was too tempting to miss.

"Could I stay here, somewhere?" he asked. Determined that she should not mistake his motives, he added, "I wouldn't bother you. I mean, you wouldn't have to be scared or anything."

"I wouldn't be frightened," she said. "I don't think I could ever be frightened again. I'll see what I can do about Philippe's room."

Left to himself, Craig poured out a glass of wine and leaned back in his chair. An overwhelming tiredness suddenly took hold of him. Pushing the plates away from in front of him, he put his arms on the table and dropped his head on to them. In a moment, he was asleep.

Some twenty minutes later, the woman was shaking him awake.

"The room's ready," she said, gently, and led him upstairs. The climb up the stairs cleared his drowsy mind. She left him at the door and went into the adjoining room.

Craig could see that the woman had taken some trouble to clean up her husband's room. The floor had been swept, the desk and chairs had been dusted and fresh sheets and pillow cases had been placed upon the bed.

Craig took off his boots, socks, trousers and shirt. He crawled between the sheets wearing only his underclothes. He lay on his back and luxuriated in the touch of fresh linen and the sensation of having his clothes off. It seemed months since he had felt his own naked thighs and legs touching each other. He took a cigarette from the packet on the table beside him and smoked.

He vaguely thought about the woman in the room next door. What would she do if he made a pass at her? The prospect of a woman's body made him think of his wife, Anne. She had been living with his parents in Scranton, Pennsylvania, ever since he went overseas. But it couldn't be much fun for her staying with an elderly retired coal-miner. Her letters didn't complain, but he could detect the boredom between the lines. He'd get her a real smart place after the war. Near one of the big camps. He'd be at least a staff-sérgeant when this was all over. Maybe even an officer. The country would have proper respect for professional soldiers this time. There'd be good pay and a decent pension. And Anne. He thought of her large, comforting breasts and the feel of her wide, fleshy buttocks. But he was too tired to be excited by his thoughts. Sighing comfortably, he snuffed out the cigarette and, turning over, went to sleep.

He opened his eyes and wondered what had awakened him so quickly. Instinctively he grabbed the rifle which he had left beside the bed and raising himself on one elbow called out, "Who's there?"

He had no idea how long he had slept but it must have been a considerable time since his mind was clear and unfatigued. The artillery was in full cry, the slam and thud of guns filling the night. Muzzle-flashes seared intermittently across the gaping window-space, and in one of the flashes that lit the room, he could see the Frenchwoman in a far corner of the room, pressed against the walls.

She was on her knees, dressed only in a white slip, her hands pressed to her mouth quivering with terror. The house shook under the inferno of sound and blast, and each successive reverberation made her wince with fear. Tears stained her cheeks and she could barely control her trembling lips enough to speak.

"I'm sorry," she whimpered. "I didn't want to disturb you, but I'm frightened. I just wanted to stay here... near somcone."

Craig listened to the shattering noise outside. He had slept through hundreds of bombardments of this kind. They had become a routine background of his life.

"Those are our guns, I think," he said.

All the noises of the night seemed to roar around the house, shaking it but failing to gain entry, so that the bedroom seemed like a little black cell of silence in which, however quietly they spoke, their voices sounded loud and unfamiliar.

"It's not the guns, it's the planes." Her voice cracked with desperation as she tried to fight back her hysteria. "They were bombing till a moment ago. And you never woke up. I slept for a while, and then I woke up, and I haven't been able to sleep since. I've been sitting here for hours frightened to death. I was determined not to wake you. I thought you must surely wake up with all the noise, but you slept. My God, how you slept! And in all that noise! I don't know how you can sleep with all that...Oh, I can't be alone. I just can't stand it any more." Her teeth began to chatter. She cringed, an abject heap. "Oh, please I want to stay here. I can't stand any more. I won't bother you...Please..."

Craig could now distinguish a new noise added to the din outside. The bombers were coming back. Their droning swelled. Into the uproar pierced the whistle of bombs. The bombs roared, the earth shook and all the shutters of the house rattled.

Conscious only of the need to give comfort Craig drew aside his blanket and motioned her into his bed. Slowly she rose and then eagerly, almost like a child, she ran from her corner into his bed. She huddled against him, her head on his chest, and sobbed bitterly.

It was some time later that he asked, "Do you feel better?" He could feel the movement of her cheek against his skin as she nodded. He felt no more desire for her now than he had the evening before; only an elementary pleasure in her warmth, and the deep primal consciousness of human companionship in the weight, the movements, the pressure of her limbs mingled with his in the darkness. He stroked her firm sharp breasts because it seemed the natural thing to do.

Suddenly her lips were clamped to his. He could feel her fingernails digging into his shoulders and the violence of her embrace. She took possession of him with sharp and urgent movements, assailing him in the darkness like a demonic little animal. She uttered a little sound of release in her throat. A few moments later she whispered—this cultivated Frenchwoman, lying against the half-washed body of an unknown man, with the flash and roar of death all around and death prowling the sky overhead in search of her—"All the same, this is better than the purity of Non-Being."

He could only hold her and wonder.

She awoke first. Morning sunlight filled the room. All the guns had stopped and the silence was a balm. She was only dimly aware of her surroundings. Across her chest lay an outstretched male arm. She could hear a faint snoring.

Stupid with sleep, she opened her eyes on the hairy arm without seeing its blue tattooing of twin hearts and names. Sinking back into sleep, she turned her back towards the man, muttering, "C'est un rêve. Dors, Philippe. Dors."

Craig stirred but did not waken. She closed her eyes and joined him in exhausted slumber.

* * *

Overnight the war left them behind. They lay down in the dark, filthy and tired after thirty hours of "hedge-hopping"—clearing the enemy from one deadly hedgerow after another, preparing the way for other troops to break out of the Normandy bridgehead. They were in another one of those endless orchards. A battery of mediums moved into a field nearby at the same time and banged away from beneath draped camouflage netting, but it did not stop them from sleeping.

They woke up next morning and everything was quiet. The sky was clear and blue. The guns had limbered up and gone off, leaving a litter of cartridge cases and boxes. For a few days the whole American Army seemed to be passing on the road by their field, tanks, guns, tanks, guns, infantry; and the whole U.S. Air Force seemed to be overhead. Then the pursuit passed them by. The sky was empty. The road was empty except for an occasional lorry that roared past, like a repentant straggler, and vanished in a cloud of white dust.

It was uncanny. They were spared, reprieved. They read the daily battle-reports from the front, but they could not even hear the fighting. There was only the vast quietness, the intermittent mumble of invisible aircraft in the sky, the sun, the deserted road, and the Company busy with light hearts at domestic chores.

The old and the wise, who by now were few, knew that they were being rested, and that one day at short notice they would be shovelled into the furnace again. But most of the men seemed to accept the illusion that the Company had been forgotten, mislaid, as it were, by the Army; that it might be here for months before the Brass remembered it again.

Of course, rumours thrived. New ones came up with every ration delivery. The Germans were going to surrender. The Germans were collecting armour for a big drive to throw the Allies back into the sea. The unit was going to be sent to the States for a long rest. The unit was going to be shipped out to the Pacific. The British were doing fine. The British were in a bad state. Eisenhower was going to be replaced by Georgie Patton. Georgie Patton—ah, who cared?

They were happy. War was for some other guy. They relaxed in the shade of the orchard. Occasionally a local farmer would turn up ready to trade eggs or Calvados for cigarettes or K-rations. Sometimes one of the men would mysteriously acquire a chicken or a pig and nobody asked any questions as they ate their share of this loot.

Trower spotted him first. The boy was leaning against a shed, with his legs crossed, watching the squad lining up for breakfast. At first glance he looked like a small German. He wore a German soldier's tunic so long that it almost reached his knees. The sleeves had been rolled up several inches to allow his hands to protrude. His khaki trousers had been crudely scissored to his length and had a gaping tear at the left knee. He wore army boots and a big-peaked Afrika Korps cap.

He was thirteen or fourteen years old and his face was so delicately moulded that he might have been a girl. He had brooding, dark eyes, a straight nose and full, pouting lips. He watched the men warily as they shuffled, mess tins in hand, past two cooks who were filling their plates with porridge and their tin cups with coffee.

Trower, just behind Chase in the food queue, thought the boy looked hungry. He was just a kid and there was plenty of food around. Hell, the American army could afford it!

"Hey, kid!" he shouted. "Viens ici."

The boy, carrying a pathetic bundle of belongings, trotted across to the canteen, his diffidence gone, a lift of bravado now showing in his stride. He greeted Trower with a broad, impudent grin. Even Chase, who was in front of Trower, could not help being amused by his looks and his manner.

"Avez-vous faim?" said Trower.

"You bet. Plenty." The boy's English was surprisingly good.

"Where did you learn to speak English?" said Trower, one eye on the boy beside him and one eye on the moving breakfast line in front of him.

"With soldier. Me all the time with soldiers. Germans. English. Canucks. Yanks." The boy kept up with Trower as he advanced towards the steaming pots of food.

"Germans, eh? And Yanks," said Chase, joining in the conversation. "You're a busy little guy, aren't you?"

"Sure."

"Whose food you like the best?" asked Chase.

"Oh, English and Canucks good. Yanks better. Plenty manger, plenty cigarettes, plenty chocolate. Plenty."

The shuffling line had stopped for a moment. Trower put his hand on the boy's shoulder. He liked the boy's openness.

"Well, you'd better get in line with us then."

"Okay," said the boy, his wariness all gone and now replaced by a cocky brightness and assurance. He edged into the line between Chase and Trower. Around his waist were tied, on a piece of string, a mess-tin and cup. A second's fumbling and he was holding out the kitchen utensils like someone very familiar with army routine. Trower took a fork from his tunic pocket and offered it to him.

"Oh no, thank you," said the boy, indicating he had his own fork in his pocket. "Yanks very good. Yanks best gentlemen. Toujours gentlemen. You got cigarettes?"

"Not before breakfast," Chase said, giving the boy a nudge. "Keep moving."

When they reached the men serving up the food, one of the servers hesitated at the sight of this strange boy holding out his mess kit. It was strictly against regulations to hand out Army food to civilians.

"Go on, give the kid some," said Chase in a bantering tone. "He's just changed sides. Come on. Come on."

The cook was still doubtful.

"You heard." The brusque bite of authority in Trower's voice amused Chase. He remembered his friend from way back. Now Corporal Trower was an old and terrible man to the changing stream of newcomers who formed the majority of the Company. War had carved grooves down from the corners of his mouth. Many experiences looked out from behind his eyes. His letters home were brief; there was nothing about the war in them any more. The server shrugged his shoulders and filled the boy's plate.

They squatted in the shade of an apple tree to eat their breakfast. Trower and Chase watched the boy wolfing his food with unashamed hunger. The lad's bravado, his naive cunning and his disenchanted acceptance of life was beginning to appeal to the lone wolf in Chase.

"Hey, Jacko," he called out to the boy. "Not so fast. You'll lose a couple of fingers."

The boy grinned and continued eating.

"What's your name?" asked Trower.

"Jean-Pierre."

"Where are you from?" said Chase.

The boy pointed to the hills behind them.

"Courcelle."

Chase and Trower looked at each other, somewhat surprised.

"That's twenty miles back. This kid's a traveller," said Chase. "How do you expect to get home tonight, John Peter?"

"I no go home." Jean-Pierre's answer was fierce with impatience. "No more home. Big fighting. Boom, boom."

"There's been no fighting back there in weeks," said Chase.

The boy paid no attention to Chase's remark.

"No home," he insisted. "Papa and mama go away. I stay with soldiers. Good with soldiers."

The men glanced at each other over the boy's head. He was going to be a problem. His story was not a novel one. They had often come across boys, particularly in Italy, who had become detached from their families. Some of them had been tiny waifs of six or seven who wandered across the plain like little prairie dogs from one group of soldiers to another.

"After breakfast," said Trower, trying to be his most

persuasive, "how'd you like a nice ride back in a real U.S. Army jeep?"

"No! No go back!"

"Don't be silly. You have to go back."

Jean-Pierre leaped to his feet trembling with temper. He clenched his fists, shaking them in front of him, and stamped his feet. Tears sprang to his eyes.

"No! Never! I never go back!"

Chase and Trower were taken aback by the fury of the boy's outburst.

"Hey, hey, relax! Eat," said Chase, pushing the boy down to the ground again and handing him the mug and plate he had dropped in his temper. He took some food from his own plate and heaped it on the boy's. "If you want to be a soldier, you have to learn to eat when you can. Most important thing in the army."

The extra food seemed to mollify the boy. He took a gulp of coffee from his cup.

"Thank you," he said. "I stay with you. You good fellers. No go with other soldiers."

"Thanks," said Chase drily.

They watched the boy as he resumed his eating. Every sign of his tantrum was gone.

Chase looked across at Trower and gave him a quick wink.

"Well, you've got to admit the kid's got good taste."

"Yeah," replied Trower, taking a deep drink from his cup, vaguely perplexed.

Throughout the day Jean-Pierre followed Chase and Trower about the camp. He walked with a happy swagger, and grinned impudently at everyone else as if advertising the fact that he was under their protection. After breakfast they sent him to a nearby stream and made him wash himself. Chase gave him a comb and he tore at his gleaming, curly hair until it was tidy. Trower gave him a spare shirt and dungarees to wear, and put those he discarded in a can of water, boiled them, scrubbed them and hung them on a branch to dry.

All the while Jean-Pierre chattered to them about his adventures with the Germans and the Canadians. The Canadians had taught him to swear in English, and he did this with enthusiasm. He spoke of the Germans so raptly and innocently that they might have been a favourite football team. He did not seem to be aware of any difference between the Germans and the Allies. They, and the Yanks and the Canucks, were soldiers, the same species; that was all; and he reported their doings as if he were some messenger carrying news from one branch of an accidentally divided family to another.

At midday Chase and Trower lay outside their two-man tent smoking and lazing. They were basking in the sun, the soft air and the luxury of having nothing to do. A loud shout of "Chow!" from the mess tent announced lunch. Chase raised himself on his left elbow and peered in the direction of the shout.

"Chow again," he said luxuriously, pushing his cap back from his eyes. "Now isn't that nice?"

He reached out to get his mess kit which was hanging on a branch overhead but before he could do so he could hear Jean-Pierre's voice crying. "No! No! No! No!"

The boy, who had been wringing out some clothes at a derelict bathtub near the men's tent, raced over and grabbed the mess kits of both men.

"I get! I get!" he said, running off in the direction of the mess tent.

Chase watched him appreciatively as the boy went jangling off with his load of mess tins. He liked being waited on.

"Now that's the way an army always should be," he said.

Trower frowned. "We ought to be getting him back to Courcelle."

"What for?" said Chase, taking out some cutlery from his tunic pocket. "What's the hurry? Couldn't this team use a mascot?"

"Sure. But what are we going to do when we leave? Shoot him? He ought to be home with his family."

"He's happy, isn't he? What's the problem?"

Trower shook his head doubtfully.

"Where'll he sleep?"

"With us," said Chase, pointing his knife at the two-man tent behind them. "Plenty of room in the Waldorf."

Jean-Pierre returned, whistling, with two mess kits brimming with food. Handing them to the two men, he hovered like a fussy little waiter, to hear their verdict on the food.

"Is good? Is okay?" he asked, eagerly.

"C'est bon," said Trower, nodding his head.

"Yeah. Is fine," said Chase, crooking his finger in a gourmet's gesture. "Just one thing. On your way back, get a little salt and pepper, hm?"

"Du sel! Du poivre! Oui!" said Jean-Pierre, delighted to be of service, and dashing off again in the direction of the canteen.

"Oui," said Chase, settling back comfortably against a tree, and looking across at Trower. "And you want to send that nice little boy back to starvation. I'm surprised at you, Corporal."

Trower dug into the brown stew on his plate and said nothing.

Evening came, and the camp prepared for sleep. Chase had told the boy that he would be sleeping with them in their two-man tent.

"Sure," he had answered, with a sly grin and a confiding drop of the voice. "I go with you. You good fellers. No go with other soldiers."

Chase and Trower had decided that the boy would

sleep between them. They had two blankets, one beneath them and the other as a covering.

Trower took off his boots, gaiters and combat jacket, crawled into the tiny tent first and pulled the blanket over him. Chase, waiting for Jean-Pierre to come from the latrine, called to him as he saw the boy approaching.

"Come on, John Peter. Get rid of the butt and let's go." He crawled into the tent and lay down beside Trower.

Jean-Pierre put out his cigarette by knocking it against his right foot and carefully placed the butt into his breast pocket. He followed Chase through the triangular entrance of the tent and knelt on the blanket at their feet. He slipped off his shirt and let his shorts fall to his knees. He stood up, kicked them away and went down on his knees again.

Trower, lying on his side, could see the boy's shadowy movements through half-closed eyes. Kneeling there, pale and slender in the transparent darkness, he had a posture that puzzled Trower faintly, the graceful and compliant posture of a girl crouching on a bed.

Jean-Pierre looked from Chase to Trower as if making some sort of choice. Then he lay down between them, turned towards Chase, and lifting his face voluptuously, put his arms round Chase's neck. Chase, too drowsy at first to take in what was happening, felt the boy's warm cheek brushing against his ear and the boy's naked leg pressing against his thigh. From Jean-Pierre's lips came cooing words in French in the pigeon murmur of an amorous girl.

Chase's angry snarl of surprise was explosive. He leaped up out of the blankets, blundered about in booming collisions with the wall of the tent, tore open the flap and bodily threw the boy out into the night. His clothes went flying after him.

"Did you ever see anything like it?" Chase was muttering to himself as he emerged from the tent in a fury. All his accustomed casualness and flippancy were gone. "The dirty little bastard!" The words were sticking in his throat. There was a film of sweat gleaming on his face.

"Did you ever see anything like it? Did you see that?" Chase said to Trower who had followed him out of the tent and was standing beside him. "Do you know what he thought we were after?" Apparently it was less Jean-Pierre's actions than what the boy thought to be in his mind that angered him. "Why, the dirty little...He deserves to be...A kid of that age? It's unbelievable!"

It was a few moments before Trower fully understood, and when he did he was bewildered. He was a young man in whom, after more than two years of war, innocence was always breaking through.

The two men could see Jean-Pierre near one of the sheds, fumbling with his clothes as he dressed. He was sobbing quietly.

"What do we do with him now?" asked Trower.

"Shoot him for all I care!"

"And wake up the whole camp?" said Trower, drily, setting off towards the boy.

After a moment's hesitation, Chase followed him. The night air had cooled his anger and he was beginning to realize that his indignation was a betrayal of his chosen character.

Jean-Pierre was leaning against the shed when they came up to him. His face was marred with tears. He had tried to light up the cigarette stub in his pocket but he had no matches. He put it away and tried to look defiant.

"We don't...What gave you the idea...?" said Trower, stumbling for words.

Jean-Pierre took no notice of him, but looked at Chase

with his face screwed up in an expression of baffled bitterness.

"Why you do this? What I do"? he asked Chase. "I think you like me."

Chase's anger flared again.

"What do you mean?"

"Surc we like you," said Trower, patiently trying to explain their feelings. "But not like that. It's wrong."

"Wrong!" Jean-Pierre shrugged his shoulders derisively and shaped his mouth in a disbelieving pout. "The Germans like me. English like me. Ah," he burst out, his anger gathering momentum, "the Germans good. Strong. Brave. The Germans good fighter. They not afraid of Yanks. They laugh at Yanks. Hm, the Americans." He filled his mouth with saliva and spat. They could hear the breath quickening and catching in his throat, and see the tremor in his shoulders as he was seized again by the smart of rejected affection.

They did not know how to talk to him. To Jean-Pierre any kind of morality was as incomprehensible as to a young animal. He did what he had been taught to do, and it was natural to him. It was impossible to chasten him, only to hurt him. All Chase and Trower had done in throwing him out of their tent was to outrage him. They did not know what else they could have done. They, too, were bewildered, outraged, upset. They stood over him helplessly.

All the same, both men knew that they could not leave him there alone, bruised and ashamed by his experience. Chase went back to the tent and began taking out their blankets and a ground sheet. Trower took off his jacket and placed it gently round the shivering boy.

"Let's go," he said, indicating the direction of the tent.

"No." The boy made an obstinate, defiant gesture with head and shoulders.

"Come on. Let's go," said Trower firmly gripping him by the shoulder and pushing him towards the tent. The boy resisted no longer and when he got to the tent gave one final, tear-stained look at Chase, before crawling in.

Silently, the two men prepared a sleeping place for themselves out in the open under one of the trees. Before lying down under his blanket, Chase turned to Trower.

"He goes back first thing in the morning." He spoke like a man who, even if his friend had the stripes, had the ultimate, natural authority.

Trower looked at him wryly and lit the butt of a cigarette. He looked up at the dark sky and its mysteries. He finished his cigarette, gave up wondering about all mysteries, turned his back on Chase and went to sleep.

In the morning Jean-Pierre was a boy again. He ran about as if the sunlight had touched him with a beneficent magic. He washed himself and proudly showed Trower his clean neck. He got their breakfast, scoured out the mess tins, and looked them both openly and innocently in the eye, as if no memory of the previous night remained with him.

After breakfast he went climbing to the very tops of the trees gathering apples which he put into Trower's helmet. Meanwhile Chase, who could fix anything, had gone to the transport lines to borrow a jeep.

When Chase returned, Jean-Pierre was sitting beside Trower, energetically polishing apples on his shirt and offering them to Trower to eat. "Merveilleuse," he exulted, taking a luscious bite into an apple. "Like sugar."

The boy saw Chase and ran towards him with an apple in each hand.

"I pick. I pick," he cried, holding up his gifts. Chase hesitated, and took one.

"It's okay, no!"

"Yes. Fine," said Chase, without enthusiasm.

"It's good. Eat! Eat!" insisted the boy pushing at

the arm holding the apple. Chase took a bite of the apple. The expression on his face remained sombre.

"I got a jeep," he said to Trower. "Let's go."

"Okay," said Trower nodding and taking hold of the boy's arm. He spoke to the boy as firmly and gently as he could. "We're taking you home, Jean-Pierre."

"No." Startled, the boy stopped walking and stared at the ground in front of him.

"You have to go home. Anyway you can't stay here with us any longer."

"But why? Is danger. Is fighting in Courcelle."

Trower tugged at the reluctant boy.

"Not any more. That was a long time ago."

Jean-Pierre pulled himself free from Trower's grip.

"I no live in Courcelle. I tell lie." The words were sullen.

"We'll find out when we get there."

"I no go. I go away from here."

"You're going to Courcelle with us," said Trower with a firmness that put an end to all further argument.

Jean-Pierre turned to Chase in despair.

"Please, please!" he cried, seizing Chase's forearm with both hands. "Let me stay. I want to live with soldier. I happy with soldier. Please..."

"You've got to go home," said Chase, without looking at the boy.

Suddenly, without warning, Jean-Pierre darted away. Surprised, Chase and Trower started after him.

"Hey! Stop that kid!" shouted Chase to a group of soldiers amongst whom Jean-Pierre was zig-zagging in his attempt to get out of the farm. He was easily caught and held, squirming and kicking, until Chase and Trower arrived to take hold of him.

"Kid finally got tired of working for you, eh?" said one of the soldiers, grinning. "Ever hear about the Child Labour Law?"

Chase was in no mood for jokes.

"Yeah, I heard about it," he said, sourly, yanking the struggling boy away to the jeep.

It was not until the jeep was travelling at a fair speed that Trower let go his arm. Chase was driving, Trower and Jean-Pierre shared the rear seat. Trower spoke to the boy several times during the journey, but he would not answer. He sat as if he were going to prison.

The road twisted and undulated as they drove back towards the coast. They passed their former battle-grounds, where marks of recent fighting scarred the countryside. Cottages were ruined, burned-out vehicles were tipped into the ditches, and the clusters of graves, British, American and German, grew larger and more frequent.

For the first time Jean-Pierre took an interest in his surroundings, gazing around him with a frank, apprecia-tive expression as if he were enjoying a visit to a fair. Once he pointed, and said, "Look, there are some Yanks dead. Not buried. Four. Let's stop."

"Why?"

"I think machine-gun do it. The way they lie. I should like to see." He spoke in the bright voice of a boy telling his father how his toy aeroplane works. "Maybe, also, they have cigarettes in pockets." He looked at Trower, clear-eyed and hopeful.

Trower did not answer.

Jean-Pierre looked forward again, along the road they were travelling, and became silent as the growing numbers of houses indicated the nearness of Courcelle. He hunched himself up in his former wooden, brooding posture and said nothing.

"Listen, when you get home..." said Trower, trying to cheer him up. But the boy would not be consoled. He shrugged off Trower's attempts at conversation.

Courcelle was in sight; a grey village at the foot of the

next hill. There was a field on their left, sloping uphill for about three hundred yards and ending against the skyline in two small knolls. At the verges of the road stood signboards in English, German and French warning that the field had not yet been cleared of mines. A two-strand wire fence bordered the field.

Just as Chase slowed down for a bend, he felt the jeep vibrate and there was a grinding under the bonnet. He cursed the transport men who had foisted a defective vehicle on to him, steered the car to the side of the road and stopped. Chase went round to the front of the car to investigate. Trower, unthinking, leaped out of the jeep and joined him.

With a bound, Jean-Pierre was out of the jeep and running towards the open field on their left. Trower yelled "Come back," but the boy was already climbing the wire-fence leading into the mined field.

The boy was already several yards into the field by the time the two men reached the wire fence and stopped at a "Warning—Mines" signboard.

Trower was calling, "Jean-Pierre! No! No! Stop!"

Chase yelled, "Stand still! Mines! Stop, you little fool!" The boy ran on up the slope.

Trower gripped the barbed wire, moving to follow. Chase pulled him back. The boy ran on. They shouted and waved at him. Then they waited, numbly, for him to blow up. Unharmed he reached the top of the knoll and paused for breath.

He turned and looked back at them for a few seconds. He looked small and alone, but somehow full of dignity, as he stood there silhouetted on the hill against the skyline. They called after him but heard only their own voices floating on the heat waves as if someone else was shouting. Jean-Pierre turned away and trotted over the hilltop, going away from Courcelle, down into the far valleys, passing finally out of their sight.

FIVE

Coliseum News bring the world to your doorstep... Here are the most eagerly awaited pictures of the war, as American troops reach the boundary of Germany itself. At last the Reich feels the tread of conquering armies, cutting through the first outposts of the vaunted Siegfried Line.

We capture the town of Eupen, on the Belgian border but with a mainly German population. The Nazis tried desperately to hold this sector, but they failed. There's a long, long way to go to Berlin, but the Allies are on the way!

* * *

THE closer the Allied advance came to the German border, the more stubborn was the Wehrmacht's resistance. The folks at home seemed to believe that the war was nearly over. So they said in their loving, fatuous letters. The men of the Company read the letters aloud amid jeers, and tore them up. For the soldiers the time of misery had set in.

The Company was dug in along a canal east of Aachen. It had been raining for a week. They were soaked and freezing. Mud and rain had sucked the mechanized equipment of the Americans to a standstill and the foot soldiers were left, face to face with an enemy maddened by the danger to his Fatherland, to endure a trench warfare that brought to mind the fading nightmare legends of World War One.

It was night. Craig's squad were hunched in two-man foxholes with the rain drumming on their helmets and capes. They had put all the boards and bricks they could find in the bottom of their pits but as these sank in the mud, the icy water crept up to penetrate their boots. There was mud on their backs and shoulders where they leaned against the side of their holes. White blinks of gunfire waxed and waned behind the landscape, and not far on their left they could hear a steady clamour of small arms fire. Towards their hardships they had schooled themselves to apathy; but they listened to the nearby gunfire with a feeling of gratitude that someone else was getting it, not them. All they had to do was watch, as well as they could with the rain beating into their eyes and cascading from their helmets.

Craig was in fact the only one watching. He was content to let his men huddle down. Night after night he or his sentries watched the patchy darkness across the canal in case the enemy came. It was still over there now. Nothing could be heard behind the noise of the rain. But men might come out of that darkness and Craig, however idly he leaned back in his pit, kept his eyes over the parapet. Grogan, his trenchmate, split a cigarette in half. The Sergeant watched his vain attempts to light it. Grogan grimaced in disgust and fumbled under his raincape to put the sodden inch of cigarette back into a small tin box.

Chase and Trower were in the next foxhole. Chase was slumped down at one end of the pit, unconscious and shivering. One of his fits of malaria was on him. Ever since Italy it had recurred from time to time. He would never report sick. He said he felt safer with the squad than with the thieving medics.

Trower forced an atabrine tablet into Chase's mouth, then pulled his canteen from under his cape and put it to Chase's lips. Chase opened his eyes and swallowed water. For a moment his eyes were dull, then recognition came into them. He managed a grin. His eyes closed, his head lolled, and he sank back on his friend's arm, fast asleep in the pouring rain, like an utterly trusting child.

The clenched fist of his right hand, outflung from under his cape like a corpse's, relaxed and came open. A gleam dropped out of it. Trower scrabbled in the mud with his fingers and brought up a chain with a medal on it. When he had wiped it he saw that it was a Saint Christopher medal. He mused over it, a glimpse into the depth of his self-sufficient friend. He turned it over casually. On the reverse side was a Jewish Star of David. He smiled wryly. That was more like Frank Chase: the man who liked to fix things with everybody. He put the medal back into Chase's open palm and the sleeper's fingers closed over it, tightly.

* * *

There were nine of them on patrol. The rain had stopped, the sun had brought a fresh, dry crispness to the Hürtgen Forest, and the Germans, after a bloody struggle, were in retreat again. The patrol, moving in two lines of four, straddled the hard, dirt road and advanced with caution. Tall pine-trees grew thickly on either side of the road out of a deep carpet of fern. Trower was in front with his rifle at the ready. Craig was at the rear marching between the two columns.

From somewhere behind the trees came a dull, steady thudding. It was none of the familiar sounds of war, only a muffled thud...thud...thud...

They walked like cats, weapons ready, watching to the left in the direction of the road.

* * *

A half-a-mile away, invisible to the patrol, was a clearing in the forest, and in this clearing was a camp.

The thud-thud-thud was the sound made by a telephone pole carried by twenty or thirty creatures in what looked like dirty striped pyjamas as they battered it against the inside of a huge, locked gate. These creatures were men; or rather, male skeletons with skin stretched over them.

A crowd of other skeletons lay about in the main yard of the camp. Some were raised feebly on their elbows, some crawled feebly about, while feebly, intermittently, the holders of the battering ram tottered at the gate.

Many of the human skeletons did not move at all. They were dead. They had starved where they lay in the week since the S.S. guard of this concentration camp had locked the gates and fled, no doubt to have lost themselves by now in civilian clothes among the German crowd.

The gates creaked, straining at the locks. The sound was a miracle that gave strength to the beings who held the ram. They ran forward again, and yet again, and the protesting sounds of the gate intoxicated them to try once more, and yet once more. The men on the ground watched silently, mouths open, eyes burning in their fleshless faces, some with wild excitement, others hopeless and disbelieving.

The gates were beginning to give. The men with the ram made a last, desperate effort. The gates swung open.

For a moment the men stood rooted where they were, staring out at freedom. No-one else moved. Then the ram thudded to the ground. Men were running. Some lurched like drunkards out through the gate into the forest. Some, still exhausted, tottered back to comrades lying on the ground. A few, then more, of the men on the ground started to crawl toward the gateway.

Men ran through the trees desperately, as if the death in which they had lived might reclaim them. They separated and vanished among the trees.

* * *

The thudding sounds had stopped a few minutes ago. The patrol moved on. The sound had been a menace but now the silence was a greater menace. No man wanted to die at a war's end, and death might be stalking the patrol from among these dense-growing pines.

They strained for a sound, a movement among the pines. They only heard their own soft tread. Warily they moved on down the road.

A new noise alerted them, a distant rush and scuffle among the ferns. Trower, the point man, halted like a hunter's dog. Far ahead a human figure had appeared for a moment and disappeared into the trees. Without need for an order the whole patrol dispersed in an instant to take up fire positions among the trees. Every man watched the road.

Three more figures appeared from the forest. One seemed to be supported between two others. Craig's rifle cracked a warning shot. They heard Craig's harsh, "Halt!"

The three distant men had stopped. They had seen uniforms, helmets, weapons—death. On a reflex the three prisoners stopped and waited dully for death.

Trower moved out and went cautiously towards them. Chase and Grogan followed. The rest of the patrol were only visible as rifle-muzzles peeping from behind trees, waiting to give cover.

Trower could make out the striped filthy garb now;

then the dreadful skeletal bodies; then the faces, thawing into heartbreaking smiles.

The shortest of the three prisoners pulled away from the sick man he had been helping to support. He began to stumble forward. Now it was the soldiers who stood still, incredulous. The man ran, falling forward, towards the Americans. Trower had seen soldiers riddled with bullets running forward like that, the steps more and more aimless, as the dying man ran into the ground. But this man did not run into the ground. All the hope that he had never dared to hope lifted him up. He even managed to stretch out his arms in greeting. His hollow, stubbled face was smiling in such an ecstasy that he might have been seeing God's archangels.

The man stopped in front of Trower. He stood there, panting, staring to assure himself once more that this vision was real. He sank to his knees, seized Trower's left hand and kissed it, sobbing. Gently, Trower lifted him to his feet.

* * *

The left flank of the Allied advance was bogged down in Holland, Luxembourg and the Rhineland. The dash from France had petered out. The war that might have been over by Christmas was going to drag on into the spring of 1945 and maybe even longer. As the days shortened, the dank chill and drizzle of Flanders ate into the men's bones. Their energy and enthusiasm drained away. The marks of war-weariness appeared on many faces. Desertions by the thousands plagued the Allied armies. It was a worrying, unheroic time.

The Flemish towns and hamlets were crowded with shabby, tired soldiers, shapelessly bundled in jerkins, stained greatcoats and clumsy raincapes. The flooded countryside was deserted. Along the straight, raised roads that intersected it, an occasional patrol might be seen trudging with sullen step, the slow reluctant pace betraying the fear rather than the hope of a hostile encounter.

Men on leave were able to go to Ostend or Brussels or Liége for a few days' rest, and it was only during these interludes that they were able to feel any pleasure in living, or even any warmth in their flesh.

There was nothing much to do in Ostend but it was better than a foxhole. Chase and Trower had been wandering about in the blackout, peering into dimly-lit bars for some company and excitement. An illuminated sign, the letters shining from behind a black screen so that no light could be seen from the air, announced, "Dancing Bar." A tinny blare of jazz tempted them in.

The place was crowded with soldiers and girls. Couples shuffled on a tiny dance floor, to a lethargic three-piece band. Overhead a revolving crystal ball spun coloured lights about the dreary room. Large British and American flags were pinned to the walls and a white banner stretched overhead with the misspelt greeting, "Wellcome to Our Allies."

A waiter ushered Chase and Trower to a table beside the dance floor. They ordered brandies and tossed for the bill. Trower lost. Chase's eyes roamed over the women.

The three tired musicians stopped playing. Two of them stowed their instruments away and stepped down from the small platform. The pianist remained on his stool, head bowed, hands resting in his lap.

A girl came out of a side door and walked on to the dais. She carried a violin case. Her face was grave, aquiline, not unattractive. She opened the case, brought out her violin, and adjusted the strings, thoughtfully, as if unaware of the chattering crowd milling about the room. She nodded to the pianist. They began to play.

The tune was *Humoresque*. The fragile, banal notes

filtered through the laughter and chatter. She played it competently, but with a curious air, at once absorbed and completely uninterested. Her bow and fingers moved mechanically as if she were unaware of them. She seemed unaware, too, of the absurd and inappropriate uniform she wore: long black stockings and tightly fitting briefs beneath a white silk shirt and black bolero.

No one in the room seemed to be listening, except Trower. He was enchanted, not only by her face, which was delicately moulded and serious, but by her attitude, so full of a grace that he had almost forgotten. Her head was bowed over the instrument, and the listening remoteness of her eyes, the slight flowing movements of her arms, the touch of her fingers on the strings, the relaxed stillness of her body, mirrored like ballet the sweet, gentle melody she was playing.

Chase had decided that the girl's legs were not bad. He glanced at Trower.

"You like that?" he said.

"What?" said Trower, startled, "Yes. Yes, I do."

"Ask her over for a drink."

"Yes...I will." He noticed Chase's face. "What's so funny?"

"Nothing, Corporal," said Chase. "Nothing. Relax."

Trower called a waiter, slipped some money into his hand and spoke to him.

When she had finished playing, the waiter whispered to her. She looked over her shoulder towards the two soldiers and shrugged. She put her violin into its case and, carrying it, came towards their table.

"Better have another drink, quick," said Chase.

"You're a funny man," said Trower.

He rose, somewhat awkwardly, to his feet as the girl arrived at the table. Chase co-operatively followed suit. She inclined her head slightly in greeting, and said quietly "Good evening, messieurs."

Trower said, "Good evening." Chase nodded to her.

Trower said, "Please sit down." As she seated herself, he said, "You speak English?"

"A little."

"What would you like to drink?"

"Nothing, thank you." She sounded tired.

"Are you sure?" asked Trower. "Maybe later. Cigarette?"

"Thank you," she said. She put the cigarette between her lips, Trower lit it.

"I enjoyed your playing," he said. "It's too bad you can't play somewhere nice where people listen."

"Where?" With a faint derision.

"There are other places."

"I have never played in any."

"But you play as if you had real training."

"Yes. I study in Conservatoire in Brussels until I stop."

"Why did you give it up?"

She shrugged her shoulders.

"Why don't you go back?" She looked at him negligently.

Trower said, "I'm sorry. Are my questions annoying you?"

"No, I am not annoyed. There is no use to go back."

Chase had been looking on with amusement. He said to the girl, "How old are you?"

"Twenty-one."

"Where's your family?"

"Deported."

Chase nodded and settled over his drink again.

Trower said, "When I was in Naples they had opera. They gave shows for the troops. Do you like opera?"

He waited as if for the response to a password. But the girl was glancing up at someone approaching behind him. The soldier who stopped at their table was named Eldridge.

"Hi, Chase," he said, "Hi, Trower. I'll buy the drinks.

Trower said, "No thanks."

Eldridge was in one of the other platoons of their Company. He was up for a medal. He had cleaned out a nest of six Germans in a farmhouse, killing them all.

"Am I intruding?"

"Yeah."

Eldridge had a bad name in the Company. He was said to be in the black market. When he got drunk he was savage. He had once roamed through a town shooting bottles off the shelves in a succession of bars. An indulgent commanding officer had let him off with a light penalty because he was up for a medal.

More recently, he had announced, on the crowded staircase of a brothel, that he would set up an attendance record in a period of seven days, if other soldiers would provide the money, at two bucks a time. He had found enough backers to set up an impressive score—rumours varied as to exactly how many. At the end of the week Eldridge had challenged anyone in the Company to ask the girls if they didn't believe him.

"Ah, come on," he said, and turning to Trower, "The Corporal doesn't mind, do you Corp?" He turned to the girl. "What's your name, baby?"

"Régine."

He put his hand on her knee. "You like jig-a-jig?"

She sat still and indifferent. Chase rose and said to Eldridge, "Come over to the bar and I'll buy you a drink."

"What's wrong with here?"

"I said the bar," said Chase, taking Eldridge by the arm.

"I never say no," said Eldridge.

Eldridge got up. He bent down and kissed Régine lightly on the cheek. "I'll see you again, honey. When I'm in the mood," he said. He let Chase pull him towards the bar.

Trower watched him go with hatred and with envy of his confidence. He stubbed his cigarette furiously into an ashtray. The scene had humiliated him and he felt the girl must have been humiliated, too.

"I'm sorry about that," he said.

She made an indifferent pout. "A soldier."

"Would you like a drink now?"

"No, thank you."

"Would you like to dance?"

"No," she said, looking at him and smiled briefly to herself. "But I answer all your questions. I was student at Conservatoire until I am seventeen. I am only child. Just after war starts, my parents bring me here and leave me with family they know and go back to Brussels. After a time, their letters stop and I hear they are taken away. I have no one else. I must work. There is no use to go some other place and it does not matter to me what I do..."

She stopped talking, her voice trailing away. Trower had been watching her, touched by her gentleness and fascinated by the line of her thin-boned, well-bred features.

"I am very tired," she said, lightly rubbing her forehead and momentarily shutting her eyes. "I think I shall go home now."

"Can I see you home?"

"As you wish," she said, getting up with her violin case.

"I'd like to," said Trower. "Where do you live?"

"At the Hotel de la Paix. Not far. Just at the other end of this street."

They left, and walked down the dark, cobbled street together. Trower held her arm as gently as he could. He couldn't think of any apt conversation. He was still embarrassed by that business with Eldridge. In the motionless, lifted poise of her head and the emptiness of her look he imagined disgust, weariness at the males who came, one after another, to sniff at her like dogs. He was afraid that if he moved too close to her or said anything too intimate the same disgust would roll out over him.

The doorway of the Hotel de la Paix was a dark slot between two shops. They paused outside and looked at each other.

"I have to go back to Liége tomorrow, on a training course," said Trower. "Is there anything I can do for you there?"

"No."

"I don't know when I can get back here again. But when I do I'd like to come to the bar again to see you. If you don't mind?"

Trower thought she was going to say something. There was a fleeting dilation of the eyes, and a second's inquiring scrutiny. Then, in a voice that suddenly seemed crushed with fatigue, she said, "As you wish."

"I wish," said Trower. He hesitated, then kissed her gently on the cheek. He reached into his pocket and gave her a packet of cigarettes. He returned to camp that evening feeling confused, happy and alive.

He looked forward with a vague, tender pleasure to his next meeting with Régine. He had little to say when Chase spoke to him about her.

It was five weeks before Trower and Chase got another pass to Ostend. They arrived in town about seven o'clock in the evening and went straight to the dancing-bar. Chase sensed Trower's excitement. He was amused, but sympathetic.

Régine was not there. The tiny band was thumping out its familiar tunes. The floor was crowded as usual. They waited at the bar for about an hour in the thick, smoke-hung room. Girls brushed invitingly past them every few moments, but they ignored them all. Chase sat on his bar stool and watched Trower quizzically.

At a few minutes before eight, the door opened. For the hundredth time Trower sat up with expectation. She entered. He was half out of his chair when he sat down again. Chase, glancing round, saw what he had seen, and said, "Don't look so tragic. Finish your drink."

She was with Eldridge. She walked across the room with her arm through his, clasping herself raptly to his side. In the crowd, she seemed to stand apart; her body seemed to be making a proclamation; her step was happy, her cheeks had assumed a full, catlike shape of contentment. Her hair, that had previously fallen about her face in soft ringlets, was now swept back and piled high in a brittle sophisticated style. She was wearing a black lace dress, cut provocatively low, with matching earrings and necklace.

Eldridge, looking more than usually expansive and pleased with himself, was smoking a cigar. He handed the cigar, with an autocratic gesture, to one of his cronies seated at a table, and joined in the dancing. As their bodies met for the dance, Régine threw both her arms lovingly around Eldridge's neck. She pressed herself close to him, her cheek to his. As they moved about the floor she almost lay upon him. She appeared unaware of anything outside his sheltering arms.

Trower watched them, sick inside with disappointment and a sense of betrayal. He was humiliated by the transformation in her, by his own failure to understand her, by the memory of his vague dreams, by the fact that the man was Eldridge. How could she? How *could* she?

"Want to go?" Chase said.

Trower, his fists on the bar counter in front of him, did not answer.

"Why don't you dance?" said Chase. "You haven't noticed but there's a nice little redhead over there who's been giving you the eye."

"You dance."

Chase called the bartender, ordered two brandies, said to Trower, "They're both for you," and went across to the redhead.

She was lolling against a wall.

"My name's Eisenhower," he said, by way of introduction. "What's yours?"

The girl sipped the drink in her hand and peered at him over the rim of the glass before answering.

"Stalin," she said.

"How are things on the Eastern Front?" he said, surveying her appreciatively.

"Getting warmer." She made the guttural Flemish accent sound attractive.

He offered her a cigarette. She leaned forward for a light, her eyes promising over the flame. Across the floor he noticed Eldridge and Régine dancing. They stopped. Eldridge was gesturing towards Trower.

Chase said, "Excuse me."

He started across the floor.

Eldridge manoeuvred the girl to the empty stool on Trower's left. He said, "Howdy-doody, Corporal. I'll buy you a drink."

Régine, putting her bag and gloves on the counter, gave Trower a passing glance of bare recognition as she sat down beside him. Eldridge, standing between and behind them, put his arms convivially round both of them.

"No, thanks. I've got these," said Trower.

"I mean a real drink. Champagne. A gentleman's drink, eh?" He called, "Hey, champagne, vite!"

Chase arrived. He seated himself on Trower's other side.

Eldridge said, "Hi, pal!"

"He wants to buy us champagne," said Trower.

"Business must be good."

Trower was mystified by Chase's remark. Eldridge uttered a happy hoot of laughter. He pulled out his wallet and riffled proudly through the bills with which it was stuffed.

"Yes, I got a good little thing going here," he said, tapping Régine appreciatively on the knee. "She's a good little worker, this kid. Hey, where's this champagne?"

Trower looked numbly at Régine. She was fixing her hair with her eyes on a compact mirror, completely uninterested in what Eldridge was saying.

Chase said, "Never mind. We're drinking brandy."

Eldridge refused to be rebuffed. "Never turn down a drink, pal. Right, Corporal?" Eldridge turned to Trower. "Hey! What's up? You look sick."

"Forget it."

"The chick, huh?" He grinned knowingly. "You had a yen for her, didn't you?" His voice was full of solicitude. "Cheer up, Corp. You can have her. Go on, take her down the road. For nothing. She's got a nice little place. Clean." He leaned over towards the girl. "What do you say, chickie? Take a walk with the Corporal, eh?"

Régine, busily powdering her face, glanced casually in Trower's direction. "If he wishes."

"No, thanks," said Trower. He started to rise. "Let's go."

He was paralyzed with misery. He had to escape from this bad dream. His ears rang with disbelief.

He had been foolish enough to expect some kind of acknowledgment in her glance; shame, perhaps, or defiance, or self-justification, or even accusation, for he knew now what had really happened between them at the door of the Hotel de la Paix. But the eyes that rested on him were careless, cold, disdainful.

"Finish your drink," said Chase to Trower. Weakness

of any kind sickened him, and his anger turned agains Trower. People looked after themselves. He did. The gir did. Eldridge did more than any of them. Trower would have to learn. "Hey, Eldridge. Have much trouble with her?"

"Nah," Eldridge leaned happily on the other men's shoulders. "After a couple of times she couldn't do without me." He chuckled. "The third night I give her the message. She don't get it at first. She sits there for about five minutes, thinking. Then she gets up, shrugs her shoulders, and out she goes. She's been as good as gold ever since. I haven't had a complaint yet."

"You're quite a guy," said Chase.

"Well, you've got to be firm. You've got to let 'em know they need you. You got to make 'em understand they're better off with you than they are on their own. No different here than back home. Like they say, it's all one world."

"I hope she appreciates all you've done for her," Chase said.

Régine ignored them, still busy with compact and lipstick.

"Ah, she's crazy about me." He patted her indulgently. "She knows who's taking care of her, don't she?"

Régine was putting away her make-up. She came to life with a pleased smile. There was nothing demonstrative in her attitude now. What Trower saw was even more painful; the matter-of-fact security, the complacent acceptance of a pleasant relationship. She took Eldridge's hand and held it in hers. Her shoulders began to sway to the music.

"She wants to dance," said Chase.

"Yeah, she likes dancing." Eldridge chuckled. "I think

ll give her a little exercise. Come on, baby. Dancey, lancey." They rose. "Stick around, fellows. We'll be back."

As they started away, with Régine already clinging to him, Chase said, conversationally, "Do us a favour and drop dead first."

Eldridge turned back to give Chase a startled look.

"What?" Then he laughed, completely unoffended. "Oh, jealous, hey? Naughty, naughty." They started to drift back towards the dance floor.

"Eldridge!" It was Trower's voice, hoarse and oddly stifled. As Eldridge turned, Trower stepped from the bar and lunged out at him with his fist. He was able to hit Eldridge once before Chase and a couple of bystanders grabbed him by the arms and pulled him back.

Eldridge was still staring, bewildered, at the struggling, frantic Corporal, when Régine launched herself at Trower. Her long fingers clawed at Trower's cheek. Eldridge grabbed her round the waist and swung her away from Trower.

Trower relaxed. He muttered, "All right, you can let me go."

He stood with Chase. Long scratches bled down his cheeks. On the dance floor, Eldridge was rubbing his chin ruefully, with no sign of ill-feeling. Régine leaned against him. She looked proudly up at him. He was smiling. She turned towards Chase and Trower and threw a harsh, scornful laugh at them.

Frank Chase saw the two smiling faces and shoved Trower towards the door. "For God's sake let's get out of here before the doorman calls the M.P.'s."

A few yards down the street, he took Trower's arm and bundled him into another bar. He ordered brandies and pushed a glass towards Trower. When he had drunk it Chase gave him another, and then another, until he was hot and stupid. He led him to their jeep, and drove him back to camp. Neither of them spoke another word that night. When they went to their beds, they did not even say "goodnight."

SIX

COLISEUM NEWS SPECIAL

Blizzards and the coldest winter in recorded history bring the war to a stand-still on the Western front, both on land and in the air! Along the entire length of the battle-front, hostilities come almost to a complete stop, as roads become useless and the countryside impassable for large-scale operations. But G.I. Joe somewhere in Belgium, can't stand inactivity for long. Deprived of the chance to fight a real war, he stages one of his own! And even if the ammunition is only snowballs, you can see that our boys have not lost their deadly aim!

* * *

Xmas Xtra!

SANTA AT THE FRONT

A Christmas party in war-torn Holland, with hospitalized Allied soldiers entertaining Dutch war orphans, on Christmas Eve. And judging by the faces of old and young, a good time is had by all!

* * *

The Management of this Theatre

Wish Everyone a

MERRY CHRISTMAS

and a

HAPPY NEW YEAR

And now, Folks, Follow the Bouncing Ball—

EVERYBODY SING!

Jingle Bells, Jingle Bells,

Jingle all the way.

Oh, what fun it is to ride,

In a one-horse, open sleigh!

* * *

THE notice on the bulletin board had said they were to report for special duty at 0600 hours. There followed the names of ten men. They sat in the back of the truck wearing greatcoats and gloves and trying to keep warm. Some of them dozed; others just sat there with folded arms and hunching their bodies in an effort to keep out the cold wind coming through the open back of the truck. There had been some desultory speculation about where they were going but it had quickly died. They were old enough hands not to waste their breath questioning orders. They'd know soon enough.

Snow lay over the countryside like some vast, soft eiderdown. The pine trees bowed stoically under their burden. It was fresh snow and everything, including sound, was muffled. The truck jostled along the rutted road like some scurrying black beetle in this unrelenting white world. Its noisy progress seemed an affront to the silence.

Craig, sitting with the driver in the cab, was re-reading the contents of the Top Secret envelope he had been handed that morning. He stuffed the paper into his pocket and stared ahead at the ribbon of road in front of him. Except for a tighter set to the line of his mouth, his face betrayed nothing.

They had been travelling for just over an hour when Craig saw ahead of him the familiar, abnormally punctilious figures of two M.P.'s. They carried flags and were signalling two trucks, that had come from the opposite direction, down a small side road. At the junction, the military policemen waved Craig's truck to follow the others. Looking behind him, Craig could see other trucks approaching. Their timing had been excellent. They had all converged at the same time at this junction and together they formed a convoy of five trucks proceeding along this narrow lane.

After a few moments of travelling along this tree-lined road—obviously private—Craig could see that they were in the grounds of a French chateau. The house rose dignified and solitary out of an expanse of snow-covered land. Beneath the snow the terraces of a French eighteenth-century landscaped garden descended from the front of the house.

Craig's truck was the last of the five. The convoy stopped in the drive that led to the chateau. Other trucks and jeeps were already there and men were being assembled and marched off through some trees to the right of the building. Two M.P.'s stood rigidly attention on either side of the open front doors of th chateau.

Craig was quickly out of the cab.

"All right! Out!" he called to the men inside. The party tumbled out and stood at the back of the vehicle in a disorderly group. The other trucks were also disgorging similar groups of G.I.'s.

The men surrounded Craig, blowing on their fingers or stamping their feet and slapping their arms in an effort to keep warm. It had been a cramping, frigid ride.

"What's happening, Sarge?" said Grogan, wiping his nose with a large brown, handkerchief.

Craig, his face set and withdrawn, ignored the question. Pulling a typewritten order from his pocket, he began to read in a quick, peremptory fashion.

"The following named enlisted men, drawn by lot, have been selected to act as witnesses to an execution for desertion. They will proceed at 0630 hours, etcetera, etcetera, etcetera." He knew the men would be uninterested in the rest of the details in the order. "I won't read your names. They're all on the list."

Before the men had time to react, ask any questions, demand more information, Craig shouted, "Fall in!"

They moved in a disciplined shuffle into two lines and waited. All around them the forecourt of the chateau was alive with N.C.O's lining up small groups of men and marching them away. The frozen hush of the morning was being splintered by incisive, staccato commands. "Detail!...Fall in!...Attention!...On the Double!... Left Face!" The barks of the Sergeants to their squads warred in a hubbub that contradicted the orderly movement of the many small parties moving black against the snow to compose one meaningful pattern.

To Chase, Trower and the rest, the occasion was still somewhat bizarre and unreal. An American G.I. being ɔt for desertion! They'd never thought it possible. f course, they had all heard the rumours of massive .esertions that had followed on the German offensive in :he Ardennes. More than one in the party could name someone who had disappeared, usually the night before a big attack. Some expressed anger against the men who ratted and left their comrades to bear the burden. Others professed a negligent sympathy for the veteran soldier who decided he had had enough. The war would be over at the latest in the spring. Why get killed now? If he was caught, it would only mean a prison sentence and probably a quick reprieve once the Armistice had been signed.

The prospect of being shot for desertion had never seriously occurred to any of them. The American public wouldn't stand for it! There would be hell to pay in Congress! Standing out there in the cold waiting to see a fellow-American being shot was an unnerving experience. But they were too numbed by the cold and surprised by their situation to be able to think coherently.

"Attention!" It was Craig's voice. "Left face! March!"

The squad tagged on to the other groups marching through the trees to the rear of the chateau. Nothing could now be heard but the rhythmic crunch of boots as they trod on the crisp snow. Their progress made an eerie, crackling sound, as if they were marching through a field of cornflakes. They moved in a slightly bent position as they trudged through the snow.

Once through the trees, they continued to march on through the deep snow until they came to a small frozen lake.

At the far end of the lake an isolated wooden post about six feet high had been driven into the ice. It looked gaunt and stark.

Facing the post were about a hundred soldiers drawn up in two lines. Sergeants were barking their groups to a

SEVEN

Coliseum Special

BIG THREE MEETING AT YALTA

To the Big Three Conference in the Crimea go not only the leaders of the three Allied Powers but also the hopes and faith of all men who look to a future free from war.

The site for this most momentous conference of the entire war is the old city of Yalta, summer resort of the Russian Czars.

The three great leaders and their staffs of military and political advisers face the inevitable battery of cameras. This is the day the free world has been waiting for—the first meeting of Churchill, Roosevelt and Stalin—The Grand Alliance, face to face!

* * *

Latest in Wrestling

BATTLE ROYAL IN MOLASSES AND FEATHERS

It's the latest wrinkle in the grand old sport of grunt and groan, a battle-royal in feathers and molasses!

The Victors

Something new to tickle the paying customers, who don't seem to know just how to take it...Somehow or other these modern gladiators just can't seem to get started. Maybe it's because way down deep they're really stuck on each other, or is it the other way around?...Anyway it's all good clean fun. The winner and still champion, a very plucky fellow indeed!

* * *

CHASE watched the women in the queue. Shawled, shabby, tired and patient, they waited. They were waiting outside a baker's shop for bread. The shop was shuttered, closed.

He was on pass to Brussels for three days, with a lot of back pay in his wallet. The Regiment was not far away, a long way back from the line for the Regiment to be. From the reconnoitring of truck drivers and conversations in the bars it seemed as if the whole Division was out.

Maybe those buzz-bombs and V-2's had made Liége too hot for a rest area. Or had they stopped now? When half of life was made up of rumours, no-one could be sure.

The Regiment was training during its "rest." There were big drafts of new men to be absorbed. Fresh clothing and equipment came up. Beside the training of the new men, they took part in a good deal of mysterious exercising which seemed to be in the nature of rehearsal; for what, nobody told them. Chase had an inkling. The training involved the use of assault boats and other specialized equipment. But Chase had mastered the technique of not thinking about things like that.

In the main streets there were hotels, cafés and street cars clattering on rails, a vision of civilization for men from the front; even if there were few goods in the shops and menus in the restaurants were scanty. In these narrow, cobbled back streets there were shabby, tired people, and queues.

He strolled on. He was in no hurry. It was enough to saunter and taste life.

He came to another queue. This one was composed of men in uniform, British, Canadian, American. They lounged against the wall, chatting, tossing cigarette butts into the gutter. They looked as if they might be waiting for a movie house to open; but the queue ran to the doorway of a small hotel.

As Chase approached on the other side of the street, some of the men sent up a ragged cheer. Three girls came tittuping down the road. They wore tight skirts that showed their buttocks, and pert hats. Their faces were plastered with that exaggerated, ritual mask of make-up which marks the lower-grade Continental prostitute. The girls passed the men, with a step that waggled their bottoms. One of them began to unlock the front door.

Men were shouting to them by name, and upbraiding them for being late. Evidently their working hours were well known. The girls threw back ogling smiles and incomprehensible French badinage.

Chase was sizing up the girls. The brunette was not bad. The other two were just meat; short, thick farm wenches with homely faces, who might have been arriving at the cowhouse to milk the cattle. They seemed popular enough with the line of jesting men. Chase's tastes were too fastidious, either for the queue or for the women. He liked to find his own company, and it had to be pretty fancy to be worthy of Frank Chase.

Turning the corner, Chase happened to glance through the large, plate-glass window of a typical Brussels bar. The place was empty except for a barman and a blonde woman seated at one of the tables. She was smoking and leafing through some papers.

He stopped and inspected her. She looked up, met his eyes, and returned to her work. The place was called the Venus Bar. A large, wooden notice with the words "Off Limits" was nailed beside the entrance. He walked on a few feet more and then deliberately turned back. Again he stopped outside the window and looked in. He was about to go in when he was accosted by two M.P.'s who had come round the corner.

"Let's see your pass, buddy," said one of them.

"Delighted, Sarge," said Chase, taking out the form from his inside pocket.

The M.P. took the pass in both hands and studied it intently.

"It's not on there but my rifle number is 321579," said Chase, with a sweet smile.

"Yeah," said the M.P., handing back the pass. "And this place," waving his truncheon at the Venus Bar, "is off-limits."

"I never would have guessed. Thanks, Sarge."

"All right, wise guy." A note of authoritative menace crept into the M.P.'s voice. "We know your face."

Chase touched his cap with an off-hand gesture and sauntered away. The two M.P.'s watched him for a few moments and then walked off in the opposite direction and turned the corner.

Chase waited in a doorway for a minute or so to see if the M.P.'s intended to come back. Then he returned to the Venus Bar and went in.

Now that he was closer to her, Chase was even more interested. She had blonde hair down to her shoulders and a small, cold, clever face. She was beautiful; but what stirred excitement in Chase was her upright, controlled poise, her air of calculation, the hint of menace in her composure. The one kind of danger he liked was in women's faces. He had always prided himself on having the best, but this woman was of a class he had only aspired to in the past.

She wore a black leather dress with a tightly pulled-in belt that outlined her lithe body. She looked elegant, relaxed yet full of authority.

"Bonjour, madame," said Chase, unbuttoning his coat and throwing it on a chair. She ignored his greeting, got up from the table and walked over to the bar. Chase went to the bar and spoke to the waiter.

"A glass of beer, s'il vous plaît," and turning to the woman, "and perhaps I can buy the lady a drink."

She looked at him, coldly.

"If you want a girl the waiter will get you one." Her English was good. The accent was unfamiliar.

"I'm sorry, ma'am," he said, "you've misunderstood me. I've got three days to spend here and I thought you might be able to give me a little advice about the town."

Her voice remained cold. "The waiter is a well-informed man."

"I'm sure he is," said Chase, "but I'd still like to buy you a drink."

"I'm the owner," she said, leaning forward with hands together on the bar counter. She did not look at him. There was a moment's silence and then she continued in a hard voice. "You know this place is off limits."

"Yeah. I noticed."

"I would like you to leave at once," she said, not troubling to look at him. "I obey the authorities in all respects. Please go."

"Far be it from me to involve you with the authorities," he said drily. "I bid you good day."

But before he could reach the door, the woman called out after him, "And tell your friends in the Military Police not to waste their time in the future."

Chase turned round with a look of amused astonishment on his face.

"My what?" he said, at a complete loss for words. He walked back to the bar. "Lady, you were never more wrong in your life. In fact, if you knew me better..."

She had been leaning with her back against the bar, surveying him with clinical detachment.

"Let me see your hands," she said, brusquely.

"My hands?" Chase was genuinely puzzled, but he gave her his right hand.

She turned it palm upwards and examined it quickly.

"I was wrong," she said, dropping his hand. "The police have no callouses on their hands. You are only an ordinary soldier after all. Goodbye."

Except for a slight lifting of her eyebrows, she remained indifferent. From an open cigarette pack, she took a cigarette and put it between her lips.

"Permettez," said Chase, lighting it for her. "Ordinary is another word you wouldn't use if you knew me better." He put on his cap. "Do you believe in luck? Well, this is the unluckiest day in your life. This is the day you let Frank Chase slip through your fingers."

He moved towards the door, picking up his coat.

"One moment." Again at the last moment the woman spoke. He turned round. "Will you have a drink with me?"

Chase grinned. His opinion of himself was restored. "Thank you." He came back to her. She was smiling.

"Not here," she said. In an alcove, hidden from the view of any passing police patrol, she called the waiter. He bobbed a bow.

"Deux cognacs."

"Oui, Madame Magda," said the waiter, hurrying away.

Chase, sitting back with both hands on the table, echoed the name as he studied her. "Magda." She looked at him questioningly and said, "You were reckless to come here."

"Nothing is reckless if the stakes are high enough."

She smiled tolerantly, but her eyes were scrutinizing him with interest. "Why is your place out of bounds?"

"Your police are prejudiced against me."

"Why?"

"Because the Gestapo let me stay open when the Germans were here."

"Why shouldn't the Gestapo have let you stay open?"

"I am Polish." That explained her accent. "They could have sent me to a labour camp but I paid them well. Soon I shall pay your police, too. Then I will not be off-limits."

"I see." The waiter came with the brandy. Chase fondled his glass. "Well, that's the nice thing about money...everybody understands it." He lifted his glass to her. "May your endeavours be crowned with success."

She sipped her cognac in acknowledgment of his toast.

"You could do better for yourself," Magda said, putting her glass down. Her eyes studied his uniform with its conspicuous absence of badges of rank.

"For example?"

"Clever men stay warm and safe. In the army or out of it. There are plenty of fools to march and freeze and die in the fields. For a man with brains there is always something better." She fell silent again, facing him across the table with her cold, level look.

"Yeah," said Chase. "Eisenhower's been neglecting my talents something awful. F.D.R. ought to be told about it."

Magda allowed a suspicion of a smile to flit across her face.

'Is my conversation interesting to you?" she asked.

"Sure. It's about me, isn't it?"

"You are interesting to me, too. Would you like to dine with me tonight?"

It was a second before he recovered from his surprise. "Very much."

"I invite you."

"I accept."

He picked her up at the Venus Bar later that evening. They walked through the dark, cobbled streets and stopped outside a shuttered house. Magda knocked. The door was opened slightly by a man who inspected Chase, then saw Magda and greeted her with a welcoming gesture. As they entered the man bowed to her.

A dark hall and another doorway led to the restaurant. They could hear the sound of a piano and an animated murmur of conversation. An attendant took their coats.

Magda without her coat was a revelation. She was wearing a dark velvet dress with a neat gold collar. The dress was so subtly cut and so smoothly moulded to her body that it could only have been the work of an expensive designer. Her hair was elaborately dressed into a golden plait ringing the crown of her head and separating the fringe in front from the blonde tresses that fell to the back of her neck.

An obsequious head waiter was poised at the entrance to the restaurant to lead them to their table. On seeing her come in, the pianist interrupted his playing and with a flourish broke into the opening chords of Chopin's

Waltz Polonaise. He continued until they were seated at a wall table in a discreet corner of the restaurant. Magda nodded to the pianist, acknowledging his gesture, and he returned to the tune he had been playing before her entrance.

To Chase, who had spent the past weeks trudging in the mud and huddling in cold, lamplit tents, eating his meals cold, in drizzling rain, out of a mess tin, this was like some dream of a forbidden paradise. Forbidden it certainly was, for in those day of severe rationing, places like this were outside the law, hidden from the knowledge of the hungry and the law-abiding.

To have walked into a room like this with a woman like this, to such a greeting, was a supreme experience for him.

Chase looked around the room hardly believing his eyes. The restaurant was small but discreetly and lavishly furnished. The walls were panelled in subdued, brown mahogany with wooden pillars topped with graceful, gilded ornaments. Large oil portraits, heavily framed, gave the place an aura of quiet distinction, as did the elaborately carved and painted ceiling. A discreet chandelier and small, scallop-shaped lamps on the tables provided the subdued lighting. The small tables dotted about the room were covered with spotless tablecloths of white damask that hung in thick folds almost to the floor. Glinting glasses and dazzling cutlery were tastefully laid. Almost all the tables were occupied.

In the centre of the room was a sideboard heaped high with the kind of food Chase had only ever seen before in the pages of luxury magazines. A sucking pig, caviar, salmon, turkey, a small barrel of oysters, lobsters, an assortment of pâté, pineapples, satiny peaches, grapes, tangerines—a gourmet's delight.

Among the people who sat at the other tables were a

few British officers, mostly of senior rank, who glanced at Chase curiously and then looked away. There were many of the smart, hard, mercenary girls he had seen in the more expensive bars; and there were men in civilian clothes who were of two kinds.

Some of them were middle-aged, big and prosperous men, who entered in heavy but beautifully cut overcoats, whose faces, as they moved from the shadows into the soft circles of light around their tables, were sleek and strong, and whose soft controlled voices, as they bowed with an air of mocking courtesy to their women, were full of shrewdness, sensuality and cynicism. They were men who seemed to be pricing everything and everyone they looked at; and the even murmur of their conversation always seemed to have overtones of business. The rest were young men, with firm, sharply profiled faces and alert, watching eyes, most of whom were loudly dressed and all of whom seemed to be sitting in a kind of tigerish, nervous silence while their girls chattered to them.

It was a strange contrast, all this, to the world outside, where the shawled women queued for hours, in icy rain, for bread and where, a few miles further away, the soldiers crept along the dykes or lay in foxholes like sodden rats under the same wet freezing lash.

Two waiters hovered at Magda's table with large menus. The head waiter, still bowing and nodding, spoke a few discreet words to Magda in French. He straightened up, snapped his fingers at the other waiters, and vanished. A wine waiter appeared carrying a bottle of white wine in a silver ice bucket. Hs displayed its label to Magda, she nodded, and he filled their glasses before restoring the bottle to its cooler.

"You don't by any chance own this place, too?" asked Chase.

"I do." She offered him a cigarette.

"And I was feeling sorry for you. You must be rich."

"Ach!" It was a sound of impatience. "The real money is in the black market."

"Well, why don't you get into it then?"

"I am."

Chase studied her. His curiosity was increased rather than diminished by every moment he spent with her.

"I should have known," he said, shaking his head.

Their talk was interrupted by the arrival of a waiter carrying a whole lobster on a silver tray. Chase and Magda heaped their plates with round, juicy slices from the body and went on to open the bright red claws with silver nutcrackers. Then came delicate little spring chickens, roasted all crisp and golden in delicious gravy. Plates of artichokes followed. At the sight of the huge, tender steaks that came next, Chase leaned back in his chair and looked bemusedly at Magda.

"They'll never believe it," he said, wagging his head slowly from side to side. "They'll never believe it. Never. Never. Never."

A little later the waiter came with cheeses on a trolley. Chase thought that this was the end of the meal, but Magda explained that the cheese was to cleanse his mouth of the taste of the meat, before the dessert was served. There were two dessert courses; first a pudding of thick cream full of liqueur and preserved fruits, with which a champagne was served; and then pancakes covered with burning rum. Apart from the champagne, four wines were served with the meal—there was even a separate wine for the cheese—and afterwards there was coffee and old brandy.

After dinner, while he was smoking a cigarette, Magda said to him, "You know there are deserters in this room."

"Americans?" Chase was in a complacent stupor. He was pleased with everyone.

"Americans. British. And Germans, too," said Magda. "The war is almost over. The armies are crumbling at the edges like stale cake."

Chase looked around him with interest. At that time, it seemed natural to come across deserters. In that dreary winter thousands had deserted and it was one of the great topics of discussion among soldiers. It was a common occurrence, in bars, canteens and restaurants behind the lines, for the orchestra suddenly to stop playing and a raiding group of Military Police to inspect the documents of the men who sat silently at their tables.

"You've got a couple of crumbs left over from the last war, too," he said, nodding in the direction of a table of elderly, rich-looking civilians.

"They are business men."

"Business must be good."

Magda smiled at him through her balloon glass of brandy.

"Business is always good in a war if you know how to live."

Chase was still looking round the room.

"I saw a deserter shot once..." he said. He drank his brandy and they talked of other things.

He went home with Magda. Her flat was lavishly but showily furnished. The flower-patterned wallpaper, the many mirrors, the prints of nudes on the walls, the ostentatious femininity of it all, indicated wealth rather than taste.

They made love violently. There was a serpentine cunning about her love-making that took him beyond all his previous experiences. He was taken aback by her demands; at times he felt he was being consumed. But, looking down afterwards at her sleeping face, it occurred to him that not once in that long night had a flicker of genuine feeling disturbed its cruel calm.

They slept late the next morning, and a middle-aged housekeeper brought their lunch to them in bed. In the morning, Magda's manner towards him was more relaxed than it had been. She no longer spoke to him and watched him in the same, controlled, cat-and-mousehole way as on the previous evening. She walked about the room, talking in a higher, clearer voice than before, the words coming more rapidly, her guard dropped. Like a wife, she talked when she had her back to him, not ceasing when she was letting a garment fall over her head. She told him how they were to spend the day with the sharp, clear confidence of one giving orders without fear of demur.

He only half-listened to the attractive guttural sound of her voice. He was lolling in a huge, white bath with only his head and toes emerging like islands in a sea of foaming bubbles. His eyes wandered round the pink-tiled walls and the soft fur rug on the floor and he could not help congratulating himself on his luck.

He had always been sure that he was meant for the big-time, in spite of a hard and unstable childhood. His father, a small-time building contractor, had lived on the move from State to State to find work and escape debt-collectors. His mother, resentful of her faded looks and fugitive life, had nagged incessantly at her husband and her six children. Chase blamed his scrappy education, made up of interrupted spells at a dozen schools, for his own failure to make the big-time.

He had been smart, bold, persuasive with men, successful with women, a good dresser, never short of a buck, an enjoyer of life, a man of the world; yet not one of his enterprises had brought him any nearer to the golden prize, the big killing that would give him ease and position. The jobs with big prospects had all died on him, right up to the last stroke of ill-luck when he was drafted.

It was curious that now, of all times, by a freak of the

hated war, he should find himself in the big-time. Everything that he wanted was in his grasp. He would not even let himself think of those freezing foxholes again. He wanted to hold on to his dream, to have more of it, more girls as elegant as Magda, more champagne, more bowing waiters, more bubble baths as grand as Hollywood.

He had what it took to earn these things. He was looking down with complacency at the body which had earned him these things when Magda came and knelt beside the bath. She was wearing a pastel-coloured shirt and slacks that flattered the elegant line of her thighs and legs. She handed him a small glass of brandy.

"You know, when I was a kid I always wished I had a fairy godmother," said Chase, lifting his chin out of the soap bubbles. "Now I've got one."

She smiled.

"I used to wish for a fairy godfather to come and take me away."

"From where?"

"From Warsaw."

"Why? I always thought that was a great town."

Magda lifted a large bar of soap out of the bath and began to soap Chase's chest and shoulders.

"I was born in a section that is very well known. It has the highest rate of crime in all Europe. Even the police stayed away at night."

"Nice neighbourhood, eh?" muttered Chase, enjoying the caress of her palms on his chest.

"I told you it is very well known."

"And did a fairy godfather ever come?"

"Oh, yes. He used to come two or three times a year to look over the crop. Finally my turn came when I was fifteen."

"And where did he take you?"

"To Hamburg. The waterfront."

"At fifteen!"

"I was lucky and clever." She had talked without a trace of emotion. It was only now that some evidence of real feeling came into her voice; a note of complacent pride in her achievements. "A business man from Berlin fell in love with me and bought me out." She had stopped washing him and was drying her hands on a huge, soft towel. "I saved the money he gave me and after a year I left him. I have been on my own ever since, and as you can see I have done very well."

Chase sat up in the tub.

"And to what do you attribute your success?"

Magda thought for a moment. She reached for a cigarette and lit it.

"Never to depend upon anyone," she said, slowly. "Never to fall in love with anyone—you have no idea how stupid some girls are—and never to give anything away that can be sold."

"That's a philosophy I've run across once or twice before," said Chase. "Can I have a cigarette, please?"

"No," she said. "But I will sell you one."

Chase looked at her, taken aback. She leaned towards him smiling. Her fingers played across his neck and shoulder as she put her lips to his and kissed him fiercely.

That afternoon they went down to the Venus Bar. Chase watched from the alcove while she checked accounts with the barman and dealt with business contacts. In the evening they went dancing, then to the restaurant for another sumptuous dinner. After that, a second night of Magda's cold, accomplished lust.

The next day, after they had made their routine call to the Venus Bar, they returned to Magda's flat. Rain was falling, not the sleety drizzle of the preceding days, but a battering, continuous downpour. Magda started to change into a short, dark cocktail dress covered in sequins. Like all her clothes, it was expensive and provocative.

Chase sprawled on the settee trying to make sense out of the sports pages of a French newspaper. A warm fire blazed in the fireplace and the comfort was beginning to grip him like a drug. These had been the three best days of his war, perhaps the best in his entire life. He refused to think beyond them.

Magda, who was painting her fingernails at her bedroom dressing table, called out to him and asked for the time. It was a quarter past five.

"Is it still raining?" she asked.

Chase took his feet off the sofa and walked to the window. Parting the curtains, he at first could see nothing at all. The glass was thickly misted with rivulets of rain.

"It's still raining," he called to her. He stayed at the window. He was looking down at the street.

Soldiers were marching past. Every few minutes another little phalanx came marching down the cobbled street. The soldiers moved calf-deep through a blur of bouncing raindrops, whose hiss mingled with the quick crash of their boots and the splash of water they threw up. The men were as bulky as cattle with their gleaming-wet raincapes spread over their packs and weapons. Stooping under the weight of their burdens, packed in a close, surging huddle, with lowered heads, they poured through the narrow street like steers into a casting-pen. The rain rattled on their steel helmets and streamed off their capes. Their swift and regular movement, the crash of their boots, set up a brisk, rhythmic tempo like a drumbeat hastening them out of the living world.

They were Americans. Infantry. He peered through the glass more intently. Here and there he recognized a face amongst the marching men.

"I think we're moving out," he said to Magda.

"What?"

"I said I think we're moving out. The whole regiment."

"Good." Magda's voice sounded matter-of-fact and pleased.

Chase was puzzled by its tone.

"Why?" he asked.

"Don't act like a virgin," said Magda. There was scorn in the remark. "You know you are not going back. You know you are going to stay and work for me. What do you think I've been trying to show you these last three days?"

Chase did not answer. She continued to talk through the open door between the bedroom and living-room while she chose her jewellery for the evening.

"You don't think I'm a Sister of Charity, do you? You've been living in the world of fools. Those men," she indicated the marching men outside the window. "Their world. It's for nobodies. Not for people with brains. Why did I tell you about my business and my plans? Why?"

She was trying on ear-rings and judging their effect in the mirror of her dressing-table.

"I need someone like you. Someone clever. Someone lucky. And I know when people are lucky. Someone not afraid to take chances. Because this is the time to make money. Everything is gold these days—bread, meat, blankets, medicine, gasoline—everything your armies are bringing in."

She rose and surveyed herself in the mirror, smoothing out the wrinkles in her dress.

"I need someone who can get into the supply dumps, and out again. Someone like you who can pass as an officer. I can get you any papers you need." Giving her hair a final pat, she walked out of the bedroom. "And now with your regiment gone, you'll be completely safe. And you'll make money with me."

No sound had come from Chase all this time. She came into the living-room. He was standing in front of the open wardrobe door. His tie was on and he was putting on his jacket. She glared at him. A slight flush came to her cheeks.

"You are afraid?" She was controlling herself.

"Yeah. I guess I am."

"Why?" Magda came closer to him. "Because you saw a man get shot once? That will never happen again. One of your own officers told me you have more than forty thousand deserters already."

Turning towards the cupboard, Chase deliberately took out his overcoat and cap. He did not look at her as he spoke.

"No. No. Anytime you got tired of me all you'd have to do is turn me in to the police."

"How could I?" Magda's voice was now a blend of supplication and anger. She kneeled on the settee and took hold of his left hand. "You would know everything about me." The words now tumbled out in a desperate rush. "I'll pay you ten thousand francs a week—what's that, two hundred and fifty dollars isn't it, in your money? And a percentage on every deal. I'll find you a beautiful flat. If it's girls you want, I have the best in the country. I'm offering you the biggest chance of your life. Anyway, the war is over. They don't need you."

He stood with his back to her, looking towards the window. She left him with his thoughts. The longer he

America's Sweetheart

SHIRLEY TEMPLE WEDS

Eleven years ago she was Little Miss Marker. Today she's Mrs. John Agar. After a five-month engagement, Hollywood's famed Shirley Temple becomes the bride of Aviation Engineer Sergeant John Agar, Junior. Crowds outside Wilshire Methodist Church get hard to handle as the couple leave for the wedding reception. At Shirley's Brentwood home, friends offer their congratulations. Sergeant Agar, on a seven-day furlough to wed his 17-year-old bride, will head for overseas as soon as he completes his basic training. But for the future, a fond world wishes them health and happiness.

* * *

The Victors

A REPLACEMENT named Weaver joined the squad. He looked absurdly young among the others, although he was no younger than Trower and Chase had been when they came to the Regiment. Everything about him looked new; his rifle, his uniform, the topcoat that seemed too large for him, and his baffled face.

Private Weaver was ignored. He had come at a time when the squad no longer welcomed newcomers. He trudged about the camp on his own, his collar turned up against the incessant thin rain, his hands in his pockets, the big skirts of his coat flapping about his legs. The camp was a dreary waste-land, tents and tarpaulin shelters leaning in a sea of mud. The lines looked deserted, except for an occasional man hurrying from one tent to another or the scream of engines as trucks fought their way on to a firm road. It must all have been sad and disappointing to him. He always looked a little hurt, for he was a willing boy and proud to be with a veteran combat unit that was waiting to go into the front line.

One day a dog came loping into the Company area. It lifted its head and looked at the passing soldiers with liquid, imploring eyes. It nosed at the flaps of the tents and made hungry mewing sounds.

The squad was crowded into a big tent. The dog trotted into the tent and stood in the doorway, trembling with the cold, looking up at the men. Grogan struck at it with a slat of wood and it scurried out.

The dog stood in the rain for a few moments, puzzled by his reception, then he trotted back into the tent. Again he was driven out. This time some G.I.'s, who were laying rubble on the road to strengthen it for trucks, threw stones at the dog. He bolted for a hundred yards, slowed down to a dejected, road-sniffing trot and vanished from sight.

Private Weaver, sitting on his own in a corner of the tent, watched all this, wondering. He did not know that Grogan, the son of a Missouri policeman, the former college footballer whose hulking, fast-moving body had got him into university on an athletic scholarship in spite of his slow mind, had once had a dog of his own. He did not know that only a year ago these soldiers had given dogs the run of their camps, stolen them sometimes, kept them as mascots. But that had been a year ago.

Private Weaver went for a walk and came back with the dog inside the breast of his topcoat. The large tent was packed with men. Five of them were playing poker. They seemed bored with the game. Grogan lay on some blankets reading a paperback. Trower sat with a pad on his knees, writing a letter. Hanging oil lamps lit the tent dimly. The air reeked of kerosene and the smell of wet clothing.

Weaver went over to his bed and began to dry the dog with his towel. In his hands the animal seemed smaller than ever. Grogan had lowered the book and was watching him. Weaver dried the dog's head and paws with gentle care, then put it down. The dog went over to Grogan and nosed about his feet.

"Hey, replacement," said Grogan, pushing the dog away, "get this dog out of here."

"He's not bothering anyone," said Weaver, in a low, obstinate voice.

"It's bothering me. We don't want any dogs in here."

"Why not? He's only a pup."

"They're dirty. They carry fleas. They make dirt." Grogan's voice was edged with impatience and irritation. "Now if I get one louse on me, I'll break your back."

He pushed his foot at the dog and sent it sprawling

amongst the poker players. One of them, Barnsby, put down his cards, picked up the dog by the scruff of its neck and flung it through the tent flaps with all his might. From the dog came a yelp as it was hurled into the wet evening.

Weaver looked uncomprehendingly around him. The poker game had already re-started. Grogan was unconcernedly reading his book and Trower was writing. Without a word, he turned up his collar and went out into the rain, slipping and stumbling on the muddy ground.

He did not return till after dark. The men were asleep. He entered the tent as quietly as he could, bent low and picking his way cautiously over the recumbent bodies. He pulled off his sodden overcoat and lay down on his blankets with his back to the others. The dog's head was peeping out from under his sweater. Weaver tried to keep the dog still by communicating his own stillness. But the warmth and the comfort brought forth squeaks of canine pleasure from the small creature. Weaver tried to stifle the yelps. But it was too late. This time both man and dog were flung out into the mud. His coat was tossed out after him.

Together they wandered in the rain looking for shelter. He found the chapel of a ruined church which could still boast of a door and a bit of roof. Weaver prowled down the stone stairs and under a stained glass window, still miraculously undamaged, he found a dry spot. He tied the dog to a stone and fed it some of his K-rations. That night he slept on a stone floor that was wet and filthy. Rain dripped through the bare slat of the ceiling and was borne in through the gaping windows and walls by each gust of cold wind. Here he established a home for himself and the dog.

The next day some of the men discovered his secret. They jeered at him and called him Doggy. He did not answer, but went about his duties with a blank, lowered expression. There was no hope in his white, thin face. He could not understand why the men resented him so and how they could work up so much antagonism against a dog. He could not appreciate their antipathy towards him just because he was a fellow-American bearing the derogatory epithet of "replacement." He could not accept the fact that they considered him an outsider.

When he was away from the bombed-out church, Weaver kept the dog tied up, with plenty of food and water and a nest of sacking to sleep in. He dared not let the dog loose, for it would have come prowling into the camp after him, to its peril.

It was a couple of days later that Weaver approached Trower. The Sergeant was sitting at a table in front of a tent filling out forms and jotting in a notebook.

"Sergeant," said Weaver.

"If it's about the dog," said Trower, not looking up from his writing, "don't bother me."

"But it's a shame to keep a dog tied up all day long."

Trower continued writing.

"Let him go."

"But he's only a puppy. Don't you feel sorry for him?"

"Sure, I feel sorry for him. I feel sorry for everybody. I feel sorry for myself, too."

"But everybody likes a dog."

"Well, my men don't."

"They don't like me either. I never did anything to any of them. I didn't ask to be sent here."

Trower stopped writing and looked up at Weaver. There was no humour in the Sergeant's smile.

"Well, neither did they," said Trower. "Maybe they don't like you because you're fresh from home. You've been back there all this time, they've been here."

"That's not my fault."

"Doesn't matter whose fault. But they've got enough to worry about. And anyway they want it, is good enough for me. And I don't want to hear any more about it." His voice took on a more brittle tone. "I mean it."

Trower waved the young soldier away. Weaver turned to go, hopelessly.

"Hey, Weaver," said Trower, putting down his notebook and standing up. "We don't keep dogs any more because when we move out we have to shoot them, otherwise they'd starve to death. You see?...Now I'll give you some advice. It's different out here. It's not like back home at all. If you want to stay healthy, don't...don't make any trouble. Don't get on anybody's nerves. You understand?"

Weaver stared at Trower, shocked by the quiet menace in Trower's voice. The young soldier turned and walked away. Trower looked after him for a few moments and then went back to his work.

A few days later the order came to move. Sergeants lurched along the muddy paths calling their squads together. Men packed their equipment and pulled down their tents and tarpaulins and heaved the paraphernalia of existence on to vehicles. For a couple of hours the camp swarmed with movement; then the men, bulky as bears in their greatcoats and packs, clustered round the lined-up trucks, and where the camp had been there was only a waste of grey mud, churned, rutted and littered with refuse.

Weaver was the last of the squad lining up to take their place in one of the trucks. He was burdened like everyone else, but looked even bulkier. Trower was at the rear of the vehicle supervising the men getting into the truck.

As Weaver went to climb into the truck, there was an excited heaving from beneath the lapels of his greatcoat. The conspicuous bulge near his chest revealed itself as the wriggling, imprisoned dog. Trower could see the dog's muzzle trying to thrust itself out to freedom and the shine of its brown eyes. He pulled open Weaver's coat, grabbed the dog and dropped it on the ground.

"Stupid idiot, I'm fed up with you," he said, shoved the young soldier over the tail-gate into the back of the truck, and went forward to the cab. Weaver sat miserably at the rear.

The truck began to move. It lurched through the mud, pulled out on to the road and took its place in the convoy as the next truck, fifty yards behind, pulled out of the camp and followed.

The men sat along the sides of the truck, looking out over the tail-gate apathetically. Grogan, who was sitting opposite Weaver, said "Look at that crazy dog." The dog was chasing the truck, his legs trotting tirelessly under him. He leaped over ruts and zig-zagged round puddles in his determination to keep up with the truck. The men watched idly, Weaver intently.

The truck gathered speed. The dog scampered more rapidly, then, with its open mouth indicating its exhaustion, lost hope and ran out to the roadside, where he stood and watched the vehicle speeding away.

Grogan's face registered disappointment. "Ah, that's too bad." he said. He looked back over his shoulder to Weaver. "Hey, give him a whistle."

Weaver's features expanded in bewildered relief at the friendly tone in Grogan's voice. Leaning over the tail-gate, he put his fingers in his mouth and called the dog with a long, fluting whistle. The dog gathered itself up and shot down the road after the truck. Weaver cried, "There he comes," and looked round at the soldiers, beaming. He must have thought that now at last, when he was going up the line, all his trials were over.

Grogan turned to Barnsby, who was sitting beside him.

"Fifty bucks?" he said. It was an offer any betting man would understand.

Weaver seemed to understand only slowly. His smile persisted, then became fixed and silly.

"You got yourself a bet," said Barnsby. He dropped on one knee, raised his rifle and, swaying with the truck, took a shot at the scampering dog. Weaver seemed to deflate. He sagged back against the taut hood of the truck, his head lolling on one side so that, still watching the dog, he appeared sightless. The only tension was in his hands, tightly gripping the barrel of the rifle that stood between his knees.

The dog had not noticed the shot, and was still bolting after the truck.

"Call yourself a soldier?" said Grogan. He took Barnsby's rifle, raised it, and fired from a standing position. The dog was lifted backwards into the air, turned over in a somersault and hit the road.

Grogan handed back the rifle to Barnsby. "There," he said, "That's fifty you owe me. Takes a soldier to do that."

Weaver sat silent and slumped with his head bowed upon the muzzle of his rifle.

* * *

"Only light resistance," the papers from home said. The Allies were roaring into the heart of Germany.

Well, the last part was true. The maps showed the great wedge of the Allied armies being hammered into the body of Germany.

But the war correspondents who talked about "light resistance" should have been with the Company when it faced a village garrisoned with fanatical S.S.

An American tank, killed by a Nazi mine, keeled on one broken track at the entrance to the village street. The infantry had been following and three corpses lay like bundles in the road. The rest of the men were in cover.

Two more American tanks stayed farther back, hull

down behind rising ground. The infantry commander directed their fire and their guns banged methodically. They knocked the quaint old spire off the quaint old village church, and killed the enemy's observers. They knocked jagged holes into old-fashioned houses where windows had been, a sniper at each window.

Then the infantry crept forward along the walls and cleared out the houses. Jagged S.S. signs shaped like lightning bolts were whitewashed on some walls. The infantry killed S.S. men as they crouched with sub-machine-guns at the back of shadowy rooms or tried to leap out of windows; and some of the infantry died doing it.

For the Company, the war was as angry as ever. "Resistance is light"—but the next village might be garrisoned by another fanatical detachment of S.S. or paratroops whose only hope and aim was to kill as many of the conquerors as possible.

The village was cleared. Sergeant Trower turned a body over with his foot. The face that stared up at him was of a seventeen-year-old boy.

G.I's were roaming to and fro across the street. A crack sounded from nowhere and Knofke fell. Chase ran to him. Knofke was dead. Around a scorched hole in his coat the smallest stain of blood splotched over his heart. Men had flung themselves into doorways and were looking around in bewilderment for the source of the fire.

A bullet screeched off the roadway. Chase heard Trower yelling, "Get down, Frank! Hit the dirt! The tank! The tank!"—and he was already running for a doorway when something hit his right side and spun him round. He fell, facing the tank, and the only pain he knew was when the back of his head hit the roadway. He heard his helmet rolling away.

Numbed, he heard shouting, then, twice, the whoof of an American bazooka. From where he lay he saw the wrecked American tank, in which the last German sniper had hidden himself, catch fire.

He was shipped to England and spent eight weeks in a hospital bed with a broken hip. The doctors told him he was lucky that there had been no splintering, and did wonders repairing the bone with pins.

After two months he was walking and a week later he could manipulate his crutches so successfully that he was given an afternoon pass out of the hospital.

He wanted to go to Blanton, a nearby village where there was another military hospital. Staff-Sergeant Craig was there, also recovering from wounds. Chase had a gift for the Sergeant in his pocket, a bottle of wine.

"You won't overdo it now, will you?" said the middle-aged English nurse as he hobbled past her down the hospital corridor.

"Just a couple of sets of tennis before tea, that's all," he said. The nurse wagged an admonitory finger at him and he gave her a friendly grimace in return.

Slowly he made his way out of the hospital grounds into the deserted Sunday streets. It was a good half-mile to the nearest bus stop and, unused to his crutches, he was very tired when he reached it. He leaned with some relief against the post and lit a cigarette. The printed time-table above his head indicated that the bus to Blanton would soon be along.

A Sabbath serenity had settled over this typical working-class street. A soft, sullen greyness indicated the imminent approach of rain. The houses were small brick boxes, one joined to another in rows that made long, monotonous perspectives. The sunken doorsteps were scrubbed spotless. Chase could see nothing but row after row of doors shut and blank against strangers.

It began to drizzle. Chase wondered whether to return to the hospital and give up his attempt to visit Craig. A woman, pushing a baby carriage, and with two young boys beside her turned the corner and hurried down the street towards Chase. They entered the doorway a few yards away from the bus standard. One of the boys stared at Chase until his mother pushed him through the open door. The street was deserted and silent again. Not a vehicle had passed Chase in twenty minutes.

He had just about abandoned his vigil when the door which the woman and children had entered opened again. A short, sturdy man came out. He was in his middle fifties. He wore a grey cardigan over his Sunday waistcoat. He came towards Chase and tapped him on the shoulder. He held an open umbrella over his head.

"Excuse me," he said in a polite, North-country voice. "If you're waiting for the bus to Blanton, I'm afraid it isn't due for another two hours."

Chase pointed wearily to the printed time-table.

"Yes, that was before the war. I'm afraid they never got around to changing it. I'm sorry."

Chase appreciated the stranger's efforts to be helpful. He had seen enough of war-time England not to be surprised by road signs and traffic directions that were years out of date.

"It's not your fault," he said. "Is there a movie around here somewhere? I mean, a cinema?"

"It doesn't open till this evening. Why don't you come in and have a cup of tea?"

"No, thanks." Chase resented any suspicion of pity.

"It's no trouble," urged the man. "My wife's just making it. Please...we'd like to have you." Chase was beginning to feel awkward in rejecting the man's obvious sincerity. "Anyway, there's nothing else open. Come on...come in."

Chase gave in. "Thanks very much," he said, moving towards the house under the shelter of the man's umbrella.

The street door opened directly into a living-room, small, spotless and full of furniture. On one of the chairs sat the young woman whom Chase had seen entering the house a few minutes before. She was holding the baby in her lap. On the sofa were the two small boys, sitting up stiff with self-conscious embarrassment at this confrontation with a stranger.

"He'll have a cup of tea," said the man, closing the door and putting down his umbrella.

A pleasant-faced, grey-haired woman, wearing an apron round her waist, came out of the kitchen and greeted Chase with a quiet smile.

"I'm glad you came in," she said. "The buses are terrible these days."

"Thank you. My name's Frank Chase." He felt awkward, leaning on his crutches in the middle of the room, facing the silent, staring boys.

"Pleased to meet you, Frank," said the man, cheerfully. "It wasn't easy to get him out of the rain, but I talked him into it." He pointed to the elderly woman. "This is my wife Joan," and then he introduced the others. "This is our son's wife, Eileen. And the boys are Tom, after his father, and William. The little one is Fiona. She came after Tom's last leave. And my name's Dennis."

Chase nodded to them all, wiping the rain from his face with a handkerchief.

"Let me take your mac," said Dennis, helping Chase take off his rain coat. "You must be soaking." He led Chase to a chair beside the fireplace where a great red bank of coals was blazing behind the bars of the grate.

"Now you just sit here beside the fire and make yourself comfortable." The whistle of a kettle could be heard coming from the kitchen. The two women could be heard setting out the paraphernalia of an English tea—teapots, cups and saucers, jugs of hot water, plates of bread and cake, dishes of jam.

"I'll help with the tea," said Dennis, leaving Chase alone in the room with the two boys. After fidgeting uncomfortably on the sofa in unaccustomed silence, the youngest boy, William, followed his grandfather into the kitchen.

Chase was touched by the natural and unassuming hospitality that he was being given. He relaxed in front of the fire and was warmed by a state of mellow contentment. The oldest boy, Tom, was still sitting on the settee staring at Chase. He had been fascinated by Chase's crutches and uniform.

"Going to be a soldier when you grow up?" asked Chase, making conversation.

"No," said the boy, squirming uneasily at the prospect of having to talk. "Me Dad don't like it."

Chase grinned.

"Good for him," he said, lighting another cigarette and closing his eyes.

The tea arrived. The table was laid with a spotless white cloth, a rose-painted tea service and a set of gleaming cutlery. Tea turned out to be a generous meal with inch-thick slices cut from a fresh loaf of bread, smoked haddock served swimming in melted butter, a cut-glass dish of jam full of real strawberries and a home-baked fruit cake.

They talked in a homely, amiable way while they ate. Chase told them he was going to Blanton to see a wounded friend. Dennis said he was a foundry worker and he talked about the foundry, their married children and what diversions there were to be found in the town on a weekday. They asked him no questions, except of the most polite kind, and when the dishes had been cleared away, Joan said, "Shut your eyes if you want to. Don't mind us." Chase answered that he was not tired but—out of sheer contentment and the soporific warmth of the tea and fire—he fell asleep.

He was awakened by Dennis gently shaking his arm.

"Your bus will be along soon," Dennis said.

"Oh," said Chase, sitting up and taking a few seconds to realize where he was. "Oh...I'm sorry."

Dennis was handing him his crutches.

"It did you good. You were tired. But you don't want to miss your bus, do you?"

"No," said Chase, rising from his chair and feeling embarrassed that he had fallen asleep.

"The rain's stopped," said Dennis, handing him his coat and his cap.

"Good," said Chase, adjusting the crutches under his arms and flinging the coat over his shoulder. "Thank you." He saw Joan and Eileen standing at the entrance to the kitchen. "Well, I was the life of the party, wasn't I?" He hobbled over to the two women. "Oh, thank you for the tea. It was very kind."

"No, it wasn't," said Joan, firmly brushing away his gratitude. "You're welcome."

"I hope your husband gets home soon," Chase said to Eileen.

"Better hurry!" cried Dennis, who was at the open door looking down the street. There was a flurry of awkward handshakes and they all followed him out as he limped his way to the bus stop.

The bus had just arrived and waited at the stop with its engine running. Chase shook hands with Dennis.

"Thanks very much," he said. "Goodbye."

"Look after yourself," said Dennis. "And if you're by this way again, please come."

"I will, thanks. Next time I'll try to keep awake."

The small boy, Tom, came running forward with a bowl of apples. He held the glass bowl out and in the boy's innocent stance, the way he offered the apples, Chase caught an image of another boy who had offered him apples. Jean-Pierre! The image brought back its instinctive reaction. He shook his head, rejecting Tom's gift, and stepped aboard the bus.

The bus driver waited until he was seated before starting up. Looking back over his shoulder, he saw his new-found friends, all in a row, smiling and waving to him. He returned their wave until the corner was turned and thcy were out of view.

He settled back in his seat, warmed by the memory of their simple friendliness. Reaching into his upper breast pocket, he took out a packet of Camel cigarettes. In amongst the cigarettes, he noticed a folded bit of brown and white paper. He took it out, unfolded it, and found that it was a crisp, fresh ten-shilling note. He stared at the gift, visibly touched by this further gesture of Dennis's kindness. He looked back over his shoulder but the working-class street was well out of sight. He shook his head ruefully and carefully re-folded the note. Two dollars. A big gift, by English standards, for poor people. It was a souvenir he was determined to keep.

It was not a long drive to Blanton. The bus stopped in front of the country mansion that had been converted into a hospital. There was a large sign at the entrance to the grounds with the words, "Blanton Rehabilitation Center. U.S. Military Hospital."

No one questioned him as he made his way through the large doors into the hushed atmosphere of the spacious hall. He consulted a slip of paper on which he had written Craig's room number and slowly progressed along the quiet corridor checking the appropriate numbers.

Chase speculated about the nature of Craig's injuries as he hobbled along the gleaming, polished floors. He knew they were serious because Craig had been wounded many weeks before Chase. He recalled Trower telling him about it. Craig had seen the body of a dead American soldier floating in a canal. When Craig reached over to fish it out, the body exploded. It had been booby-trapped. They had speculated upon why someone of Craig's experience had been fooled by such a trick. They agreed that it must have been the fact that the body was in the water that had tricked Craig into acting without his normal caution. Most booby-traps worked on a wire or spring that needed a firm anchorage in the ground; not this one. Chase had asked, "What happened to him?" Trower had answered only, "He was a mess."

A few moments later Chase had found the right room number. There was a small white card on the closed door on which were written the words "S/Sgt. J. R. Craig." He took out of his raincoat pocket the bottle of wine he had brought as a gift and knocked on the door with the bottle.

"Sarge!" he called out, listening for a sign of movement inside the room.

"Who's there?" The voice was undeniably Craig's.

With his free hand, and leaning on his crutches, he turned the door handle and entered.

"Hi, Sarge!" he said, boisterously, standing at the foot of the bed and looking at the man propped up against the pillows. The joyous greeting died in his throat.

This was not Craig; at least, it was not the face of Craig. It was a mass of pink, blotched scar tissue that was all that remained of Craig's features. There was no nose, only two black holes acting as nostrils; the cheeks had been sheared away as if slashed by a knife; the eyebrows had been burnt off leaving the flickering eyes eerily alive in this dead face; the ears were crumbled knots of twisted skin.

The creature on the bed spoke again.

"Get out of here, you stupid idiot!"

The familiar abuse spoken in the old familiar way jerked Chase back to reality. He stared at the mutilated face. He walked up to the head of the bed.

"Hi, Sarge," he said, and opened the bottle of wine.

NINE

Coliseum News Special!

GERMANY SURRENDERS!

"A memorable day" says President Harry S. Truman in the White House. "This is a solemn but glorious hour. I only wish that Franklin D. Roosevelt had lived to see this day."

* * *

"A day of thanksgiving" says Winston Churchill. "But let us not forget for a moment the toils and efforts that lie ahead. Japan with all her treachery and greed remains unsubdued. The injuries which she has inflicted upon Great Britain, the United States and other countries and her detestable cruelties call for justice and retribution."

* * *

A day of reckoning for the master race, beaten, homeless and hungry. With their power-mad leaders killed or captured, these once proud conquerors are now reduced to begging, looting and pillaging, just as their blitzkrieg bully boys once did in conquered countries, but now they do it in their own backyard—until the Allies officially take over.

* * *

A glorious day for the victorious Allies who have marched the whole length of Europe to meet for the first time in the heart of Germany itself. East meets West as joint victors and friends!

* * *

A day to remember the prophetic words of the late, martyred President Franklin Delano Roosevelt already dying on his return from the Crimean conference a few short months ago.

"Never before have major Allies been more closely united, not only by their war aims, but also in their peace aims, and they're determined to continue to be united—to be united with each other and with all peace-loving nations so that the ideal of lasting peace will become a reality and I am confident that the Congress of the American people will accept the results of this conference as the beginnings of a permanent structure for peace, from which we can begin to build, under God, that better world in which our children and grandchildren, yours and mine, the children and grandchildren of the whole world must live and can live."

TEN

FIRST PICTURES!

ATOM BOMB DROPPED ON HIROSHIMA

From an escorted B.29 is loosed the greatest explosion ever caused by man. The planes manoeuvre away from the terrible concussion, as a pillar of fire and smoke which shot up 10,000 *feet at the instant of the blast, continues to rise. Mounting from the devastated city below, this column, like a giant geyser—its head mushrooming out, has in a few moments reached an altitude of* 45,000 *feet. These are official Signal Corps pictures.*

Hiroshima, first target of atomic destruction, loosed when the Emperor of Japan refused to surrender! From a lone B.29 the single atomic bomb was dropped by parachute, exploded a quarter of a mile above the ground—now hardly a building stands. Thirty-three thousand of its people were killed immediately, and equal numbers are still classified as missing.

The Victors

Never in the history of the world has such destruction been wrought.

Hiroshima, great Jap Army deployment centre, had a population of a half a million people, as big as Denver. Hiroshima today has virtually ceased to exist.

* * *

THE war in Europe had been over six months. Some men had already gone home; others were waiting for available troopships to get them back. Only two of the squad that had originally stormed the beaches in Sicily—Grogan and Trower—were still in uniform. Death, wounds and fatigue had claimed the rest. Grogan was a Sergeant in London; Trower was a Staff-Sergeant in Berlin. It was only a matter of weeks before they, too, would be back home. They had all been promised Christmas in the States.

Trower was in a long line of people waiting at the check-point before entering the Russian sector of Berlin. The people waited patiently while two bored Russian sentries checked their papers.

It was nearly four years since he had enlisted. He had looked since then into the stunned, uncomprehending eyes of dying men, he had known the sickening clutch of fear in his bowels, he had suffered the misery of dysentery and malaria, he had felt the numbing deadness of his legs knee-deep in icy Flanders water, he had seen friends die, promises and slogans fade. Four irrecoverable years of his life had vanished like a day. His face showed it.

A biting wind swept through the open square as Trower waited for the two Russian sentries at the check-point to reach him. The Russians were taking their time, meticulously surveying each document presented to them. He had been through this procedure many times before. Ever since he met Helga, he had been an almost nightly visitor to the Eastern sector.

The stories Helga had told him about the Russians, and these nightly irritations at the hands of the sentries had frayed the good-will he had once felt for his Russian allies. When he first arrived in Berlin, he was still full of admiration for their stand at Stalingrad. He had looked forward to meeting them. But he had only seen soldiers alien, hostile in their attitude, insulting, arrogant, primitive—men who could leave a barracks fouled with excrement like a stable, and who were said to have raped the young and the old like wild beasts.

By the time his turn came to have his papers checked, Trower was cold and impatient. He recognized the sentry to whom he held out his wallet with his identification card showing. The sentry knew him well, having let him pass into the Eastern sector on many nights, yet he still persisted in going through this official scrutiny of Trower's papers. A look of mutual antipathy flashed between them.

Instead of merely checking Trower's card, the sentry began to look through the rest of the papers in Trower's wallet. Furiously, Trower snatched the wallet away, deliberately took out the identification card and handed it to the sentry. Their eyes met again in hostility.

The sentry accepted Trower's challenge. He looked up and down between the photograph on the card and Trower's face with maddening slowness. Then he walked over to the second sentry and whispered something in his ear. The second sentry, suppressing a smile, glanced towards Trower and then proceeded to check the card against a list of names hanging on the wall.

Trower, knowing he was being baited, controlled his anger. They went on with their game.

"Oh, for Pete's sake..." he broke out.

The sentries glanced at him as if they had scored a point and went on pretending to scrutinize his papers. Eventually the second sentry handed Trower his card. But this was only a stage in the game. The other sentry reached for Trower's small carry-all as if to examine its contents. Trower, with a furious gesture, jerked the carry-all out of his grasp. The Russian angrily reached for it again, but the second sentry restrained him, tired of the game, and motioned Trower to move on. Firmly stuffing the carry-all under his arm, Trower entered the Eastern zone, swearing under his breath.

He tramped through the devastated Berlin streets no longer awed or impressed by the totality of the ruins around him. The jagged remnants of buildings as far as the eye could see, looked like a rocky desert. No street lamps worked, but the ruins were blanketed by moonlight.

He came to a section in which the streets still had recognisable shape. Civilians, faces down against the wind, hurried past him.

He had met Helga Metzger at a P.X. She was one of the clerical staff needed for work connected with German civilians. She also did a little translating. In spite of the non-fraternization rule everybody else, from Generals down, was going to bed with frauleins so why should he be fussy?

The flat that the Metzgers occupied was in one of those houses that had been partially bombed yet miraculously could still be lived in. He walked up two flights of stairs and rang the bell. As always he was puzzled by a narrow slit of unpainted wood, about two inches long, on the wooden framework around the door. He was not to know that a mezzuzah had once been nailed to that spot indicating the presence of orthodox Jews. The mezzuzah was gone and only its scar remained.

The door was opened by Herr Metzger, a man in his

middle fifties wearing a small moustache and steel-rimmed glasses. He had pleasant features and his brow was wrinkled in a perpetual frown. His clothes seemed a little large for him, as if he had either shrunk or they were not his own.

The anxious look on his face changed into a broad smile as he recognized Trower.

"Ah, der Herr Sergeant. Guten abend, Herr Sergeant."

"Good evening, Herr Metzger," said Trower.

"Kommen sie herein," said Metzger, nodding effusively and taking Trower's hat and coat. "Mutter," he called to the kitchen, "Herr Sergeant."

The living room, although sparsely furnished, was clean and tidy. The furniture was solid and respectable with a few family photographs on the mantelpiece. It was warm and friendly.

Frau Metzger, a small, plump, dumpling of a woman, came into the room from the adjoining kitchen, smiling and bowing. Her fair, round face was still rosy from the heat of the oven. She added her enthusiastic welcome in German.

"Is cold, yah?" said Herr Metzger. "Winter coming, yah." It was obvious his range of conversation in English was limited.

"Your English is coming along, too," said Trower, approvingly. "Is Helga home?"

Metzger was still busily hanging up Trower's coat with the humility and obsequiousness of a porter. He quickly turned to Trower to answer his question.

"Helga. Nein. Nein. She is coming. . ." He groped for the next word in English, was unable to find it and reached for a pocket dictionary in his jacket.

"Soon?" said Trower, smiling.

"Yah, yah, soon. She is coming soon." He laughed at his linguistic clumsiness.

Trower picked up his carry-all and went into the

kitchen. He walked over to the large stove and sniffed at the bubbling saucepan.

"Hey, that smells good," he said, nodding appreciatively. "Wonderful. Sehr gut."

Frau Metzger beamed at the compliment.

Trower carried the hold-all to the kitchen table and proceeded to take from it a variety of tins and packages of food—breakfast cereal, coffee, jam, butter, tinned soup and vegetables. The Metzgers watched him with speechless gratitude. Unable to contain herself, Frau Metzger, her eyes moist with emotion, took hold of his hands and began to kiss them.

The display of effusive gratitude for such paltry gifts embarrassed him. He pulled his hands away from her.

"Please, don't do that," he said.

She continued to thank him in German with her head bobbing up and down. From the bag, he lifted out a portable radio.

"For Helga," he said, holding it up.

Frau Metzger poured out effusive thanks in German.

"She says when you go home, she sad in heart," said Herr Metzger, carefully doing his best to translate his wife's words.

"Who's going home? They've forgotten all about me." Trower was now picking out the last tin from his bag.

Herr Metzger, holding his dictionary in his right hand, dutifully translated Trower's remark. Frau Metzger spoke again, her face screwed up with doleful foreboding.

"Mama say what a shame to keep a boy away from home when the war is over," said Herr Metzger. "But if Americans go, who would" (he had to search for the word in the dictionary) "protect us from the Russians?"

"Yeah." Curtly. The door-bell rang.

"Hey, that's Helga," he said, going to the door in the living room and opening it.

It wasn't Helga at the door. The girl was in her middle

twenties, over-blonde and wearing an elaborate, bushy fur coat that might have been bear-skin. On her head was a white fox-fur beret. Her pert features stared at him with a cynically assured expression.

"The boy friend, yah?" she said in English, looking at the Metzgers who were standing behind Trower.

She brushed past Trower and kissed her mother and father, greeting them formally in German. She turned to Trower, "I come at a bad time, yes? I tell my parents not to worry, you won't run away from them. It's Helga you like, not them."

The girl's parents stood in embarrassed silence at the entrance to the kitchen. Trower was puzzled by the tension in the room.

The girl laughed at the Metzger's evident consternation and walked into the kitchen. They all followed her in.

She went to the kitchen table and disdainfully picked up the tins that Trower had brought.

"So nice," she said, "This one is very generous. And I have brought you so very little." She drew out of her bag two eggs and held them up sardonically. "Two little German eggs...only two little German eggs."

She put the eggs on the table and turned to Trower. She spoke in a tone of deliberate challenge.

"I am sister of Helga."

"How do you do?"

She pulled back a chair and sat down, inspecting him with irony. Her parents had shrunk into unhappy silence in the background. He sat down opposite her at the table.

"They are ashamed from me," she said, throwing her head back in the direction of her parents. "I have a Russian boy friend. A Captain." There was a note of defiant pride in her voice.

"That's nice," said Trower, quietly. He noted that her parents had now turned their backs on her and were washing up at the sink.

"He give me this," she said, standing up and pirouetting to show her coat, "and this," she held out her right arm to display an expensive-looking wrist-watch.

"Congratulations," said Trower.

From her bag, she took out a large box of Russian cigarettes and offered them to Trower. He shook his head. She held out the open box to her father.

"Go on, papa, take," she said. "The Sergeant don't care. He will give you some American cigarettes, too, and you sell them and get rich."

"Nein, danke," said Herr Metzger, his eyes fixed on the floor.

The girl defiantly put one of the cigarettes in her mouth and shook away Trower's offer to light it. She lit it with a large lighter of her own. Herr Metzger shuffled over to the table with an ash-tray and returned to the sink.

"You are speaking German?" she said to Trower.

"No, not much."

"French?"

"No. Not really."

"My Captain speaks four languages." She was obviously determined to bait Trower. "Your people have no culture. You see this flat? My Captain. Otherwise they would live in camp. But they are ashamed from me."

"I don't think they are ashamed of you."

"Oh, yah!" There was a grating harshness in her laugh. "They don't like Russians. But they take...How long you go with Helga?"

"Quite a while now."

"She'll make you crazy. She has Russian boy friend too, once."

The girl realized she had taken him by surprise.

"She don't tell you from him? He is friend of my Captain. He is Captain, too. Very handsome. He has very nice girl friend now, much more pretty from Helga.

Actress. Was in movies. Very nice. I think Helga is sorry now."

Trower's lips tightened in suppressed anger. He knew she wanted him to lose his temper. She was obviously enjoying his discomfiture.

"You let Helga go out with other soldiers?"

"Sometimes."

"My Captain don't let me go with nobody."

"Good for him."

"You get Helga job in P.X.?"

"No, I didn't."

"My Captain gave me job. In office."

Trower was starting to hate her. He heard a motorcycle stopping outside the building. Without a word to Helga's sister, he got up and went to the window and parted the curtains. He just managed to catch sight of a motorcycle, driven by an American soldier, disappearing down the street. A minute later the living-room door opened and Helga came in.

Flushed with cold, she was younger and she looked pretty with an innocence that her sister lacked. Her blonde hair was done up in the plaited style of the German mädchen and she was wearing a simply-cut skirt and khaki army shirt which managed to look successfully feminine on her. Yet in the childish face her eyes were knowing.

As she came into the kitchen, she saw her sister and stood as if she comprehended all.

"Ach, Trudi..." she said. She recovered her aplomb, blew a kiss to Trower who was still at the window, and formally kissed her parents.

Slipping off her coat and tossing it on a chair, she said, "Die Frau Kapitan ist hier," and to Trower, "We are honoured tonight." Although Trower could barely understand German, he sensed the deep hostility between the two sisters. Their parents made up a silent and uneasy audience.

"You're looking tired," said Trudi, in English, puffing cigarette smoke disdainfully in the air. "Is hard work in P.X., yes?"

"No, is easy," said Helga. Their use of English enabled them to be frigidly remote as well as maintaining a veneer of politeness to each other in front of Trower.

Helga, having adjusted to her sister's presence, was now determined to be aggressively affectionate to Trower.

"Hello, darling," she said, putting her arms around his neck and kissing him ostentatiously. Trower realized uncomfortably that the embrace was more for Trudi's benefit than for his. He could only manage a stiff response.

At that moment Helga saw the radio on the table.

"Oh, honey!" she said, picking it up and examining it eagerly, "Exactly what I asked for." She held it out to Trudi, bubbling over with provocative enthusiasm. "Nice, yes? American is best, yah?"

Trower watched their verbal scratching with increasing discomfort.

Helga, clutching the radio to her bosom, danced over to the draining board where she plugged it into a socket over the sink. The small ivory box burst into a loud explosion of dance music.

"Prima, yah?" said Helga, looking at her sister.

Trudi made a sour grimace and put her hands over her ears.

"It's too loud," she complained.

Helga, who had come back to the kitchen table, shrugged off her complaint.

"I like it," she said, defiantly.

Trudi, with an elaborate gesture, looked at her wrist-watch.

"I have to go," she said, getting up. "We have a party tonight. Goodbye."

Helga, examining the tins of food on the table, did not look at her sister as she casually replied, "Bye bye."

Trudi paused for a moment, studying her sister, and then said goodbye to her parents. "Auf wiedersehen, Sergeant," she called out before leaving.

"Goodbye," said Trower, thankful she was going at last.

There was an uncomfortable silence for a moment on Trudi's exit from the kitchen. It was broken by a petulant outburst in German from Helga.

"What are we waiting for? He's hungry. So am I. Why don't we eat?" Trower could just interpret the key words.

Her parents, startled into obedient action by her words, began silently to lay the table and prepare the serving of the meal.

Trudi, however, had not yet gone. With a jaunty smile, she was back at the kitchen door, looking at Helga.

"Helga," she said, "I say hello for you to everybody."

She did not wait for Helga to reply. They knew she was gone because they heard the outside door slam.

Helga sensed the fact that Trudi's parting gibe had made its impact on Trower.

"Cow!" she said, almost spitting the word. "You know why she comes tonight? She wants me to go to party with her. With Russians."

She got up from the table and pulled out the plug of the radio which had been swamping the kitchen with over-loud jazz. She carried the radio into the living-room and Trower followed her.

"Would that be so unusual?" he said, his jealousy aroused by Trudi.

Helga turned on him, angrily.

"What you talk about?"

"Well, she said you had a Russian boy friend once. A Captain."

"She said this?" Helga's voice was lifted in outrage. "Me with Russians. After what they do to me? You believe crazy thing like that?"

She folded her arms, staring at him with frigid fury.

"Well, that's what she said," answered Trower, retreating before her anger.

"Pappi," cried Helga, storming into the kitchen and calling to her father in German with hurt indignation. Trower heard her rapid, high-pitched protest. He caught the words "rüssisch...freund...schwein..."

The Metzgers, startled by Helga's outburst, obeyed energetically.

"Never, Sergeant, never," said Herr Metzger, coming out of the kitchen, his face a picture of pained remonstrance. "She is good girl. Never with Russians."

"Never mind," Trower said, trying to calm them all down. "It doesn't matter. I didn't believe her anyway."

Frau Metzger began to weep. She lamented and wrung her hands in her apron.

Her husband put his arm around her heaving shoulders, trying to comfort her. Helga seemed to have lost interest in the subject. She was on her knees plugging the radio into a new socket in a corner of the living room.

"What's she saying?" asked Trower, baffled by Frau Metzger's tears.

Helga shrugged her pretty shoulders, obviously bored by this display by her parents.

"Oh, she says how they came to the house and took everything away and put us in the street."

"How could they do that?"

"I don't know. They just did." She was on her knees trying to get the radio going. "They say the house is too big for us."

"Well, they gave you this place according to your sister."

"That's right," said Helga, unperturbed. The radio was now transmitting another gay tune, this time in French.

"Listen, darling," she cried. "Paris. Come on." She got up and put her arms around Trower. They began to dance and their differences were momentarily forgotten. The Metzgers watched them for a moment or two and then went back to the kitchen to get the meal ready.

Frau Metzger's cooking was both tasteful and ample. The unpleasantness of Trudi's appearance was forgotten as they relaxed before the fireplace after dinner. Frau Metzger had socks to darn, her husband intensely studied a chess problem, while Helga and Trower held hands as they listened to records on the Armed Forces programme. The young people were gently dozing, Helga's head on Trower's lap, when a crescendo of finale music indicated that the radio station was shutting down for the night. Helga opened her eyes and switched off the radio.

"Come on, sweetie," she said, pulling him out of his chair.

Trower smiled drowsily at her.

"Where?" he asked.

Helga indicated the bedroom.

"Oh, we changed rooms today," she said. "From today I sleep in bedroom."

She recognized the look of puzzled concern in Trower's face.

"Don't forget, I work," she said, trying to explain away the fact that they were depriving her parents of their bed. "I need rest. Don't worry about them. They eat good." She glanced impatiently at her parents and said, "Gute nacht."

As ever, the Metzgers revealed nothing but polite pleasure at whatever happened to them. They bowed and

smiled at their daughter as if it were perfectly normal [illegible]
they should be sleeping in the living-room while [illegible]
daughter took her lover to bed in their bedroom. [illegible]
had suffered too much, this elderly pair, they had [illegible]
crushed too often, they were too used to obeying.

"Come on, darling," said Helga, opening the [illegible]
door. "Come on."

The cold indifference of Helga to the [illegible]
her own parents embarrassed Trower. Although he [illegible]
made love to Helga often, there had always been, [illegible]
now, at least the pretence that they had not. They [illegible]
shared the couch in the living room while her [illegible]
had discreetly retired. The blatant recognition of [illegible]
relationship in Helga's own home made him [illegible]
awkward.

Trying to somehow make amends, he handed [illegible]
father an almost full packet of cigarettes.

"Keep those," he said. The gesture did not [illegible]
his sensation of guilt. "I have another packet."

Herr Metzger eagerly took the cigarettes and [illegible]
them into the pocket of his cardigan.

"Danke schön. Danke sehr," he said, [illegible]
Trower. "Gute nacht."

Trower, still uncomfortable, nodded to the [illegible]
and followed Helga into the bedroom. Passing [illegible]
mantelpiece he saw, not for the first time, a [illegible]
bordered in black crepe. The picture was of two [illegible]
men in German uniform, boys really, smiling, [illegible]
and almost classically Nordic-looking. He knew that [illegible]
were Helga's brothers. He entered the bedroom.

Helga, closing the door behind Trower, turned to [illegible]

"Please don't give papa so much cigarettes," she [illegible]
"If he has cigarettes to sell, he don't have to work."

Helga spoke with casual detachment. She [illegible]
was completely unconcerned about her parents. [illegible]
turned on the light near the bed and plugged in the [illegible]

JULIUS CAESAR

JULIUS CÆSAR
S.P.Q.R
POMP

JULIUS CAESAR

BY

WILLIAM SHAKESPEARE

1870 EDITION

ORIGINALLY WRITTEN IN 1599

ILLUSTRATED by H. C. SELOUS

ILLUSTRATED PLAYS OF
WILLIAM SHAKESPEARE
PUBLISHED BY

EDITION INFORMATION
The illustrations are by H. C. Selous. The cover is based on an 1805 painting entitled "The Assassination of Julius Caesar" by Vincenzo Camuccini.

PERMISSIONS
The 16 illustrations appearing in this publication, including the frontispiece, are courtesy of Michael John Goodman, The Victorian Illustrated Shakespeare Archive, January 20, 2019. They are drawn by H.C. Selous and appeared in the 1870 Cassell & Company printing of *The Plays of William Shakespeare.*

SeaWolf Press
P.O. Box 961
Orinda, CA 94563
Email: support@seawolfpress.com
Web: http://www.SeaWolfPress.com

CONTENTS

ACT I

ACT II

ACT III

ACT IV

ACT V

Dramatis Personæ

JULIUS CAESAR
OCTAVIUS CAESAR, Triumvir after his death.
MARCUS ANTONIUS, Triumvir after his death.
M. AEMILIUS LEPIDUS, Triumvir after his death.
CICERO, PUBLIUS, POPILIUS LENA, Senators.
MARCUS BRUTUS, Conspirator against Caesar.
CASSIUS, Conspirator against Caesar.
CASCA, Conspirator against Caesar.
TREBONIUS, Conspirator against Caesar.
LIGARIUS, Conspirator against Caesar.
DECIUS BRUTUS, Conspirator against Caesar.
METELLUS CIMBER, Conspirator against Caesar.
CINNA, Conspirator against Caesar.
FLAVIUS, tribune
MARULLUS, tribune
ARTEMIDORUS, a Sophist of Cnidos.
A Soothsayer
CINNA, a poet.
Another Poet.
LUCILIUS, TITINIUS, MESSALA, young CATO, and VOLUMNIUS,
Friends to Brutus and Cassius.
VARRO, CLITUS, CLAUDIUS, STRATO, LUCIUS, DARDANIUS,
Servants to Brutus
PINDARUS, Servant to Cassius
CALPHURNIA, wife to Caesar
PORTIA, wife to Brutus

The Ghost of Caesar
Senators, Citizens, Soldiers, Commoners, Messengers, and Servants.

SCENE: *Rome, the conspirators' camp near Sardis, and the plains of Philippi.*

JULIUS CAESAR

ACT I

SCENE I. *Rome. A street.*

Enter FLAVIUS, MARULLUS *and a throng of Citizens.*

FLAVIUS.

Hence! home, you idle creatures, get you home.
Is this a holiday? What, know you not,
Being mechanical, you ought not walk
Upon a labouring day without the sign
Of your profession? Speak, what trade art thou?

CARPENTER.

Why, sir, a carpenter.

MARULLUS.

Where is thy leather apron and thy rule?
What dost thou with thy best apparel on?
You, sir, what trade are you?

COBBLER.

Truly, sir, in respect of a fine workman, I am but, as you would say, a cobbler.

MARULLUS.

But what trade art thou? Answer me directly.

COBBLER.

A trade, sir, that I hope I may use with a safe conscience, which is indeed, sir, a mender of bad soles.

MARULLUS.

What trade, thou knave? Thou naughty knave, what trade?

COBBLER.

Nay, I beseech you, sir, be not out with me; yet, if you be out, sir, I can mend you.

MARULLUS.

What mean'st thou by that? Mend me, thou saucy fellow!

COBBLER.

Why, sir, cobble you.

FLAVIUS.

Thou art a cobbler, art thou?

COBBLER.

Truly, sir, all that I live by is with the awl; I meddle with no tradesman's matters, nor women's matters, but with awl. I am indeed, sir, a surgeon to old shoes: when they are in great danger, I recover them. As proper men as ever trod upon neat's leather have gone upon my handiwork.

FLAVIUS.

But wherefore art not in thy shop today?
Why dost thou lead these men about the streets?

COBBLER.

Truly, sir, to wear out their shoes, to get myself into more work. But indeed, sir, we make holiday to see Caesar, and to rejoice in his triumph.

MARULLUS.

Wherefore rejoice? What conquest brings he home?
What tributaries follow him to Rome,
To grace in captive bonds his chariot wheels?
You blocks, you stones, you worse than senseless things!
O you hard hearts, you cruel men of Rome,
Knew you not Pompey? Many a time and oft
Have you climb'd up to walls and battlements,
To towers and windows, yea, to chimney tops,
Your infants in your arms, and there have sat
The livelong day with patient expectation,
To see great Pompey pass the streets of Rome.
And when you saw his chariot but appear,

Have you not made an universal shout,
That Tiber trembled underneath her banks
To hear the replication of your sounds
Made in her concave shores?
And do you now put on your best attire?
And do you now cull out a holiday?
And do you now strew flowers in his way,
That comes in triumph over Pompey's blood?
Be gone!
Run to your houses, fall upon your knees,
Pray to the gods to intermit the plague
That needs must light on this ingratitude.

FLAVIUS.

Go, go, good countrymen, and, for this fault
Assemble all the poor men of your sort,
Draw them to Tiber banks, and weep your tears
Into the channel, till the lowest stream
Do kiss the most exalted shores of all.

Exeunt Citizens.

See whether their basest metal be not mov'd;
They vanish tongue-tied in their guiltiness.
Go you down that way towards the Capitol;
This way will I. Disrobe the images,
If you do find them deck'd with ceremonies.

MARULLUS.

May we do so?
You know it is the feast of Lupercal.

FLAVIUS.

It is no matter; let no images
Be hung with Caesar's trophies. I'll about
And drive away the vulgar from the streets;
So do you too, where you perceive them thick.
These growing feathers pluck'd from Caesar's wing
Will make him fly an ordinary pitch,
Who else would soar above the view of men,
And keep us all in servile fearfulness.

Exeunt.

SCENE II. *The same. A public place.*

Enter, in procession, with music, CAESAR; ANTONY, *for the course;* CALPHURNIA, PORTIA, DECIUS, CICERO, BRUTUS, CASSIUS *and* CASCA; *a great crowd following, among them a* SOOTHSAYER.

CAESAR.

Calphurnia.

CASCA.

Peace, ho! Caesar speaks.

Music ceases.

CAESAR.

Calphurnia.

CALPHURNIA.

Here, my lord.

CAESAR.

Stand you directly in Antonius' way,
When he doth run his course. Antonius.

ANTONY.

Caesar, my lord?

CAESAR.

Forget not in your speed, Antonius,
To touch Calphurnia; for our elders say,
The barren, touched in this holy chase,
Shake off their sterile curse.

ANTONY.

I shall remember.
When Caesar says "Do this," it is perform'd.

CAESAR.

Set on; and leave no ceremony out.

Music.

SOOTHSAYER.

Caesar!

CAESAR.

Ha! Who calls?

CASCA.

Bid every noise be still; peace yet again!

Music ceases.

CAESAR.

Who is it in the press that calls on me?
I hear a tongue shriller than all the music,
Cry "Caesar"! Speak. Caesar is turn'd to hear.

SOOTHSAYER.

Beware the Ides of March.

Cassius. Will you go see the order of the course?
Brutus. Not I. *Act I. Scene II.*

CAESAR.

What man is that?

BRUTUS.

A soothsayer bids you beware the Ides of March.

CAESAR.

Set him before me; let me see his face.

CASSIUS.

Fellow, come from the throng; look upon Caesar.

CAESAR.

What say'st thou to me now? Speak once again.

SOOTHSAYER.

Beware the Ides of March.

CAESAR.

He is a dreamer; let us leave him. Pass.

Sennet. Exeunt all but BRUTUS *and* CASSIUS.

CASSIUS.

Will you go see the order of the course?

BRUTUS.

Not I.

CASSIUS.

I pray you, do.

BRUTUS.

I am not gamesome: I do lack some part
Of that quick spirit that is in Antony.
Let me not hinder, Cassius, your desires;
I'll leave you.

CASSIUS.

Brutus, I do observe you now of late:
I have not from your eyes that gentleness
And show of love as I was wont to have.
You bear too stubborn and too strange a hand
Over your friend that loves you.

BRUTUS.

Cassius,
Be not deceived: if I have veil'd my look,
I turn the trouble of my countenance
Merely upon myself. Vexed I am
Of late with passions of some difference,
Conceptions only proper to myself,
Which give some soil perhaps to my behaviors;
But let not therefore my good friends be grieved
(Among which number, Cassius, be you one)
Nor construe any further my neglect,
Than that poor Brutus, with himself at war,
Forgets the shows of love to other men.

CASSIUS.

Then, Brutus, I have much mistook your passion;
By means whereof this breast of mine hath buried
Thoughts of great value, worthy cogitations.
Tell me, good Brutus, can you see your face?

BRUTUS.

No, Cassius, for the eye sees not itself
But by reflection, by some other things.

CASSIUS.

'Tis just:
And it is very much lamented, Brutus,
That you have no such mirrors as will turn
Your hidden worthiness into your eye,
That you might see your shadow. I have heard
Where many of the best respect in Rome,
(Except immortal Caesar) speaking of Brutus,
And groaning underneath this age's yoke,
Have wish'd that noble Brutus had his eyes.

BRUTUS.

Into what dangers would you lead me, Cassius,
That you would have me seek into myself
For that which is not in me?

CASSIUS.

Therefore, good Brutus, be prepared to hear;
And since you know you cannot see yourself
So well as by reflection, I, your glass,
Will modestly discover to yourself
That of yourself which you yet know not of.
And be not jealous on me, gentle Brutus:
Were I a common laugher, or did use
To stale with ordinary oaths my love
To every new protester; if you know
That I do fawn on men, and hug them hard,
And after scandal them; or if you know
That I profess myself in banqueting,
To all the rout, then hold me dangerous.
Flourish and shout.

BRUTUS.

What means this shouting? I do fear the people
Choose Caesar for their king.

CASSIUS.

Ay, do you fear it?
Then must I think you would not have it so.

BRUTUS.

I would not, Cassius; yet I love him well,
But wherefore do you hold me here so long?
What is it that you would impart to me?
If it be aught toward the general good,
Set honor in one eye and death i' the other,
And I will look on both indifferently;
For let the gods so speed me as I love
The name of honor more than I fear death.

CASSIUS.

I know that virtue to be in you, Brutus,
As well as I do know your outward favour.
Well, honor is the subject of my story.
I cannot tell what you and other men
Think of this life; but, for my single self,
I had as lief not be as live to be
In awe of such a thing as I myself.
I was born free as Caesar; so were you;
We both have fed as well, and we can both
Endure the winter's cold as well as he:
For once, upon a raw and gusty day,
The troubled Tiber chafing with her shores,
Caesar said to me, "Dar'st thou, Cassius, now
Leap in with me into this angry flood,
And swim to yonder point?" Upon the word,
Accoutred as I was, I plunged in,
And bade him follow: so indeed he did.
The torrent roar'd, and we did buffet it
With lusty sinews, throwing it aside
And stemming it with hearts of controversy.
But ere we could arrive the point propos'd,
Caesar cried, "Help me, Cassius, or I sink!"
I, as Aeneas, our great ancestor,
Did from the flames of Troy upon his shoulder
The old Anchises bear, so from the waves of Tiber
Did I the tired Caesar. And this man
Is now become a god; and Cassius is
A wretched creature, and must bend his body,

If Caesar carelessly but nod on him.
He had a fever when he was in Spain,
And when the fit was on him I did mark
How he did shake: 'tis true, this god did shake:
His coward lips did from their colour fly,
And that same eye whose bend doth awe the world
Did lose his lustre. I did hear him groan:
Ay, and that tongue of his, that bade the Romans
Mark him, and write his speeches in their books,
Alas, it cried, "Give me some drink, Titinius,"
As a sick girl. Ye gods, it doth amaze me,
A man of such a feeble temper should
So get the start of the majestic world,
And bear the palm alone.

Shout. Flourish.

BRUTUS.

Another general shout?
I do believe that these applauses are
For some new honors that are heap'd on Caesar.

CASSIUS.

Why, man, he doth bestride the narrow world
Like a Colossus, and we petty men
Walk under his huge legs, and peep about
To find ourselves dishonorable graves.
Men at some time are masters of their fates:
The fault, dear Brutus, is not in our stars,
But in ourselves, that we are underlings.
"Brutus" and "Caesar": what should be in that "Caesar"?
Why should that name be sounded more than yours?
Write them together, yours is as fair a name;
Sound them, it doth become the mouth as well;
Weigh them, it is as heavy; conjure with 'em,
"Brutus" will start a spirit as soon as "Caesar."
Now in the names of all the gods at once,
Upon what meat doth this our Caesar feed,
That he is grown so great? Age, thou art sham'd!
Rome, thou hast lost the breed of noble bloods!
When went there by an age since the great flood,
But it was fam'd with more than with one man?
When could they say, till now, that talk'd of Rome,

That her wide walls encompass'd but one man?
Now is it Rome indeed, and room enough,
When there is in it but one only man.
O, you and I have heard our fathers say,
There was a Brutus once that would have brook'd
Th' eternal devil to keep his state in Rome,
As easily as a king!

BRUTUS.

That you do love me, I am nothing jealous;
What you would work me to, I have some aim:
How I have thought of this, and of these times,
I shall recount hereafter. For this present,
I would not, so with love I might entreat you,
Be any further mov'd. What you have said,
I will consider; what you have to say
I will with patience hear; and find a time
Both meet to hear and answer such high things.
Till then, my noble friend, chew upon this:
Brutus had rather be a villager
Than to repute himself a son of Rome
Under these hard conditions as this time
Is like to lay upon us.

CASSIUS.

I am glad that my weak words
Have struck but thus much show of fire from Brutus.

Enter CAESAR *and his Train.*

BRUTUS.

The games are done, and Caesar is returning.

CASSIUS.

As they pass by, pluck Casca by the sleeve,
And he will, after his sour fashion, tell you
What hath proceeded worthy note today.

BRUTUS.

I will do so. But, look you, Cassius,
The angry spot doth glow on Caesar's brow,
And all the rest look like a chidden train:
Calphurnia's cheek is pale; and Cicero
Looks with such ferret and such fiery eyes
As we have seen him in the Capitol,
Being cross'd in conference by some senators.

Brutus. The games are done, and Cæsar is returning.
Cassius. As they pass by, pluck Casca by the sleeve.
Act I. Scene II.

CASSIUS.

Casca will tell us what the matter is.

CAESAR.

Antonius.

ANTONY.

Caesar?

CAESAR.

Let me have men about me that are fat,
Sleek-headed men, and such as sleep o' nights:
Yond Cassius has a lean and hungry look;
He thinks too much: such men are dangerous.

ANTONY.

Fear him not, Caesar; he's not dangerous;
He is a noble Roman and well given.

CAESAR.

Would he were fatter! But I fear him not:
Yet if my name were liable to fear,
I do not know the man I should avoid
So soon as that spare Cassius. He reads much,
He is a great observer, and he looks
Quite through the deeds of men. He loves no plays,
As thou dost, Antony; he hears no music.
Seldom he smiles; and smiles in such a sort
As if he mock'd himself and scorn'd his spirit
That could be mov'd to smile at anything.
Such men as he be never at heart's ease
Whiles they behold a greater than themselves,
And therefore are they very dangerous.
I rather tell thee what is to be fear'd
Than what I fear; for always I am Caesar.
Come on my right hand, for this ear is deaf,
And tell me truly what thou think'st of him.

Exeunt CAESAR *and his Train.* CASCA *stays.*

CASCA.

You pull'd me by the cloak; would you speak with me?

BRUTUS.

Ay, Casca, tell us what hath chanc'd today,
That Caesar looks so sad.

CASCA.

Why, you were with him, were you not?

BRUTUS.

I should not then ask Casca what had chanc'd.

CASCA.

Why, there was a crown offer'd him; and being offer'd him, he put it by with the back of his hand, thus; and then the people fell a-shouting.

BRUTUS.

What was the second noise for?

CASCA.

Why, for that too.

CASSIUS.

They shouted thrice: what was the last cry for?

CASCA.

Why, for that too.

BRUTUS.

Was the crown offer'd him thrice?

CASCA.

Ay, marry, was't, and he put it by thrice, every time gentler than other; and at every putting-by mine honest neighbors shouted.

CASSIUS.

Who offer'd him the crown?

CASCA.

Why, Antony.

BRUTUS.

Tell us the manner of it, gentle Casca.

CASCA.

I can as well be hang'd, as tell the manner of it: it was mere foolery; I did not mark it. I saw Mark Antony offer him a crown; yet 'twas not a crown neither, 'twas one of these coronets; and, as I told you, he put it by once: but, for all that, to my thinking, he would fain have had it. Then he offered it to him again: then he put it by again: but, to my thinking, he was very loath to lay his fingers off it. And then he offered it the third time; he put it the third time by; and still, as he refus'd it, the rabblement hooted, and clapp'd their chopt hands, and threw up their sweaty night-caps, and uttered such a deal of stinking breath because Caesar refus'd the crown, that it had, almost, choked Caesar, for he swooned, and fell down at it. And for mine own part, I durst not laugh, for fear of opening my lips and receiving the bad air.

CASSIUS.

But, soft! I pray you. What, did Caesar swoon?

CASCA.

He fell down in the market-place, and foam'd at mouth, and was speechless.

BRUTUS.

'Tis very like: he hath the falling-sickness.

CASSIUS.

No, Caesar hath it not; but you, and I,
And honest Casca, we have the falling-sickness.

CASCA.

I know not what you mean by that; but I am sure Caesar fell down. If the tag-rag people did not clap him and hiss him, according as he pleased and displeased them, as they use to do the players in the theatre, I am no true man.

BRUTUS.

What said he when he came unto himself?

CASCA.

Marry, before he fell down, when he perceived the common herd was glad he refused the crown, he pluck'd me ope his doublet, and offer'd them his throat to cut. And I had been a man of any occupation, if I would not have taken him at a word, I would I might go to hell among the rogues. And so he fell. When he came to himself again, he said, if he had done or said anything amiss, he desir'd their worships to think it was his infirmity. Three or four wenches where I stood cried, "Alas, good soul!" and forgave him with all their hearts. But there's no heed to be taken of them: if Caesar had stabb'd their mothers, they would have done no less.

BRUTUS.

And, after that, he came thus sad away?

CASCA.

Ay.

CASSIUS.

Did Cicero say anything?

CASCA.

Ay, he spoke Greek.

CASSIUS.

To what effect?

CASCA.

Nay, and I tell you that, I'll ne'er look you i' the face again. But those that understood him smil'd at one another and shook their heads; but for mine own part, it was Greek to me. I could tell you more news too: Marullus and Flavius, for pulling scarfs off Caesar's images, are put to silence. Fare you well. There was more foolery yet, if I could remember it.

CASSIUS.

Will you sup with me tonight, Casca?

CASCA.

No, I am promis'd forth.

CASSIUS.

Will you dine with me tomorrow?

CASCA.

Ay, if I be alive, and your mind hold, and your dinner worth the eating.

CASSIUS.

Good. I will expect you.

CASCA.

Do so; farewell both.

Exit CASCA.

BRUTUS.

What a blunt fellow is this grown to be!
He was quick mettle when he went to school.

CASSIUS.

So is he now in execution
Of any bold or noble enterprise,
However he puts on this tardy form.
This rudeness is a sauce to his good wit,
Which gives men stomach to digest his words
With better appetite.

BRUTUS.

And so it is. For this time I will leave you:
Tomorrow, if you please to speak with me,
I will come home to you; or, if you will,
Come home to me, and I will wait for you.

CASSIUS.

I will do so: till then, think of the world.

Exit BRUTUS.

Well, Brutus, thou art noble; yet I see,
Thy honorable metal may be wrought
From that it is dispos'd: therefore 'tis meet
That noble minds keep ever with their likes;
For who so firm that cannot be seduc'd?

Caesar doth bear me hard, but he loves Brutus.
If I were Brutus now, and he were Cassius,
He should not humour me. I will this night,
In several hands, in at his windows throw,
As if they came from several citizens,
Writings, all tending to the great opinion
That Rome holds of his name; wherein obscurely
Caesar's ambition shall be glanced at.
And after this, let Caesar seat him sure,
For we will shake him, or worse days endure.

Exit.

SCENE III. *The same. A street.*

Thunder and lightning. Enter, from opposite sides, Casca *with his sword drawn, and* Cicero.

Cicero.

Good even, Casca: brought you Caesar home?
Why are you breathless, and why stare you so?

Casca.

Are not you moved, when all the sway of earth
Shakes like a thing unfirm? O Cicero,
I have seen tempests, when the scolding winds
Have riv'd the knotty oaks; and I have seen
Th' ambitious ocean swell and rage and foam,
To be exalted with the threatening clouds:
But never till tonight, never till now,
Did I go through a tempest dropping fire.
Either there is a civil strife in heaven,
Or else the world too saucy with the gods,
Incenses them to send destruction.

Cicero.

Why, saw you anything more wonderful?

Casca.

A common slave, you'd know him well by sight,
Held up his left hand, which did flame and burn
Like twenty torches join'd, and yet his hand,
Not sensible of fire remain'd unscorch'd.
Besides, I ha' not since put up my sword,
Against the Capitol I met a lion,

Who glared upon me, and went surly by,
Without annoying me. And there were drawn
Upon a heap a hundred ghastly women,
Transformed with their fear; who swore they saw
Men, all in fire, walk up and down the streets.
And yesterday the bird of night did sit,
Even at noonday upon the marketplace,
Hooting and shrieking. When these prodigies
Do so conjointly meet, let not men say,
"These are their reasons; they are natural";
For I believe, they are portentous things
Unto the climate that they point upon.

CICERO.

Indeed, it is a strange-disposed time.
But men may construe things after their fashion,
Clean from the purpose of the things themselves.
Comes Caesar to the Capitol tomorrow?

CASCA.

He doth, for he did bid Antonius
Send word to you he would be there tomorrow.

CICERO.

Goodnight then, Casca: this disturbed sky
Is not to walk in.

CASCA.

Farewell, Cicero.

Exit CICERO.

Enter CASSIUS.

CASSIUS.

Who's there?

CASCA.

A Roman.

CASSIUS.

Casca, by your voice.

CASCA.

Your ear is good. Cassius, what night is this!

CASSIUS.

A very pleasing night to honest men.

CASCA.

Who ever knew the heavens menace so?

CASSIUS.

Those that have known the earth so full of faults.
For my part, I have walk'd about the streets,
Submitting me unto the perilous night;
And, thus unbraced, Casca, as you see,
Have bar'd my bosom to the thunder-stone;
And when the cross blue lightning seem'd to open
The breast of heaven, I did present myself
Even in the aim and very flash of it.

CASCA.

But wherefore did you so much tempt the Heavens?
It is the part of men to fear and tremble,
When the most mighty gods by tokens send
Such dreadful heralds to astonish us.

CASSIUS.

You are dull, Casca; and those sparks of life
That should be in a Roman you do want,
Or else you use not. You look pale and gaze,
And put on fear and cast yourself in wonder,
To see the strange impatience of the Heavens:
But if you would consider the true cause
Why all these fires, why all these gliding ghosts,
Why birds and beasts, from quality and kind;
Why old men, fools, and children calculate,
Why all these things change from their ordinance,
Their natures, and pre-formed faculties,
To monstrous quality; why, you shall find
That Heaven hath infus'd them with these spirits,
To make them instruments of fear and warning
Unto some monstrous state.
Now could I, Casca, name to thee a man
Most like this dreadful night,
That thunders, lightens, opens graves, and roars,
As doth the lion in the Capitol;
A man no mightier than thyself, or me,
In personal action; yet prodigious grown,
And fearful, as these strange eruptions are.

CASCA.

'Tis Caesar that you mean; is it not, Cassius?

CASSIUS.

Let it be who it is: for Romans now
Have thews and limbs like to their ancestors;
But, woe the while! our fathers' minds are dead,
And we are govern'd with our mothers' spirits;
Our yoke and sufferance show us womanish.

CASCA.

Indeed, they say the senators tomorrow
Mean to establish Caesar as a king;
And he shall wear his crown by sea and land,
In every place, save here in Italy.

CASSIUS.

I know where I will wear this dagger then;
Cassius from bondage will deliver Cassius:
Therein, ye gods, you make the weak most strong;
Therein, ye gods, you tyrants do defeat.
Nor stony tower, nor walls of beaten brass,
Nor airless dungeon, nor strong links of iron,
Can be retentive to the strength of spirit;
But life, being weary of these worldly bars,
Never lacks power to dismiss itself.
If I know this, know all the world besides,
That part of tyranny that I do bear
I can shake off at pleasure.

Thunder still.

CASCA.

So can I:
So every bondman in his own hand bears
The power to cancel his captivity.

CASSIUS.

And why should Caesar be a tyrant then?
Poor man! I know he would not be a wolf,
But that he sees the Romans are but sheep:
He were no lion, were not Romans hinds.
Those that with haste will make a mighty fire
Begin it with weak straws. What trash is Rome,
What rubbish, and what offal, when it serves
For the base matter to illuminate
So vile a thing as Caesar! But, O grief,

Where hast thou led me? I, perhaps, speak this
Before a willing bondman: then I know
My answer must be made; but I am arm'd,
And dangers are to me indifferent.

CASCA.

You speak to Casca, and to such a man
That is no fleering tell-tale. Hold, my hand:
Be factious for redress of all these griefs,
And I will set this foot of mine as far
As who goes farthest.

CASSIUS.

There's a bargain made.
Now know you, Casca, I have mov'd already
Some certain of the noblest-minded Romans
To undergo with me an enterprise
Of honorable-dangerous consequence;
And I do know by this, they stay for me
In Pompey's Porch: for now, this fearful night,
There is no stir or walking in the streets;
And the complexion of the element
In favour's like the work we have in hand,
Most bloody, fiery, and most terrible.

Enter CINNA.

CASCA.

Stand close awhile, for here comes one in haste.

CASSIUS.

'Tis Cinna; I do know him by his gait;
He is a friend. Cinna, where haste you so?

CINNA.

To find out you. Who's that? Metellus Cimber?

CASSIUS.

No, it is Casca, one incorporate
To our attempts. Am I not stay'd for, Cinna?

CINNA.

I am glad on't. What a fearful night is this!
There's two or three of us have seen strange sights.

CASSIUS.

Am I not stay'd for? tell me.

CINNA.

Yes, you are. O Cassius, if you could
But win the noble Brutus to our party—

CASSIUS.

Be you content. Good Cinna, take this paper,
And look you lay it in the praetor's chair,
Where Brutus may but find it; and throw this
In at his window; set this up with wax
Upon old Brutus' statue: all this done,
Repair to Pompey's Porch, where you shall find us.
Is Decius Brutus and Trebonius there?

CINNA.

All but Metellus Cimber, and he's gone
To seek you at your house. Well, I will hie,
And so bestow these papers as you bade me.

CASSIUS.

That done, repair to Pompey's theatre.

Exit CINNA.

Come, Casca, you and I will yet, ere day,
See Brutus at his house: three parts of him
Is ours already, and the man entire
Upon the next encounter, yields him ours.

CASCA.

O, he sits high in all the people's hearts!
And that which would appear offence in us,
His countenance, like richest alchemy,
Will change to virtue and to worthiness.

CASSIUS.

Him, and his worth, and our great need of him,
You have right well conceited. Let us go,
For it is after midnight; and ere day,
We will awake him, and be sure of him.

Exeunt.

ACT II

SCENE I. *Rome. Brutus' orchard.*

Enter BRUTUS.

BRUTUS.

What, Lucius, ho!
I cannot, by the progress of the stars,
Give guess how near to day.—Lucius, I say!
I would it were my fault to sleep so soundly.
When, Lucius, when? Awake, I say! What, Lucius!

Enter LUCIUS.

LUCIUS.

Call'd you, my lord?

BRUTUS.

Get me a taper in my study, Lucius:
When it is lighted, come and call me here.

LUCIUS.

I will, my lord.

Exit.

BRUTUS.

It must be by his death: and for my part,
I know no personal cause to spurn at him,
But for the general. He would be crown'd:
How that might change his nature, there's the question.
It is the bright day that brings forth the adder,
And that craves wary walking. Crown him?—that;
And then, I grant, we put a sting in him,
That at his will he may do danger with.
Th' abuse of greatness is, when it disjoins
Remorse from power; and, to speak truth of Caesar,
I have not known when his affections sway'd
More than his reason. But 'tis a common proof,
That lowliness is young ambition's ladder,
Whereto the climber-upward turns his face;
But when he once attains the upmost round,
He then unto the ladder turns his back,

Looks in the clouds, scorning the base degrees
By which he did ascend. So Caesar may;
Then lest he may, prevent. And since the quarrel
Will bear no colour for the thing he is,
Fashion it thus: that what he is, augmented,
Would run to these and these extremities:
And therefore think him as a serpent's egg
Which hatch'd, would, as his kind grow mischievous;
And kill him in the shell.

Enter LUCIUS.

LUCIUS.

The taper burneth in your closet, sir.
Searching the window for a flint, I found
This paper, thus seal'd up, and I am sure
It did not lie there when I went to bed.

Gives him the letter.

BRUTUS.

Get you to bed again; it is not day.
Is not tomorrow, boy, the Ides of March?

LUCIUS.

I know not, sir.

BRUTUS.

Look in the calendar, and bring me word.

LUCIUS.

I will, sir.

Exit.

BRUTUS.

The exhalations, whizzing in the air
Give so much light that I may read by them.

Opens the letter and reads.

Brutus, thou sleep'st: awake and see thyself.
Shall Rome, &c. Speak, strike, redress!

"Brutus, thou sleep'st: awake!"
Such instigations have been often dropp'd
Where I have took them up.
"Shall Rome, &c." Thus must I piece it out:
Shall Rome stand under one man's awe? What, Rome?

My ancestors did from the streets of Rome
The Tarquin drive, when he was call'd a king.
"Speak, strike, redress!" Am I entreated
To speak and strike? O Rome, I make thee promise,
If the redress will follow, thou receivest
Thy full petition at the hand of Brutus.

Brutus. The exhalations, whizzing in the air,
Give so much light, that I may read by them. *Act II. Scene I.*

Enter Lucius.

LUCIUS.

Sir, March is wasted fifteen days.

Knock within.

BRUTUS.

'Tis good. Go to the gate, somebody knocks.

Exit LUCIUS.

Since Cassius first did whet me against Caesar,
I have not slept.
Between the acting of a dreadful thing
And the first motion, all the interim is

Like a phantasma, or a hideous dream:
The genius and the mortal instruments
Are then in council; and the state of man,
Like to a little kingdom, suffers then
The nature of an insurrection.

Enter LUCIUS.

LUCIUS.

Sir, 'tis your brother Cassius at the door,
Who doth desire to see you.

BRUTUS.

Is he alone?

LUCIUS.

No, sir, there are more with him.

BRUTUS.

Do you know them?

LUCIUS.

No, sir, their hats are pluck'd about their ears,
And half their faces buried in their cloaks,
That by no means I may discover them
By any mark of favour.

BRUTUS.

Let 'em enter.

Exit LUCIUS.

They are the faction. O conspiracy,
Sham'st thou to show thy dangerous brow by night,
When evils are most free? O, then, by day
Where wilt thou find a cavern dark enough
To mask thy monstrous visage? Seek none, conspiracy;
Hide it in smiles and affability:
For if thou path, thy native semblance on,
Not Erebus itself were dim enough
To hide thee from prevention.

Enter CASSIUS, CASCA, DECIUS, CINNA, METELLUS CIMBER *and* TREBONIUS.

CASSIUS.

I think we are too bold upon your rest:
Good morrow, Brutus; do we trouble you?

BRUTUS.

I have been up this hour, awake all night.
Know I these men that come along with you?

CASSIUS.

Yes, every man of them; and no man here
But honors you; and everyone doth wish
You had but that opinion of yourself
Which every noble Roman bears of you.
This is Trebonius.

BRUTUS.

He is welcome hither.

CASSIUS.

This Decius Brutus.

BRUTUS.

He is welcome too.

CASSIUS.

This, Casca; this, Cinna; and this, Metellus Cimber.

BRUTUS.

They are all welcome.
What watchful cares do interpose themselves
Betwixt your eyes and night?

CASSIUS.

Shall I entreat a word?

They whisper.

DECIUS.

Here lies the east: doth not the day break here?

CASCA.

No.

CINNA.

O, pardon, sir, it doth; and yon grey lines
That fret the clouds are messengers of day.

CASCA.

You shall confess that you are both deceiv'd.
Here, as I point my sword, the Sun arises;
Which is a great way growing on the South,
Weighing the youthful season of the year.
Some two months hence, up higher toward the North

He first presents his fire; and the high East
Stands, as the Capitol, directly here.

BRUTUS.

Give me your hands all over, one by one.

CASSIUS.

And let us swear our resolution.

BRUTUS.

No, not an oath. If not the face of men,
The sufferance of our souls, the time's abuse—
If these be motives weak, break off betimes,
And every man hence to his idle bed.
So let high-sighted tyranny range on,
Till each man drop by lottery. But if these,
As I am sure they do, bear fire enough
To kindle cowards, and to steel with valour
The melting spirits of women; then, countrymen,
What need we any spur but our own cause
To prick us to redress? what other bond
Than secret Romans, that have spoke the word,
And will not palter? and what other oath
Than honesty to honesty engag'd,
That this shall be, or we will fall for it?
Swear priests and cowards, and men cautelous,
Old feeble carrions, and such suffering souls
That welcome wrongs; unto bad causes swear
Such creatures as men doubt; but do not stain
The even virtue of our enterprise,
Nor th' insuppressive mettle of our spirits,
To think that or our cause or our performance
Did need an oath; when every drop of blood
That every Roman bears, and nobly bears,
Is guilty of a several bastardy,
If he do break the smallest particle
Of any promise that hath pass'd from him.

CASSIUS.

But what of Cicero? Shall we sound him?
I think he will stand very strong with us.

CASCA.

Let us not leave him out.

CINNA.

No, by no means.

METELLUS.

O, let us have him, for his silver hairs
Will purchase us a good opinion,
And buy men's voices to commend our deeds.
It shall be said, his judgment rul'd our hands;
Our youths and wildness shall no whit appear,
But all be buried in his gravity.

BRUTUS.

O, name him not; let us not break with him;
For he will never follow anything
That other men begin.

CASSIUS.

Then leave him out.

CASCA.

Indeed, he is not fit.

DECIUS.

Shall no man else be touch'd but only Caesar?

CASSIUS.

Decius, well urg'd. I think it is not meet,
Mark Antony, so well belov'd of Caesar,
Should outlive Caesar: we shall find of him
A shrewd contriver; and you know, his means,
If he improve them, may well stretch so far
As to annoy us all; which to prevent,
Let Antony and Caesar fall together.

BRUTUS.

Our course will seem too bloody, Caius Cassius,
To cut the head off, and then hack the limbs,
Like wrath in death, and envy afterwards;
For Antony is but a limb of Caesar.
Let us be sacrificers, but not butchers, Caius.
We all stand up against the spirit of Caesar,
And in the spirit of men there is no blood.
O, that we then could come by Caesar's spirit,
And not dismember Caesar! But, alas,
Caesar must bleed for it! And, gentle friends,
Let's kill him boldly, but not wrathfully;

Let's carve him as a dish fit for the gods,
Not hew him as a carcass fit for hounds.
And let our hearts, as subtle masters do,
Stir up their servants to an act of rage,
And after seem to chide 'em. This shall make
Our purpose necessary, and not envious;
Which so appearing to the common eyes,
We shall be call'd purgers, not murderers.
And for Mark Antony, think not of him;
For he can do no more than Caesar's arm
When Caesar's head is off.

CASSIUS.

Yet I fear him;
For in the ingrafted love he bears to Caesar—

BRUTUS.

Alas, good Cassius, do not think of him:
If he love Caesar, all that he can do
Is to himself; take thought and die for Caesar.
And that were much he should; for he is given
To sports, to wildness, and much company.

TREBONIUS.

There is no fear in him; let him not die;
For he will live, and laugh at this hereafter.

Clock strikes.

BRUTUS.

Peace! count the clock.

CASSIUS.

The clock hath stricken three.

TREBONIUS.

'Tis time to part.

CASSIUS.

But it is doubtful yet
Whether Caesar will come forth today or no;
For he is superstitious grown of late,
Quite from the main opinion he held once
Of fantasy, of dreams, and ceremonies.
It may be these apparent prodigies,
The unaccustom'd terror of this night,

And the persuasion of his augurers,
May hold him from the Capitol today.

DECIUS.

Never fear that: if he be so resolved,
I can o'ersway him, for he loves to hear
That unicorns may be betray'd with trees,
And bears with glasses, elephants with holes,
Lions with toils, and men with flatterers.
But when I tell him he hates flatterers,
He says he does, being then most flattered.
Let me work;
For I can give his humour the true bent,
And I will bring him to the Capitol.

CASSIUS.

Nay, we will all of us be there to fetch him.

BRUTUS.

By the eighth hour: is that the uttermost?

CINNA.

Be that the uttermost; and fail not then.

METELLUS.

Caius Ligarius doth bear Caesar hard,
Who rated him for speaking well of Pompey;
I wonder none of you have thought of him.

BRUTUS.

Now, good Metellus, go along by him:
He loves me well, and I have given him reasons;
Send him but hither, and I'll fashion him.

CASSIUS.

The morning comes upon us. We'll leave you, Brutus.
And, friends, disperse yourselves; but all remember
What you have said, and show yourselves true Romans.

BRUTUS.

Good gentlemen, look fresh and merrily;
Let not our looks put on our purposes,
But bear it as our Roman actors do,
With untired spirits and formal constancy.
And so, good morrow to you everyone.

Exeunt all but BRUTUS.

Boy! Lucius! Fast asleep? It is no matter;
Enjoy the honey-heavy dew of slumber:
Thou hast no figures nor no fantasies,
Which busy care draws in the brains of men;
Therefore thou sleep'st so sound.

Enter PORTIA.

PORTIA.

Brutus, my lord.

BRUTUS.

Portia, what mean you? Wherefore rise you now?
It is not for your health thus to commit
Your weak condition to the raw cold morning.

PORTIA.

Nor for yours neither. Your have ungently, Brutus,
Stole from my bed; and yesternight at supper,
You suddenly arose, and walk'd about,
Musing and sighing, with your arms across;
And when I ask'd you what the matter was,
You star'd upon me with ungentle looks.
I urg'd you further; then you scratch'd your head,
And too impatiently stamp'd with your foot;
Yet I insisted, yet you answer'd not,
But with an angry wafture of your hand
Gave sign for me to leave you. So I did,
Fearing to strengthen that impatience
Which seem'd too much enkindled; and withal
Hoping it was but an effect of humour,
Which sometime hath his hour with every man.
It will not let you eat, nor talk, nor sleep;
And could it work so much upon your shape
As it hath much prevail'd on your condition,
I should not know you, Brutus. Dear my lord,
Make me acquainted with your cause of grief.

BRUTUS.

I am not well in health, and that is all.

PORTIA.

Brutus is wise, and, were he not in health,
He would embrace the means to come by it.

BRUTUS.

Why, so I do. Good Portia, go to bed.

Portia. Dear my lord,
Make me acquainted with your cause of grief.
Brutus. I am not well in health, and that is all.
Act II. Scene I.

PORTIA.

Is Brutus sick, and is it physical
To walk unbraced and suck up the humours
Of the dank morning? What, is Brutus sick,
And will he steal out of his wholesome bed
To dare the vile contagion of the night,
And tempt the rheumy and unpurged air
To add unto his sickness? No, my Brutus;

You have some sick offence within your mind,
Which, by the right and virtue of my place,
I ought to know of: and, upon my knees,
I charm you, by my once commended beauty,
By all your vows of love, and that great vow
Which did incorporate and make us one,
That you unfold to me, your self, your half,
Why you are heavy, and what men tonight
Have had resort to you; for here have been
Some six or seven, who did hide their faces
Even from darkness.

BRUTUS.

Kneel not, gentle Portia.

PORTIA.

I should not need, if you were gentle Brutus.
Within the bond of marriage, tell me, Brutus,
Is it excepted I should know no secrets
That appertain to you? Am I your self
But, as it were, in sort or limitation,
To keep with you at meals, comfort your bed,
And talk to you sometimes? Dwell I but in the suburbs
Of your good pleasure? If it be no more,
Portia is Brutus' harlot, not his wife.

BRUTUS.

You are my true and honorable wife,
As dear to me as are the ruddy drops
That visit my sad heart.

PORTIA.

If this were true, then should I know this secret.
I grant I am a woman; but withal
A woman that Lord Brutus took to wife;
I grant I am a woman; but withal
A woman well reputed, Cato's daughter.
Think you I am no stronger than my sex,
Being so father'd and so husbanded?
Tell me your counsels, I will not disclose 'em.
I have made strong proof of my constancy,
Giving myself a voluntary wound
Here, in the thigh: can I bear that with patience
And not my husband's secrets?

BRUTUS.

O ye gods,
Render me worthy of this noble wife!

Knock.

Hark, hark, one knocks. Portia, go in awhile;
And by and by thy bosom shall partake
The secrets of my heart.
All my engagements I will construe to thee,
All the charactery of my sad brows.
Leave me with haste.

Exit PORTIA.

Enter LUCIUS *with* LIGARIUS.

Lucius, who's that knocks?

LUCIUS.

Here is a sick man that would speak with you.

BRUTUS.

Caius Ligarius, that Metellus spake of.
Boy, stand aside. Caius Ligarius, how?

LIGARIUS.

Vouchsafe good-morrow from a feeble tongue.

BRUTUS.

O, what a time have you chose out, brave Caius,
To wear a kerchief! Would you were not sick!

LIGARIUS.

I am not sick, if Brutus have in hand
Any exploit worthy the name of honor.

BRUTUS.

Such an exploit have I in hand, Ligarius,
Had you a healthful ear to hear of it.

LIGARIUS.

By all the gods that Romans bow before,
I here discard my sickness. Soul of Rome!
Brave son, derived from honorable loins!
Thou, like an exorcist, hast conjur'd up
My mortified spirit. Now bid me run,
And I will strive with things impossible,
Yea, get the better of them. What's to do?

BRUTUS.

A piece of work that will make sick men whole.

LIGARIUS.

But are not some whole that we must make sick?

BRUTUS.

That must we also. What it is, my Caius,
I shall unfold to thee, as we are going,
To whom it must be done.

LIGARIUS.

Set on your foot,
And with a heart new-fir'd I follow you,
To do I know not what; but it sufficeth
That Brutus leads me on.

Thunder.

BRUTUS.

Follow me then.

Exeunt.

SCENE II. *A room in Caesar's palace.*

Thunder and lightning. Enter CAESAR, *in his nightgown.*

CAESAR.

Nor heaven nor earth have been at peace tonight:
Thrice hath Calphurnia in her sleep cried out,
"Help, ho! They murder Caesar!" Who's within?

Enter a SERVANT.

SERVANT.

My lord?

CAESAR.

Go bid the priests do present sacrifice,
And bring me their opinions of success.

SERVANT.

I will, my lord.

Exit.

Enter CALPHURNIA.

CALPHURNIA.

What mean you, Caesar? Think you to walk forth?
You shall not stir out of your house today.

CAESAR.

Caesar shall forth. The things that threaten'd me
Ne'er look'd but on my back; when they shall see
The face of Caesar, they are vanished.

CALPHURNIA.

Caesar, I never stood on ceremonies,
Yet now they fright me. There is one within,
Besides the things that we have heard and seen,
Recounts most horrid sights seen by the watch.
A lioness hath whelped in the streets,
And graves have yawn'd, and yielded up their dead;
Fierce fiery warriors fight upon the clouds
In ranks and squadrons and right form of war,
Which drizzled blood upon the Capitol;
The noise of battle hurtled in the air,
Horses did neigh, and dying men did groan,
And ghosts did shriek and squeal about the streets.
O Caesar, these things are beyond all use,
And I do fear them!

CAESAR.

What can be avoided
Whose end is purpos'd by the mighty gods?
Yet Caesar shall go forth; for these predictions
Are to the world in general as to Caesar.

CALPHURNIA.

When beggars die, there are no comets seen;
The heavens themselves blaze forth the death of princes.

CAESAR.

Cowards die many times before their deaths;
The valiant never taste of death but once.
Of all the wonders that I yet have heard,
It seems to me most strange that men should fear,
Seeing that death, a necessary end,
Will come when it will come.

Enter SERVANT.

What say the augurers?

Calphurnia. O Cæsar, these things are beyond all use,
And I do fear them!
Cæsar. What can be avoided
Whose end is purposed by the mighty gods?
Act II. Scene II.

SERVANT.

They would not have you to stir forth today.
Plucking the entrails of an offering forth,
They could not find a heart within the beast.

CAESAR.

The gods do this in shame of cowardice:
Caesar should be a beast without a heart
If he should stay at home today for fear.
No, Caesar shall not. Danger knows full well
That Caesar is more dangerous than he.
We are two lions litter'd in one day,
And I the elder and more terrible,
And Caesar shall go forth.

CALPHURNIA.

Alas, my lord,
Your wisdom is consum'd in confidence.
Do not go forth today: call it my fear
That keeps you in the house, and not your own.
We'll send Mark Antony to the Senate-house,
And he shall say you are not well today.
Let me upon my knee prevail in this.

CAESAR.

Mark Antony shall say I am not well,
And for thy humour, I will stay at home.

Enter DECIUS.

Here's Decius Brutus, he shall tell them so.

DECIUS.

Caesar, all hail! Good morrow, worthy Caesar.
I come to fetch you to the Senate-house.

CAESAR.

And you are come in very happy time
To bear my greeting to the Senators,
And tell them that I will not come today.
Cannot, is false; and that I dare not, falser:
I will not come today. Tell them so, Decius.

CALPHURNIA.

Say he is sick.

CAESAR.

Shall Caesar send a lie?
Have I in conquest stretch'd mine arm so far,
To be afeard to tell grey-beards the truth?
Decius, go tell them Caesar will not come.

DECIUS.

Most mighty Caesar, let me know some cause,
Lest I be laugh'd at when I tell them so.

CAESAR.

The cause is in my will; I will not come.
That is enough to satisfy the Senate.
But for your private satisfaction,
Because I love you, I will let you know:
Calphurnia here, my wife, stays me at home.
She dreamt tonight she saw my statue,
Which like a fountain with an hundred spouts
Did run pure blood; and many lusty Romans
Came smiling, and did bathe their hands in it.
And these does she apply for warnings and portents
And evils imminent; and on her knee
Hath begg'd that I will stay at home today.

DECIUS.

This dream is all amiss interpreted:
It was a vision fair and fortunate.
Your statue spouting blood in many pipes,
In which so many smiling Romans bath'd,
Signifies that from you great Rome shall suck
Reviving blood, and that great men shall press
For tinctures, stains, relics, and cognizance.
This by Calphurnia's dream is signified.

CAESAR.

And this way have you well expounded it.

DECIUS.

I have, when you have heard what I can say;
And know it now. The Senate have concluded
To give this day a crown to mighty Caesar.
If you shall send them word you will not come,
Their minds may change. Besides, it were a mock
Apt to be render'd, for someone to say,
"Break up the Senate till another time,
When Caesar's wife shall meet with better dreams."
If Caesar hide himself, shall they not whisper
"Lo, Caesar is afraid"?
Pardon me, Caesar; for my dear dear love
To your proceeding bids me tell you this,
And reason to my love is liable.

CAESAR.

How foolish do your fears seem now, Calphurnia!
I am ashamed I did yield to them.
Give me my robe, for I will go.

Enter BRUTUS, LIGARIUS, METELLUS, CASCA, TREBONIUS, CINNA *and* PUBLIUS.

And look where Publius is come to fetch me.

PUBLIUS.

Good morrow, Caesar.

CAESAR.

Welcome, Publius.
What, Brutus, are you stirr'd so early too?
Good morrow, Casca. Caius Ligarius,
Caesar was ne'er so much your enemy
As that same ague which hath made you lean.
What is't o'clock?

BRUTUS.

Caesar, 'tis strucken eight.

CAESAR.

I thank you for your pains and courtesy.

Enter ANTONY.

See! Antony, that revels long o' nights,
Is notwithstanding up. Good morrow, Antony.

ANTONY.

So to most noble Caesar.

CAESAR.

Bid them prepare within.
I am to blame to be thus waited for.
Now, Cinna; now, Metellus; what, Trebonius!
I have an hour's talk in store for you:
Remember that you call on me today;
Be near me, that I may remember you.

TREBONIUS.

Caesar, I will. *Aside.* and so near will I be,
That your best friends shall wish I had been further.

CAESAR.

Good friends, go in, and taste some wine with me;
And we, like friends, will straightway go together.

BRUTUS.

Aside. That every like is not the same, O Caesar,
The heart of Brutus yearns to think upon.

Exeunt.

SCENE III. A *street near the Capitol.*

Enter ARTEMIDORUS, *reading a paper.*

ARTEMIDORUS.

"Caesar, beware of Brutus; take heed of Cassius; come not near Casca; have an eye to Cinna; trust not Trebonius; mark well Metellus Cimber; Decius Brutus loves thee not; thou hast wrong'd Caius Ligarius. There is but one mind in all these men, and it is bent against Caesar. If thou be'st not immortal, look about you: security gives way to conspiracy. The mighty gods defend thee!
Thy lover, ARTEMIDORUS."

Here will I stand till Caesar pass along,
And as a suitor will I give him this.
My heart laments that virtue cannot live
Out of the teeth of emulation.
If thou read this, O Caesar, thou mayest live;
If not, the Fates with traitors do contrive. *Exit.*

Artemidorus. Here will I stand till Cæsar pass along,
And as a suitor will I give him this. *Act II. Scene III.*

SCENE IV. *Another part of the same street, before the house of Brutus.*

Enter PORTIA *and* LUCIUS.

PORTIA.

I pr'ythee, boy, run to the Senate-house;
Stay not to answer me, but get thee gone.
Why dost thou stay?

LUCIUS.

To know my errand, madam.

PORTIA.

I would have had thee there and here again,
Ere I can tell thee what thou shouldst do there.
Aside. O constancy, be strong upon my side,
Set a huge mountain 'tween my heart and tongue!
I have a man's mind, but a woman's might.
How hard it is for women to keep counsel!
Art thou here yet?

LUCIUS.

Madam, what should I do?
Run to the Capitol, and nothing else?
And so return to you, and nothing else?

PORTIA.

Yes, bring me word, boy, if thy lord look well,
For he went sickly forth: and take good note
What Caesar doth, what suitors press to him.
Hark, boy, what noise is that?

LUCIUS.

I hear none, madam.

PORTIA.

Pr'ythee, listen well.
I heard a bustling rumour, like a fray,
And the wind brings it from the Capitol.

LUCIUS.

Sooth, madam, I hear nothing.

Enter the SOOTHSAYER.

PORTIA.

Come hither, fellow:
Which way hast thou been?

SOOTHSAYER.

At mine own house, good lady.

PORTIA.

What is't o'clock?

SOOTHSAYER.

About the ninth hour, lady.

PORTIA.

Is Caesar yet gone to the Capitol?

SOOTHSAYER.

Madam, not yet. I go to take my stand,
To see him pass on to the Capitol.

PORTIA.

Thou hast some suit to Caesar, hast thou not?

SOOTHSAYER.

That I have, lady, if it will please Caesar
To be so good to Caesar as to hear me,
I shall beseech him to befriend himself.

PORTIA.

Why, know'st thou any harm's intended towards him?

SOOTHSAYER.

None that I know will be, much that I fear may chance.
Good morrow to you. Here the street is narrow.
The throng that follows Caesar at the heels,
Of Senators, of Praetors, common suitors,
Will crowd a feeble man almost to death:
I'll get me to a place more void, and there
Speak to great Caesar as he comes along.

Exit.

PORTIA.

I must go in.
Aside. Ay me, how weak a thing
The heart of woman is! O Brutus,

The heavens speed thee in thine enterprise!
Sure, the boy heard me. Brutus hath a suit
That Caesar will not grant. O, I grow faint.
Run, Lucius, and commend me to my lord;
Say I am merry; come to me again,
And bring me word what he doth say to thee.

Exeunt.

ACT III

SCENE I. *Rome. Before the Capitol; the Senate sitting.*

A crowd of people in the street leading to the Capitol. Flourish. Enter CAESAR, BRUTUS, CASSIUS, CASCA, DECIUS, METELLUS, TREBONIUS, CINNA, ANTONY, LEPIDUS, ARTEMIDORUS, PUBLIUS, POPILIUS *and the* SOOTHSAYER.

CAESAR.

The Ides of March are come.

SOOTHSAYER.

Ay, Caesar; but not gone.

ARTEMIDORUS.

Hail, Caesar! Read this schedule.

DECIUS.

Trebonius doth desire you to o'er-read,
At your best leisure, this his humble suit.

ARTEMIDORUS.

O Caesar, read mine first; for mine's a suit
That touches Caesar nearer. Read it, great Caesar.

CAESAR.

What touches us ourself shall be last serv'd.

ARTEMIDORUS.

Delay not, Caesar. Read it instantly.

CAESAR.

What, is the fellow mad?

PUBLIUS.

Sirrah, give place.

CASSIUS.

What, urge you your petitions in the street?
Come to the Capitol.

CAESAR *enters the Capitol, the rest following. All the Senators rise.*

POPILIUS.

I wish your enterprise today may thrive.

CASSIUS.

What enterprise, Popilius?

POPILIUS.

Fare you well.

Advances to CAESAR.

BRUTUS.

What said Popilius Lena?

CASSIUS.

He wish'd today our enterprise might thrive.
I fear our purpose is discovered.

BRUTUS.

Look how he makes to Caesar: mark him.

CASSIUS.

Casca, be sudden, for we fear prevention.
Brutus, what shall be done? If this be known,
Cassius or Caesar never shall turn back,
For I will slay myself.

BRUTUS.

Cassius, be constant:
Popilius Lena speaks not of our purposes;
For look, he smiles, and Caesar doth not change.

CASSIUS.

Trebonius knows his time, for look you, Brutus,
He draws Mark Antony out of the way.

Exeunt ANTONY *and* TREBONIUS. CAESAR *and the Senators take their* seats.

DECIUS.

Where is Metellus Cimber? Let him go,
And presently prefer his suit to Caesar.

BRUTUS.

He is address'd; press near and second him.

CINNA.

Casca, you are the first that rears your hand.

CAESAR.

Are we all ready? What is now amiss
That Caesar and his Senate must redress?

METELLUS.

Most high, most mighty, and most puissant Caesar,
Metellus Cimber throws before thy seat
An humble heart.

Kneeling.

CAESAR.

I must prevent thee, Cimber.
These couchings and these lowly courtesies
Might fire the blood of ordinary men,
And turn pre-ordinance and first decree
Into the law of children. Be not fond,
To think that Caesar bears such rebel blood
That will be thaw'd from the true quality
With that which melteth fools; I mean sweet words,
Low-crooked curtsies, and base spaniel fawning.
Thy brother by decree is banished:
If thou dost bend, and pray, and fawn for him,
I spurn thee like a cur out of my way.
Know, Caesar dost not wrong, nor without cause
Will he be satisfied.

METELLUS.

Is there no voice more worthy than my own,
To sound more sweetly in great Caesar's ear
For the repealing of my banish'd brother?

BRUTUS.

I kiss thy hand, but not in flattery, Caesar;
Desiring thee that Publius Cimber may
Have an immediate freedom of repeal.

CAESAR.

What, Brutus?

CASSIUS.

Pardon, Caesar; Caesar, pardon:
As low as to thy foot doth Cassius fall,
To beg enfranchisement for Publius Cimber.

CAESAR.

I could be well mov'd, if I were as you;
If I could pray to move, prayers would move me:
But I am constant as the northern star,
Of whose true-fix'd and resting quality
There is no fellow in the firmament.
The skies are painted with unnumber'd sparks,
They are all fire, and every one doth shine;
But there's but one in all doth hold his place.
So in the world; 'tis furnish'd well with men,
And men are flesh and blood, and apprehensive;
Yet in the number I do know but one
That unassailable holds on his rank,
Unshak'd of motion: and that I am he,
Let me a little show it, even in this,
That I was constant Cimber should be banish'd,
And constant do remain to keep him so.

CINNA.

O Caesar,—

CAESAR.

Hence! wilt thou lift up Olympus?

DECIUS.

Great Caesar,—

CAESAR.

Doth not Brutus bootless kneel?

CASCA.

Speak, hands, for me!

CASCA *stabs* CAESAR *in the neck.* CAESAR *catches hold of his arm. He is then stabbed by several other Conspirators, and at last by* MARCUS BRUTUS.

CAESAR.

Et tu, Brute?—Then fall, Caesar!

Dies. The Senators and People retire in confusion.

CINNA.

Liberty! Freedom! Tyranny is dead!
Run hence, proclaim, cry it about the streets.

CASSIUS.

Some to the common pulpits and cry out,
"Liberty, freedom, and enfranchisement!"

BRUTUS.

People and Senators, be not affrighted.
Fly not; stand still; ambition's debt is paid.

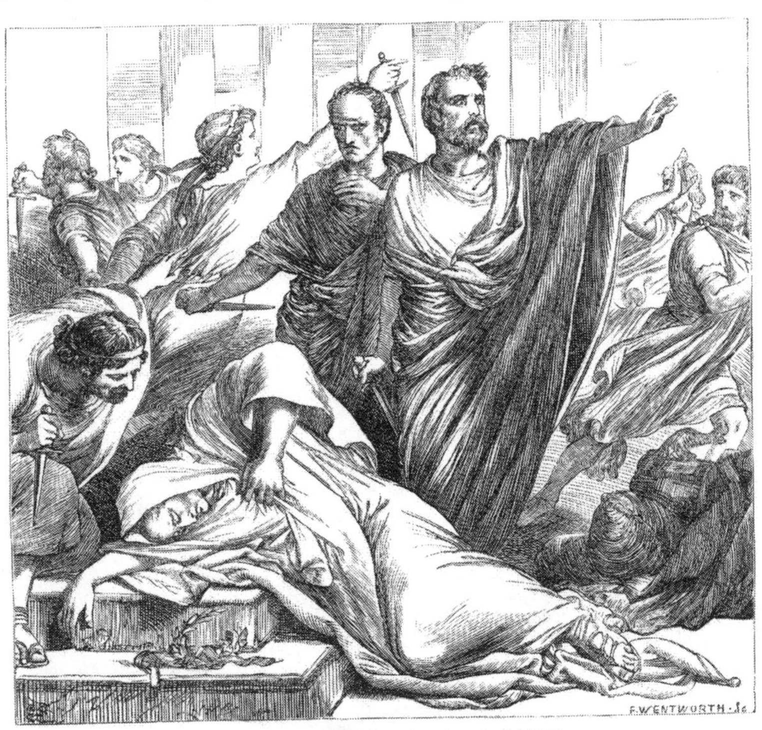

Brutus. People, and senators, be not affrighted;
Fly not; stand still:—ambition's debt is paid. *Act III. Scene I.*

CASCA.

Go to the pulpit, Brutus.

DECIUS.

And Cassius too.

BRUTUS.

Where's Publius?

CINNA.

Here, quite confounded with this mutiny.

METELLUS.

Stand fast together, lest some friend of Caesar's
Should chance—

BRUTUS.

Talk not of standing. Publius, good cheer!
There is no harm intended to your person,
Nor to no Roman else. So tell them, Publius.

CASSIUS.

And leave us, Publius; lest that the people
Rushing on us, should do your age some mischief.

BRUTUS.

Do so; and let no man abide this deed
But we the doers.

Enter TREBONIUS.

CASSIUS.

Where's Antony?

TREBONIUS.

Fled to his house amaz'd.
Men, wives, and children stare, cry out, and run,
As it were doomsday.

BRUTUS.

Fates, we will know your pleasures.
That we shall die, we know; 'tis but the time
And drawing days out, that men stand upon.

CASCA.

Why, he that cuts off twenty years of life
Cuts off so many years of fearing death.

BRUTUS.

Grant that, and then is death a benefit:
So are we Caesar's friends, that have abridg'd
His time of fearing death. Stoop, Romans, stoop,
And let us bathe our hands in Caesar's blood
Up to the elbows, and besmear our swords:
Then walk we forth, even to the market-place,
And waving our red weapons o'er our heads,
Let's all cry, "Peace, freedom, and liberty!"

CASSIUS.

Stoop then, and wash. How many ages hence
Shall this our lofty scene be acted over
In States unborn, and accents yet unknown!

BRUTUS.

How many times shall Caesar bleed in sport,
That now on Pompey's basis lies along,
No worthier than the dust!

CASSIUS.

So oft as that shall be,
So often shall the knot of us be call'd
The men that gave their country liberty.

DECIUS.

What, shall we forth?

CASSIUS.

Ay, every man away.
Brutus shall lead; and we will grace his heels
With the most boldest and best hearts of Rome.

Enter a SERVANT.

BRUTUS.

Soft, who comes here? A friend of Antony's.

SERVANT.

Thus, Brutus, did my master bid me kneel;
Thus did Mark Antony bid me fall down;
And, being prostrate, thus he bade me say:
Brutus is noble, wise, valiant, and honest;
Caesar was mighty, bold, royal, and loving;
Say I love Brutus and I honor him;
Say I fear'd Caesar, honor'd him, and lov'd him.
If Brutus will vouchsafe that Antony
May safely come to him, and be resolv'd
How Caesar hath deserv'd to lie in death,
Mark Antony shall not love Caesar dead
So well as Brutus living; but will follow
The fortunes and affairs of noble Brutus
Thorough the hazards of this untrod state,
With all true faith. So says my master Antony.

BRUTUS.

Thy master is a wise and valiant Roman;
I never thought him worse.
Tell him, so please him come unto this place,
He shall be satisfied and, by my honor,
Depart untouch'd.

SERVANT.

I'll fetch him presently.

Exit.

BRUTUS.

I know that we shall have him well to friend.

CASSIUS.

I wish we may: but yet have I a mind
That fears him much; and my misgiving still
Falls shrewdly to the purpose.

Enter ANTONY.

BRUTUS.

But here comes Antony. Welcome, Mark Antony.

ANTONY.

O mighty Caesar! Dost thou lie so low?
Are all thy conquests, glories, triumphs, spoils,
Shrunk to this little measure? Fare thee well.
I know not, gentlemen, what you intend,
Who else must be let blood, who else is rank:
If I myself, there is no hour so fit
As Caesar's death's hour; nor no instrument
Of half that worth as those your swords, made rich
With the most noble blood of all this world.
I do beseech ye, if you bear me hard,
Now, whilst your purpled hands do reek and smoke,
Fulfill your pleasure. Live a thousand years,
I shall not find myself so apt to die.
No place will please me so, no means of death,
As here by Caesar, and by you cut off,
The choice and master spirits of this age.

BRUTUS.

O Antony, beg not your death of us.
Though now we must appear bloody and cruel,
As by our hands and this our present act
You see we do; yet see you but our hands
And this the bleeding business they have done.
Our hearts you see not; they are pitiful;
And pity to the general wrong of Rome—
As fire drives out fire, so pity pity—
Hath done this deed on Caesar. For your part,

To you our swords have leaden points, Mark Antony;
Our arms in strength of malice, and our hearts
Of brothers' temper, do receive you in
With all kind love, good thoughts, and reverence.

CASSIUS.

Your voice shall be as strong as any man's
In the disposing of new dignities.

BRUTUS.

Only be patient till we have appeas'd
The multitude, beside themselves with fear,
And then we will deliver you the cause
Why I, that did love Caesar when I struck him,
Have thus proceeded.

ANTONY.

I doubt not of your wisdom.
Let each man render me his bloody hand.
First, Marcus Brutus, will I shake with you;
Next, Caius Cassius, do I take your hand.
Now, Decius Brutus, yours; now yours, Metellus;
Yours, Cinna; and, my valiant Casca, yours;
Though last, not least in love, yours, good Trebonius.
Gentlemen all—alas, what shall I say?
My credit now stands on such slippery ground,
That one of two bad ways you must conceit me,
Either a coward or a flatterer.
That I did love thee, Caesar, O, 'tis true:
If then thy spirit look upon us now,
Shall it not grieve thee dearer than thy death,
To see thy Antony making his peace,
Shaking the bloody fingers of thy foes,
Most noble, in the presence of thy corse?
Had I as many eyes as thou hast wounds,
Weeping as fast as they stream forth thy blood,
It would become me better than to close
In terms of friendship with thine enemies.
Pardon me, Julius! Here wast thou bay'd, brave hart;
Here didst thou fall; and here thy hunters stand,
Sign'd in thy spoil, and crimson'd in thy lethe.
O world, thou wast the forest to this hart;
And this indeed, O world, the heart of thee.

How like a deer strucken by many princes,
Dost thou here lie!

CASSIUS.

Mark Antony,—

ANTONY.

Pardon me, Caius Cassius:
The enemies of Caesar shall say this;
Then, in a friend, it is cold modesty.

CASSIUS.

I blame you not for praising Caesar so;
But what compact mean you to have with us?
Will you be prick'd in number of our friends,
Or shall we on, and not depend on you?

ANTONY.

Therefore I took your hands; but was indeed
Sway'd from the point, by looking down on Caesar.
Friends am I with you all, and love you all,
Upon this hope, that you shall give me reasons
Why, and wherein, Caesar was dangerous.

BRUTUS.

Or else were this a savage spectacle.
Our reasons are so full of good regard
That were you, Antony, the son of Caesar,
You should be satisfied.

ANTONY.

That's all I seek,
And am moreover suitor that I may
Produce his body to the market-place;
And in the pulpit, as becomes a friend,
Speak in the order of his funeral.

BRUTUS.

You shall, Mark Antony.

CASSIUS.

Brutus, a word with you.
Aside to BRUTUS. You know not what you do. Do not consent
That Antony speak in his funeral.
Know you how much the people may be mov'd
By that which he will utter?

BRUTUS.

Aside to CASSIUS. By your pardon:
I will myself into the pulpit first,
And show the reason of our Caesar's death.
What Antony shall speak, I will protest
He speaks by leave and by permission;
And that we are contented Caesar shall
Have all true rites and lawful ceremonies.
It shall advantage more than do us wrong.

CASSIUS.

Aside to BRUTUS. I know not what may fall; I like it not.

BRUTUS.

Mark Antony, here, take you Caesar's body.
You shall not in your funeral speech blame us,
But speak all good you can devise of Caesar,
And say you do't by our permission;
Else shall you not have any hand at all
About his funeral. And you shall speak
In the same pulpit whereto I am going,
After my speech is ended.

ANTONY.

Be it so;
I do desire no more.

BRUTUS.

Prepare the body, then, and follow us.

Exeunt all but ANTONY.

ANTONY.

O, pardon me, thou bleeding piece of earth,
That I am meek and gentle with these butchers.
Thou art the ruins of the noblest man
That ever lived in the tide of times.
Woe to the hand that shed this costly blood!
Over thy wounds now do I prophesy,
Which, like dumb mouths do ope their ruby lips
To beg the voice and utterance of my tongue,
A curse shall light upon the limbs of men;
Domestic fury and fierce civil strife
Shall cumber all the parts of Italy;
Blood and destruction shall be so in use,

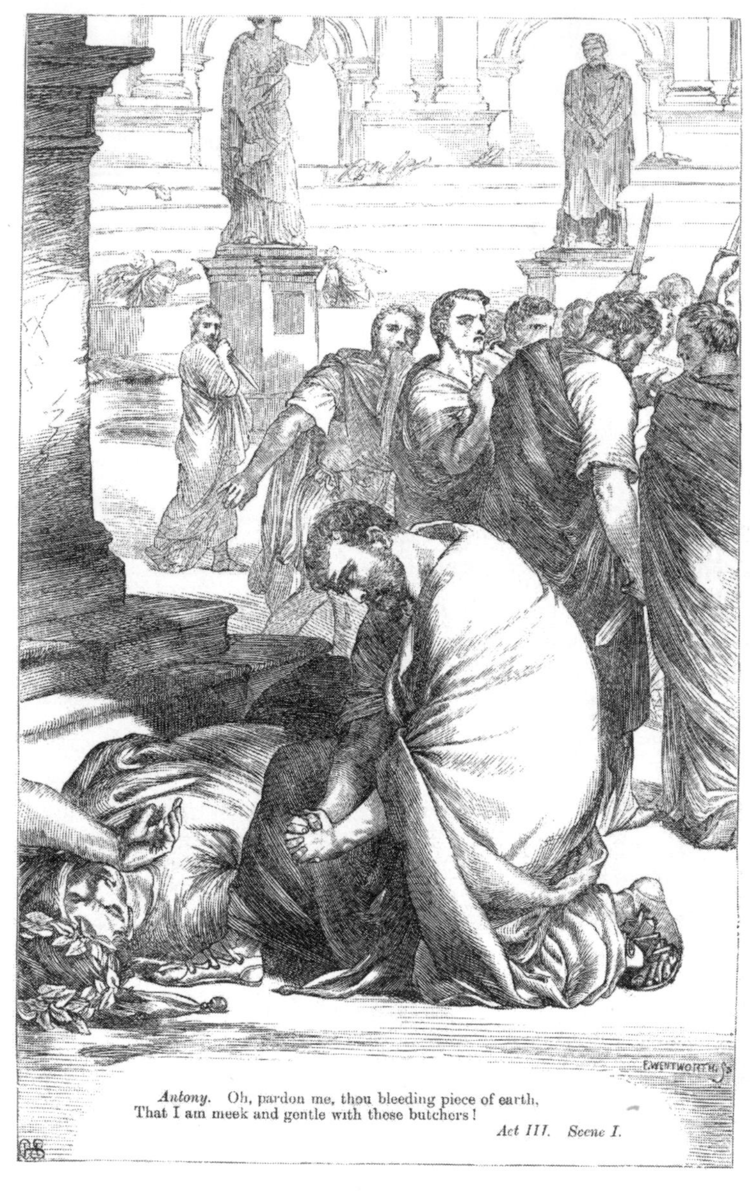

Antony. Oh, pardon me, thou bleeding piece of earth,
That I am meek and gentle with these butchers!
Act III. Scene I.

And dreadful objects so familiar,
That mothers shall but smile when they behold
Their infants quartered with the hands of war;
All pity chok'd with custom of fell deeds:
And Caesar's spirit, ranging for revenge,
With Ate by his side come hot from Hell,
Shall in these confines with a monarch's voice

Cry havoc and let slip the dogs of war,
That this foul deed shall smell above the earth
With carrion men, groaning for burial.

Enter a SERVANT.

You serve Octavius Caesar, do you not?

SERVANT.

I do, Mark Antony.

ANTONY.

Caesar did write for him to come to Rome.

SERVANT.

He did receive his letters, and is coming,
And bid me say to you by word of mouth,—
Seeing the body. O Caesar!

ANTONY.

Thy heart is big, get thee apart and weep.
Passion, I see, is catching; for mine eyes,
Seeing those beads of sorrow stand in thine,
Began to water. Is thy master coming?

SERVANT.

He lies tonight within seven leagues of Rome.

ANTONY.

Post back with speed, and tell him what hath chanc'd.
Here is a mourning Rome, a dangerous Rome,
No Rome of safety for Octavius yet.
Hie hence, and tell him so. Yet stay awhile;
Thou shalt not back till I have borne this corse
Into the market-place: there shall I try,
In my oration, how the people take
The cruel issue of these bloody men;
According to the which thou shalt discourse
To young Octavius of the state of things.
Lend me your hand.

Exeunt with CAESAR'S *body.*

SCENE II. *The same. The Forum.*

Enter BRUTUS *and goes into the pulpit, and* CASSIUS, *with a throng of Citizens.*

CITIZENS.

We will be satisfied; let us be satisfied.

BRUTUS.

Then follow me, and give me audience, friends.
Cassius, go you into the other street
And part the numbers.
Those that will hear me speak, let 'em stay here;
Those that will follow Cassius, go with him;
And public reasons shall be rendered
Of Caesar's death.

FIRST CITIZEN.

I will hear Brutus speak.

SECOND CITIZEN.

I will hear Cassius; and compare their reasons,
When severally we hear them rendered.

Exit CASSIUS, *with some of the Citizens.*
BRUTUS *goes into the* rostrum.

THIRD CITIZEN.

The noble Brutus is ascended: silence!

BRUTUS.

Be patient till the last.
Romans, countrymen, and lovers, hear me for my cause; and be silent, that you may hear. Believe me for mine honor, and have respect to mine honor, that you may believe. Censure me in your wisdom, and awake your senses, that you may the better judge. If there be any in this assembly, any dear friend of Caesar's, to him I say that Brutus' love to Caesar was no less than his. If then that friend demand why Brutus rose against Caesar, this is my answer: Not that I loved Caesar less, but that I loved Rome more. Had you rather Caesar were living, and die all slaves, than that Caesar were dead, to live all free men? As Caesar loved me, I weep for him; as he was fortunate, I rejoice at it; as he was valiant, I honor him; but, as he was ambitious, I slew him. There is tears, for his love; joy for his fortune; honor for his valor; and death, for his ambition. Who is here so base, that would be a bondman? If any, speak; for him have I offended. Who is here so rude, that would not be a Roman? If any, speak; for him have I offended. Who is here so vile, that will not love his country? If any, speak; for him have I offended. I pause for a reply.

CITIZENS.

None, Brutus, none.

BRUTUS.

Then none have I offended. I have done no more to Caesar than you shall do to Brutus. The question of his death is enroll'd in the Capitol, his glory not extenuated, wherein he was worthy; nor his offences enforc'd, for which he suffered death.

Enter ANTONY *and others, with* CAESAR'S *body.*

Here comes his body, mourned by Mark Antony, who, though he had no hand in his death, shall receive the benefit of his dying, a place in the commonwealth; as which of you shall not? With this I depart, that, as I slew my best lover for the good of Rome, I have the same dagger for myself, when it shall please my country to need my death.

CITIZENS.

Live, Brutus! live, live!

FIRST CITIZEN.

Bring him with triumph home unto his house.

SECOND CITIZEN.

Give him a statue with his ancestors.

THIRD CITIZEN.

Let him be Caesar.

FOURTH CITIZEN.

Caesar's better parts
Shall be crown'd in Brutus.

FIRST CITIZEN.

We'll bring him to his house with shouts and clamours.

BRUTUS.

My countrymen,—

SECOND CITIZEN.

Peace! Silence! Brutus speaks.

FIRST CITIZEN.

Peace, ho!

BRUTUS.

Good countrymen, let me depart alone,
And, for my sake, stay here with Antony.

Do grace to Caesar's corse, and grace his speech
Tending to Caesar's glories, which Mark Antony,
By our permission, is allow'd to make.
I do entreat you, not a man depart,
Save I alone, till Antony have spoke.

Exit.

FIRST CITIZEN.
Stay, ho! and let us hear Mark Antony.

THIRD CITIZEN.
Let him go up into the public chair.
We'll hear him. Noble Antony, go up.

ANTONY.
For Brutus' sake, I am beholding to you.

Goes up.

FOURTH CITIZEN.
What does he say of Brutus?

THIRD CITIZEN.
He says, for Brutus' sake
He finds himself beholding to us all.

FOURTH CITIZEN.
'Twere best he speak no harm of Brutus here!

FIRST CITIZEN.
This Caesar was a tyrant.

THIRD CITIZEN.
Nay, that's certain.
We are blest that Rome is rid of him.

SECOND CITIZEN.
Peace! let us hear what Antony can say.

ANTONY.
You gentle Romans,—

CITIZENS.
Peace, ho! let us hear him.

ANTONY.
Friends, Romans, countrymen, lend me your ears;
I come to bury Caesar, not to praise him.
The evil that men do lives after them,

The good is oft interred with their bones;
So let it be with Caesar. The noble Brutus
Hath told you Caesar was ambitious.
If it were so, it was a grievous fault,
And grievously hath Caesar answer'd it.
Here, under leave of Brutus and the rest,
For Brutus is an honorable man,
So are they all, all honorable men,
Come I to speak in Caesar's funeral.
He was my friend, faithful and just to me;
But Brutus says he was ambitious,
And Brutus is an honorable man.
He hath brought many captives home to Rome,
Whose ransoms did the general coffers fill:
Did this in Caesar seem ambitious?
When that the poor have cried, Caesar hath wept;
Ambition should be made of sterner stuff:
Yet Brutus says he was ambitious;
And Brutus is an honorable man.
You all did see that on the Lupercal
I thrice presented him a kingly crown,
Which he did thrice refuse. Was this ambition?
Yet Brutus says he was ambitious;
And sure he is an honorable man.
I speak not to disprove what Brutus spoke,
But here I am to speak what I do know.
You all did love him once, not without cause;
What cause withholds you then to mourn for him?
O judgment, thou art fled to brutish beasts,
And men have lost their reason. Bear with me.
My heart is in the coffin there with Caesar,
And I must pause till it come back to me.

FIRST CITIZEN.

Methinks there is much reason in his sayings.

SECOND CITIZEN.

If thou consider rightly of the matter,
Caesar has had great wrong.

THIRD CITIZEN.

Has he, masters?
I fear there will a worse come in his place.

FOURTH CITIZEN.

Mark'd ye his words? He would not take the crown;
Therefore 'tis certain he was not ambitious.

FIRST CITIZEN.

If it be found so, some will dear abide it.

SECOND CITIZEN.

Poor soul, his eyes are red as fire with weeping.

THIRD CITIZEN.

There's not a nobler man in Rome than Antony.

FOURTH CITIZEN.

Now mark him; he begins again to speak.

ANTONY.

But yesterday the word of Caesar might
Have stood against the world; now lies he there,
And none so poor to do him reverence.
O masters! If I were dispos'd to stir
Your hearts and minds to mutiny and rage,
I should do Brutus wrong and Cassius wrong,
Who, you all know, are honorable men.
I will not do them wrong; I rather choose
To wrong the dead, to wrong myself and you,
Than I will wrong such honorable men.
But here's a parchment with the seal of Caesar,
I found it in his closet; 'tis his will:
Let but the commons hear this testament,
Which, pardon me, I do not mean to read,
And they would go and kiss dead Caesar's wounds,
And dip their napkins in his sacred blood;
Yea, beg a hair of him for memory,
And, dying, mention it within their wills,
Bequeathing it as a rich legacy
Unto their issue.

FOURTH CITIZEN.

We'll hear the will. Read it, Mark Antony.

CITIZENS.

The will, the will! We will hear Caesar's will.

ANTONY.

Have patience, gentle friends, I must not read it.
It is not meet you know how Caesar loved you.

You are not wood, you are not stones, but men;
And being men, hearing the will of Caesar,
It will inflame you, it will make you mad.
'Tis good you know not that you are his heirs;
For if you should, O, what would come of it?

Citizens. The will! the testament!
Second Citizen. They were villains, murderers: the will! read the will,
Act III. Scene II.

FOURTH CITIZEN.

Read the will! We'll hear it, Antony;
You shall read us the will, Caesar's will!

ANTONY.
Will you be patient? Will you stay awhile?
I have o'ershot myself to tell you of it.
I fear I wrong the honorable men
Whose daggers have stabb'd Caesar; I do fear it.

FOURTH CITIZEN.
They were traitors. Honorable men!

CITIZENS.
The will! The testament!

SECOND CITIZEN.
They were villains, murderers. The will! Read the will!

ANTONY.
You will compel me then to read the will?
Then make a ring about the corse of Caesar,
And let me show you him that made the will.
Shall I descend? and will you give me leave?

CITIZENS.
Come down.

SECOND CITIZEN.
Descend.

He comes down.

THIRD CITIZEN.
You shall have leave.

FOURTH CITIZEN.
A ring! Stand round.

FIRST CITIZEN.
Stand from the hearse, stand from the body.

SECOND CITIZEN.
Room for Antony, most noble Antony!

ANTONY.
Nay, press not so upon me; stand far off.

CITIZENS.
Stand back; room! bear back.

ANTONY.
If you have tears, prepare to shed them now.
You all do know this mantle. I remember

The first time ever Caesar put it on;
'Twas on a Summer's evening, in his tent,
That day he overcame the Nervii.
Look, in this place ran Cassius' dagger through:
See what a rent the envious Casca made:
Through this the well-beloved Brutus stabb'd;
And as he pluck'd his cursed steel away,
Mark how the blood of Caesar follow'd it,
As rushing out of doors, to be resolv'd
If Brutus so unkindly knock'd, or no;
For Brutus, as you know, was Caesar's angel.
Judge, O you gods, how dearly Caesar lov'd him.
This was the most unkindest cut of all;
For when the noble Caesar saw him stab,
Ingratitude, more strong than traitors' arms,
Quite vanquish'd him: then burst his mighty heart;
And in his mantle muffling up his face,
Even at the base of Pompey's statue
Which all the while ran blood, great Caesar fell.
O, what a fall was there, my countrymen!
Then I, and you, and all of us fell down,
Whilst bloody treason flourish'd over us.
O, now you weep; and I perceive you feel
The dint of pity. These are gracious drops.
Kind souls, what weep you when you but behold
Our Caesar's vesture wounded? Look you here,
Here is himself, marr'd, as you see, with traitors.

FIRST CITIZEN.

O piteous spectacle!

SECOND CITIZEN.

O noble Caesar!

THIRD CITIZEN.

O woeful day!

FOURTH CITIZEN.

O traitors, villains!

FIRST CITIZEN.

O most bloody sight!

SECOND CITIZEN.

We will be revenged: revenge,—about,—seek,—burn,—fire,—kill,—slay,—let not a traitor live!

ANTONY.

Stay, countrymen.

FIRST CITIZEN.

Peace there! Hear the noble Antony.

SECOND CITIZEN.

We'll hear him, we'll follow him, we'll die with him.

ANTONY.

Good friends, sweet friends, let me not stir you up
To such a sudden flood of mutiny.
They that have done this deed are honorable.
What private griefs they have, alas, I know not,
That made them do it. They're wise and honorable,
And will, no doubt, with reasons answer you.
I come not, friends, to steal away your hearts.
I am no orator, as Brutus is;
But, as you know me all, a plain blunt man,
That love my friend; and that they know full well
That gave me public leave to speak of him.
For I have neither wit, nor words, nor worth,
Action, nor utterance, nor the power of speech,
To stir men's blood. I only speak right on.
I tell you that which you yourselves do know,
Show you sweet Caesar's wounds, poor poor dumb mouths,
And bid them speak for me. But were I Brutus,
And Brutus Antony, there were an Antony
Would ruffle up your spirits, and put a tongue
In every wound of Caesar, that should move
The stones of Rome to rise and mutiny.

CITIZENS.

We'll mutiny.

FIRST CITIZEN.

We'll burn the house of Brutus.

THIRD CITIZEN.

Away, then! come, seek the conspirators.

ANTONY.

Yet hear me, countrymen; yet hear me speak.

CITIZENS.

Peace, ho! Hear Antony; most noble Antony.

ANTONY.

Why, friends, you go to do you know not what.
Wherein hath Caesar thus deserved your loves?
Alas, you know not; I must tell you then.
You have forgot the will I told you of.

CITIZENS.

Most true; the will!—let's stay, and hear the will.

ANTONY.

Here is the will, and under Caesar's seal.
To every Roman citizen he gives,
To every several man, seventy-five drachmas.

SECOND CITIZEN.

Most noble Caesar! We'll revenge his death.

THIRD CITIZEN.

O, royal Caesar!

ANTONY.

Hear me with patience.

CITIZENS.

Peace, ho!

ANTONY.

Moreover, he hath left you all his walks,
His private arbors, and new-planted orchards,
On this side Tiber; he hath left them you,
And to your heirs forever; common pleasures,
To walk abroad, and recreate yourselves.
Here was a Caesar! when comes such another?

FIRST CITIZEN.

Never, never. Come, away, away!
We'll burn his body in the holy place,
And with the brands fire the traitors' houses.
Take up the body.

SECOND CITIZEN.

Go, fetch fire.

THIRD CITIZEN.

Pluck down benches.

FOURTH CITIZEN.

Pluck down forms, windows, anything.

Exeunt CITIZENS, *with the body.*

ANTONY.
Now let it work. Mischief, thou art afoot,
Take thou what course thou wilt!

Enter a SERVANT.

How now, fellow?

SERVANT.
Sir, Octavius is already come to Rome.

ANTONY.
Where is he?

SERVANT.
He and Lepidus are at Caesar's house.

ANTONY.
And thither will I straight to visit him.
He comes upon a wish. Fortune is merry,
And in this mood will give us anything.

SERVANT.
I heard him say Brutus and Cassius
Are rid like madmen through the gates of Rome.

ANTONY.
Belike they had some notice of the people,
How I had moved them. Bring me to Octavius.

Exeunt.

SCENE III. The same. A street.

Enter CINNA, *the poet, and after him the citizens.*

CINNA.
I dreamt tonight that I did feast with Caesar,
And things unluckily charge my fantasy.
I have no will to wander forth of doors,
Yet something leads me forth.

FIRST CITIZEN.
What is your name?

SECOND CITIZEN.
Whither are you going?

THIRD CITIZEN.
Where do you dwell?

FOURTH CITIZEN.

Are you a married man or a bachelor?

SECOND CITIZEN.

Answer every man directly.

FIRST CITIZEN.

Ay, and briefly.

FOURTH CITIZEN.

Ay, and wisely.

THIRD CITIZEN.

Ay, and truly, you were best.

CINNA.

What is my name? Whither am I going? Where do I dwell? Am I a married man or a bachelor? Then, to answer every man directly and briefly, wisely and truly. Wisely I say I am a bachelor.

SECOND CITIZEN.

That's as much as to say they are fools that marry; you'll bear me a bang for that, I fear. Proceed, directly.

CINNA.

Directly, I am going to Caesar's funeral.

FIRST CITIZEN.

As a friend, or an enemy?

CINNA.

As a friend.

SECOND CITIZEN.

That matter is answered directly.

FOURTH CITIZEN.

For your dwelling, briefly.

CINNA.

Briefly, I dwell by the Capitol.

THIRD CITIZEN.

Your name, sir, truly.

CINNA.

Truly, my name is Cinna.

FIRST CITIZEN.

Tear him to pieces! He's a conspirator.

CINNA.

I am Cinna the poet, I am Cinna the poet.

FOURTH CITIZEN.

Tear him for his bad verses, tear him for his bad verses.

CINNA.

I am not Cinna the conspirator.

FOURTH CITIZEN.

It is no matter, his name's Cinna; pluck but his name out of his heart, and turn him going.

THIRD CITIZEN.

Tear him, tear him! Come; brands, ho! firebrands. To Brutus', to Cassius'; burn all. Some to Decius' house, and some to Casca's, some to Ligarius'. Away, go!

Exeunt.

ACT IV

SCENE I. *Rome. A room in Antony's house.*

Enter ANTONY, OCTAVIUS *and* LEPIDUS, *seated at a table.*

ANTONY.

These many then shall die; their names are prick'd.

OCTAVIUS.

Your brother too must die; consent you, Lepidus?

LEPIDUS.

I do consent,—

OCTAVIUS.

Prick him down, Antony.

LEPIDUS.

Upon condition Publius shall not live,
Who is your sister's son, Mark Antony.

ANTONY.

He shall not live; look, with a spot I damn him.
But, Lepidus, go you to Caesar's house;
Fetch the will hither, and we shall determine
How to cut off some charge in legacies.

LEPIDUS.

What, shall I find you here?

OCTAVIUS.

Or here, or at the Capitol.

Exit LEPIDUS.

ANTONY.

This is a slight unmeritable man,
Meet to be sent on errands. Is it fit,
The three-fold world divided, he should stand
One of the three to share it?

OCTAVIUS.

So you thought him,
And took his voice who should be prick'd to die
In our black sentence and proscription.

Octavius. Your brother too must die; consent you, Lepidus?
Lepidus. I do consent. *Act IV. Scene I.*

ANTONY.

Octavius, I have seen more days than you;
And though we lay these honors on this man,
To ease ourselves of divers sland'rous loads,
He shall but bear them as the ass bears gold,
To groan and sweat under the business,
Either led or driven, as we point the way;
And having brought our treasure where we will,
Then take we down his load, and turn him off,
Like to the empty ass, to shake his ears,
And graze in commons.

OCTAVIUS.

You may do your will;
But he's a tried and valiant soldier.

ANTONY.

So is my horse, Octavius; and for that
I do appoint him store of provender.
It is a creature that I teach to fight,

To wind, to stop, to run directly on,
His corporal motion govern'd by my spirit.
And, in some taste, is Lepidus but so:
He must be taught, and train'd, and bid go forth:
A barren-spirited fellow; one that feeds
On objects, arts, and imitations,
Which, out of use and stal'd by other men,
Begin his fashion. Do not talk of him
But as a property. And now, Octavius,
Listen great things. Brutus and Cassius
Are levying powers; we must straight make head.
Therefore let our alliance be combin'd,
Our best friends made, our means stretch'd;
And let us presently go sit in council,
How covert matters may be best disclos'd,
And open perils surest answered.

OCTAVIUS.

Let us do so: for we are at the stake,
And bay'd about with many enemies;
And some that smile have in their hearts, I fear,
Millions of mischiefs.

Exeunt.

SCENE II. *Before Brutus' tent, in the camp near Sardis.*

Drum. Enter BRUTUS, LUCILIUS, TITINIUS *and Soldiers;* PINDARUS *meeting them;* LUCIUS *at some distance.*

BRUTUS.

Stand, ho!

LUCILIUS.

Give the word, ho! and stand.

BRUTUS.

What now, Lucilius! is Cassius near?

LUCILIUS.

He is at hand, and Pindarus is come
To do you salutation from his master.

PINDARUS *gives a letter to* BRUTUS.

BRUTUS.

He greets me well. Your master, Pindarus,
In his own change, or by ill officers,
Hath given me some worthy cause to wish
Things done, undone: but, if he be at hand,
I shall be satisfied.

PINDARUS.

I do not doubt
But that my noble master will appear
Such as he is, full of regard and honor.

BRUTUS.

He is not doubted. A word, Lucilius;
How he received you, let me be resolv'd.

LUCILIUS.

With courtesy and with respect enough,
But not with such familiar instances,
Nor with such free and friendly conference,
As he hath us'd of old.

BRUTUS.

Thou hast describ'd
A hot friend cooling. Ever note, Lucilius,
When love begins to sicken and decay
It useth an enforced ceremony.
There are no tricks in plain and simple faith;
But hollow men, like horses hot at hand,
Make gallant show and promise of their mettle;

Low march within.

But when they should endure the bloody spur,
They fall their crests, and like deceitful jades
Sink in the trial. Comes his army on?

LUCILIUS.

They meant this night in Sardis to be quarter'd;
The greater part, the horse in general,
Are come with Cassius.

Enter CASSIUS *and Soldiers.*

BRUTUS.

Hark! he is arriv'd.
March gently on to meet him.

CASSIUS.

Stand, ho!

BRUTUS.

Stand, ho! Speak the word along.

FIRST SOLDIER.

Stand!

SECOND SOLDIER.

Stand!

THIRD SOLDIER.

Stand!

CASSIUS.

Most noble brother, you have done me wrong.

BRUTUS.

Judge me, you gods; wrong I mine enemies?
And if not so, how should I wrong a brother?

CASSIUS.

Brutus, this sober form of yours hides wrongs;
And when you do them—

BRUTUS.

Cassius, be content.
Speak your griefs softly, I do know you well.
Before the eyes of both our armies here,
Which should perceive nothing but love from us,
Let us not wrangle. Bid them move away;
Then in my tent, Cassius, enlarge your griefs,
And I will give you audience.

CASSIUS.

Pindarus,
Bid our commanders lead their charges off
A little from this ground.

BRUTUS.

Lucilius, do you the like; and let no man
Come to our tent till we have done our conference.
Let Lucius and Titinius, guard our door.

Exeunt.

SCENE III. *Within the tent of Brutus.*

Enter BRUTUS *and* CASSIUS.

CASSIUS.

That you have wrong'd me doth appear in this:
You have condemn'd and noted Lucius Pella
For taking bribes here of the Sardians;
Wherein my letters, praying on his side
Because I knew the man, were slighted off.

BRUTUS.

You wrong'd yourself to write in such a case.

CASSIUS.

In such a time as this it is not meet
That every nice offence should bear his comment.

BRUTUS.

Let me tell you, Cassius, you yourself
Are much condemn'd to have an itching palm,
To sell and mart your offices for gold
To undeservers.

CASSIUS.

I an itching palm!
You know that you are Brutus that speak this,
Or, by the gods, this speech were else your last.

BRUTUS.

The name of Cassius honors this corruption,
And chastisement doth therefore hide his head.

CASSIUS.

Chastisement!

BRUTUS.

Remember March, the Ides of March remember:
Did not great Julius bleed for justice' sake?
What villain touch'd his body, that did stab,
And not for justice? What! Shall one of us,
That struck the foremost man of all this world
But for supporting robbers, shall we now
Contaminate our fingers with base bribes,

And sell the mighty space of our large honors
For so much trash as may be grasped thus?
I had rather be a dog, and bay the moon,
Than such a Roman.

CASSIUS.

Brutus, bait not me,
I'll not endure it. You forget yourself,
To hedge me in. I am a soldier, I,
Older in practice, abler than yourself
To make conditions.

BRUTUS.

Go to; you are not, Cassius.

CASSIUS.

I am.

BRUTUS.

I say you are not.

CASSIUS.

Urge me no more, I shall forget myself;
Have mind upon your health, tempt me no farther.

BRUTUS.

Away, slight man!

CASSIUS.

Is't possible?

BRUTUS.

Hear me, for I will speak.
Must I give way and room to your rash choler?
Shall I be frighted when a madman stares?

CASSIUS.

O ye gods, ye gods! Must I endure all this?

BRUTUS.

All this? ay, more: fret till your proud heart break;
Go show your slaves how choleric you are,
And make your bondmen tremble. Must I budge?
Must I observe you? Must I stand and crouch
Under your testy humour? By the gods,
You shall digest the venom of your spleen,
Though it do split you; for, from this day forth,

I'll use you for my mirth, yea, for my laughter,
When you are waspish.

CASSIUS.

Is it come to this?

BRUTUS.

You say you are a better soldier:
Let it appear so; make your vaunting true,
And it shall please me well. For mine own part,
I shall be glad to learn of noble men.

CASSIUS.

You wrong me every way, you wrong me, Brutus.
I said, an elder soldier, not a better:
Did I say better?

BRUTUS.

If you did, I care not.

CASSIUS.

When Caesar liv'd, he durst not thus have mov'd me.

BRUTUS.

Peace, peace! you durst not so have tempted him.

CASSIUS.

I durst not?

BRUTUS.

No.

CASSIUS.

What? durst not tempt him?

BRUTUS.

For your life you durst not.

CASSIUS.

Do not presume too much upon my love.
I may do that I shall be sorry for.

BRUTUS.

You have done that you should be sorry for.
There is no terror, Cassius, in your threats,
For I am arm'd so strong in honesty,
That they pass by me as the idle wind,
Which I respect not. I did send to you
For certain sums of gold, which you denied me;

For I can raise no money by vile means:
By Heaven, I had rather coin my heart,
And drop my blood for drachmas, than to wring
From the hard hands of peasants their vile trash
By any indirection. I did send
To you for gold to pay my legions,
Which you denied me: was that done like Cassius?
Should I have answer'd Caius Cassius so?
When Marcus Brutus grows so covetous,
To lock such rascal counters from his friends,
Be ready, gods, with all your thunderbolts,
Dash him to pieces!

CASSIUS.

I denied you not.

BRUTUS.

You did.

CASSIUS.

I did not. He was but a fool
That brought my answer back. Brutus hath riv'd my heart.
A friend should bear his friend's infirmities;
But Brutus makes mine greater than they are.

BRUTUS.

I do not, till you practise them on me.

CASSIUS.

You love me not.

BRUTUS.

I do not like your faults.

CASSIUS.

A friendly eye could never see such faults.

BRUTUS.

A flatterer's would not, though they do appear
As huge as high Olympus.

CASSIUS.

Come, Antony, and young Octavius, come,
Revenge yourselves alone on Cassius,
For Cassius is a-weary of the world:
Hated by one he loves; brav'd by his brother;
Check'd like a bondman; all his faults observ'd,

Set in a note-book, learn'd and conn'd by rote,
To cast into my teeth. O, I could weep
My spirit from mine eyes! There is my dagger,
And here my naked breast; within, a heart
Dearer than Plutus' mine, richer than gold:
If that thou be'st a Roman, take it forth.
I, that denied thee gold, will give my heart:
Strike as thou didst at Caesar; for I know,
When thou didst hate him worst, thou lovedst him better
Than ever thou lovedst Cassius.

BRUTUS.

Sheathe your dagger.
Be angry when you will, it shall have scope;
Do what you will, dishonor shall be humour.
O Cassius, you are yoked with a lamb
That carries anger as the flint bears fire,
Who, much enforced, shows a hasty spark,
And straight is cold again.

CASSIUS.

Hath Cassius liv'd
To be but mirth and laughter to his Brutus,
When grief and blood ill-temper'd vexeth him?

BRUTUS.

When I spoke that, I was ill-temper'd too.

CASSIUS.

Do you confess so much? Give me your hand.

BRUTUS.

And my heart too.

CASSIUS.

O Brutus!

BRUTUS.

What's the matter?

CASSIUS.

Have not you love enough to bear with me,
When that rash humour which my mother gave me
Makes me forgetful?

BRUTUS.

Yes, Cassius; and from henceforth,

When you are over-earnest with your Brutus,
He'll think your mother chides, and leave you so.

Enter POET, *followed by* LUCILIUS, TITINIUS *and* LUCIUS.

POET.

Within. Let me go in to see the generals,
There is some grudge between 'em; 'tis not meet
They be alone.

LUCILIUS.

Within. You shall not come to them.

POET.

Within. Nothing but death shall stay me.

CASSIUS.

How now! What's the matter?

POET.

For shame, you generals! What do you mean?
Love, and be friends, as two such men should be;
For I have seen more years, I'm sure, than ye.

CASSIUS.

Ha, ha! How vilely doth this cynic rhyme!

BRUTUS.

Get you hence, sirrah. Saucy fellow, hence!

CASSIUS.

Bear with him, Brutus; 'tis his fashion.

BRUTUS.

I'll know his humour when he knows his time.
What should the wars do with these jigging fools?
Companion, hence!

CASSIUS.

Away, away, be gone!

Exit POET.

BRUTUS.

Lucilius and Titinius, bid the commanders
Prepare to lodge their companies tonight.

CASSIUS.

And come yourselves and bring Messala with you
Immediately to us.

Exeunt LUCILIUS *and* TITINIUS.

BRUTUS.

Lucius, a bowl of wine.

Exit LUCIUS.

CASSIUS.

I did not think you could have been so angry.

BRUTUS.

O Cassius, I am sick of many griefs.

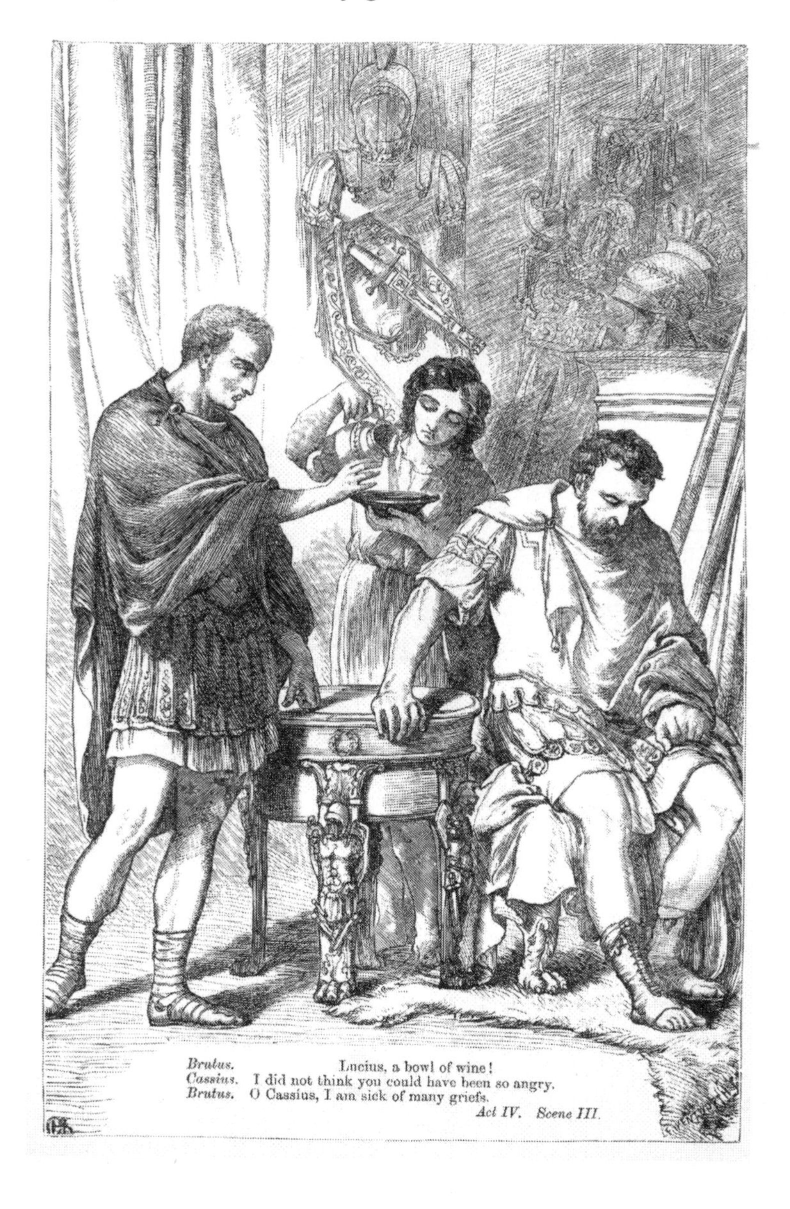

Brutus. Lucius, a bowl of wine!
Cassius. I did not think you could have been so angry.
Brutus. O Cassius, I am sick of many griefs.
Act IV. Scene III.

CASSIUS.

Of your philosophy you make no use,
If you give place to accidental evils.

BRUTUS.

No man bears sorrow better. Portia is dead.

CASSIUS.

Ha? Portia?

BRUTUS.

She is dead.

CASSIUS.

How 'scap'd I killing, when I cross'd you so?
O insupportable and touching loss!
Upon what sickness?

BRUTUS.

Impatient of my absence,
And grief that young Octavius with Mark Antony
Have made themselves so strong; for with her death
That tidings came. With this she fell distract,
And, her attendants absent, swallow'd fire.

CASSIUS.

And died so?

BRUTUS.

Even so.

CASSIUS.

O ye immortal gods!

Enter LUCIUS, *with wine and a taper.*

BRUTUS.

Speak no more of her. Give me a bowl of wine.
In this I bury all unkindness, Cassius.

Drinks.

CASSIUS.

My heart is thirsty for that noble pledge.
Fill, Lucius, till the wine o'erswell the cup.
I cannot drink too much of Brutus' love.

Drinks.

Exit LUCIUS.

Enter TITINIUS *and* MESSALA.

BRUTUS.

Come in, Titinius!
Welcome, good Messala.
Now sit we close about this taper here,
And call in question our necessities.

CASSIUS.

Portia, art thou gone?

BRUTUS.

No more, I pray you.
Messala, I have here received letters,
That young Octavius and Mark Antony
Come down upon us with a mighty power,
Bending their expedition toward Philippi.

MESSALA.

Myself have letters of the selfsame tenor.

BRUTUS.

With what addition?

MESSALA.

That by proscription and bills of outlawry
Octavius, Antony, and Lepidus
Have put to death an hundred Senators.

BRUTUS.

Therein our letters do not well agree.
Mine speak of seventy Senators that died
By their proscriptions, Cicero being one.

CASSIUS.

Cicero one!

MESSALA.

Cicero is dead,
And by that order of proscription.
Had you your letters from your wife, my lord?

BRUTUS.

No, Messala.

MESSALA.

Nor nothing in your letters writ of her?

BRUTUS.

Nothing, Messala.

MESSALA.

That, methinks, is strange.

BRUTUS.

Why ask you? Hear you aught of her in yours?

MESSALA.

No, my lord.

BRUTUS.

Now as you are a Roman, tell me true.

MESSALA.

Then like a Roman bear the truth I tell,
For certain she is dead, and by strange manner.

BRUTUS.

Why, farewell, Portia. We must die, Messala.
With meditating that she must die once,
I have the patience to endure it now.

MESSALA.

Even so great men great losses should endure.

CASSIUS.

I have as much of this in art as you,
But yet my nature could not bear it so.

BRUTUS.

Well, to our work alive. What do you think
Of marching to Philippi presently?

CASSIUS.

I do not think it good.

BRUTUS.

Your reason?

CASSIUS.

This it is:
'Tis better that the enemy seek us;
So shall he waste his means, weary his soldiers,
Doing himself offence, whilst we, lying still,
Are full of rest, defence, and nimbleness.

BRUTUS.

Good reasons must of force give place to better.
The people 'twixt Philippi and this ground
Do stand but in a forced affection;
For they have grudg'd us contribution.
The enemy, marching along by them,
By them shall make a fuller number up,
Come on refresh'd, new-added, and encourag'd;
From which advantage shall we cut him off
If at Philippi we do face him there,
These people at our back.

CASSIUS.

Hear me, good brother.

BRUTUS.

Under your pardon. You must note beside,
That we have tried the utmost of our friends,
Our legions are brim-full, our cause is ripe.
The enemy increaseth every day;
We, at the height, are ready to decline.
There is a tide in the affairs of men,
Which, taken at the flood, leads on to fortune;
Omitted, all the voyage of their life
Is bound in shallows and in miseries.
On such a full sea are we now afloat,
And we must take the current when it serves,
Or lose our ventures.

CASSIUS.

Then, with your will, go on:
We'll along ourselves, and meet them at Philippi.

BRUTUS.

The deep of night is crept upon our talk,
And nature must obey necessity,
Which we will niggard with a little rest.
There is no more to say?

CASSIUS.

No more. Good night:
Early tomorrow will we rise, and hence.

Enter LUCIUS.

BRUTUS.

Lucius! My gown.

Exit LUCIUS.

Farewell, good Messala.
Good night, Titinius. Noble, noble Cassius,
Good night, and good repose.

CASSIUS.

O my dear brother!
This was an ill beginning of the night.
Never come such division 'tween our souls!
Let it not, Brutus.

Enter LUCIUS *with the gown.*

BRUTUS.

Everything is well.

CASSIUS.

Good night, my lord.

BRUTUS.

Good night, good brother.

TITINIUS AND MESSALA.

Good night, Lord Brutus.

BRUTUS.

Farewell, everyone.

Exeunt CASSIUS, TITINIUS *and* MESSALA.

Give me the gown. Where is thy instrument?

LUCIUS.

Here in the tent.

BRUTUS.

What, thou speak'st drowsily?
Poor knave, I blame thee not, thou art o'er-watch'd.
Call Claudius and some other of my men;
I'll have them sleep on cushions in my tent.

LUCIUS.

Varro and Claudius!

Enter VARRO *and* CLAUDIUS.

VARRO.

Calls my lord?

BRUTUS.

I pray you, sirs, lie in my tent and sleep;
It may be I shall raise you by-and-by
On business to my brother Cassius.

VARRO.

So please you, we will stand and watch your pleasure.

BRUTUS.

I will not have it so; lie down, good sirs,
It may be I shall otherwise bethink me.
Look, Lucius, here's the book I sought for so;
I put it in the pocket of my gown.

Servants lie down.

LUCIUS.

I was sure your lordship did not give it me.

BRUTUS.

Bear with me, good boy, I am much forgetful.
Canst thou hold up thy heavy eyes awhile,
And touch thy instrument a strain or two?

LUCIUS.

Ay, my lord, an't please you.

BRUTUS.

It does, my boy.
I trouble thee too much, but thou art willing.

LUCIUS.

It is my duty, sir.

BRUTUS.

I should not urge thy duty past thy might;
I know young bloods look for a time of rest.

LUCIUS.

I have slept, my lord, already.

BRUTUS.

It was well done, and thou shalt sleep again;
I will not hold thee long. If I do live,
I will be good to thee.

LUCIUS *plays and sings till he falls asleep.*

This is a sleepy tune. O murd'rous slumber,
Layest thou thy leaden mace upon my boy,

That plays thee music? Gentle knave, good night;
I will not do thee so much wrong to wake thee.
If thou dost nod, thou break'st thy instrument;
I'll take it from thee; and, good boy, good night.
Let me see, let me see; is not the leaf turn'd down
Where I left reading? Here it is, I think.

Enter the GHOST *of* CAESAR.

How ill this taper burns! Ha! who comes here?
I think it is the weakness of mine eyes
That shapes this monstrous apparition.
It comes upon me. Art thou anything?
Art thou some god, some angel, or some devil,
That mak'st my blood cold and my hair to stare?
Speak to me what thou art.

GHOST.

Thy evil spirit, Brutus.

Brutus. Speak to me what thou art.
Ghost. Thy evil spirit, Brutus. *Act IV. Scene III.*

BRUTUS.

Why com'st thou?

GHOST.
To tell thee thou shalt see me at Philippi.

BRUTUS.
Well; then I shall see thee again?

GHOST.
Ay, at Philippi.

BRUTUS.
Why, I will see thee at Philippi then.

GHOST *vanishes.*

Now I have taken heart, thou vanishest.
Ill spirit, I would hold more talk with thee.
Boy! Lucius! Varro! Claudius! Sirs, awake! Claudius!

LUCIUS.
The strings, my lord, are false.

BRUTUS.
He thinks he still is at his instrument.
Lucius, awake!

LUCIUS.
My lord?

BRUTUS.
Didst thou dream, Lucius, that thou so criedst out?

LUCIUS.
My lord, I do not know that I did cry.

BRUTUS.
Yes, that thou didst. Didst thou see anything?

LUCIUS.
Nothing, my lord.

BRUTUS.
Sleep again, Lucius. Sirrah Claudius!
Fellow thou, awake!

VARRO.
My lord?

CLAUDIUS.
My lord?

BRUTUS.

Why did you so cry out, sirs, in your sleep?

VARRO AND CLAUDIUS.

Did we, my lord?

BRUTUS.

Ay. Saw you anything?

VARRO.

No, my lord, I saw nothing.

CLAUDIUS.

Nor I, my lord.

BRUTUS.

Go and commend me to my brother Cassius;
Bid him set on his powers betimes before,
And we will follow.

VARRO AND CLAUDIUS.

It shall be done, my lord.

Exeunt.

ACT V

SCENE I. *The plains of Philippi.*

Enter Octavius, Antony *and their Army.*

Octavius.

Now, Antony, our hopes are answered.
You said the enemy would not come down,
But keep the hills and upper regions.
It proves not so; their battles are at hand,
They mean to warn us at Philippi here,
Answering before we do demand of them.

Antony.

Tut, I am in their bosoms, and I know
Wherefore they do it. They could be content
To visit other places, and come down
With fearful bravery, thinking by this face
To fasten in our thoughts that they have courage;
But 'tis not so.

Enter a Messenger.

Messenger.

Prepare you, generals.
The enemy comes on in gallant show;
Their bloody sign of battle is hung out,
And something to be done immediately.

Antony.

Octavius, lead your battle softly on
Upon the left hand of the even field.

Octavius.

Upon the right hand I. Keep thou the left.

Antony.

Why do you cross me in this exigent?

Octavius.

I do not cross you; but I will do so.

March.

Drum. Enter Brutus, Cassius *and their Army*; Lucilius, Titinius, Messala *and others.*

Brutus.

They stand, and would have parley.

Cassius.

Stand fast, Titinius; we must out and talk.

Octavius.

Mark Antony, shall we give sign of battle?

Antony.

No, Caesar, we will answer on their charge.
Make forth; the generals would have some words.

Octavius.

Stir not until the signal.

Brutus.

Words before blows: is it so, countrymen?

Octavius.

Not that we love words better, as you do.

Brutus.

Good words are better than bad strokes, Octavius.

Antony.

In your bad strokes, Brutus, you give good words;
Witness the hole you made in Caesar's heart,
Crying, "Long live! Hail, Caesar!"

Cassius.

Antony,
The posture of your blows are yet unknown;
But for your words, they rob the Hybla bees,
And leave them honeyless.

Antony.

Not stingless too.

Brutus.

O yes, and soundless too,
For you have stol'n their buzzing, Antony,
And very wisely threat before you sting.

Antony.

Villains, you did not so when your vile daggers
Hack'd one another in the sides of Caesar:

You show'd your teeth like apes, and fawn'd like hounds,
And bow'd like bondmen, kissing Caesar's feet;
Whilst damned Casca, like a cur, behind
Struck Caesar on the neck. O you flatterers!

CASSIUS.

Flatterers! Now, Brutus, thank yourself.
This tongue had not offended so today,
If Cassius might have rul'd.

OCTAVIUS.

Come, come, the cause. If arguing make us sweat,
The proof of it will turn to redder drops.
Look, I draw a sword against conspirators.
When think you that the sword goes up again?
Never, till Caesar's three and thirty wounds
Be well aveng'd; or till another Caesar
Have added slaughter to the sword of traitors.

BRUTUS.

Caesar, thou canst not die by traitors' hands,
Unless thou bring'st them with thee.

OCTAVIUS.

So I hope.
I was not born to die on Brutus' sword.

BRUTUS.

O, if thou wert the noblest of thy strain,
Young man, thou couldst not die more honorable.

CASSIUS.

A peevish school-boy, worthless of such honor,
Join'd with a masker and a reveller.

ANTONY.

Old Cassius still!

OCTAVIUS.

Come, Antony; away!
Defiance, traitors, hurl we in your teeth.
If you dare fight today, come to the field;
If not, when you have stomachs.

Exeunt OCTAVIUS, ANTONY *and their Army.*

CASSIUS.

Why now, blow wind, swell billow, and swim barque!
The storm is up, and all is on the hazard.

BRUTUS.

Ho, Lucilius! Hark, a word with you.

LUCILIUS.

My lord?

BRUTUS *and* LUCILIUS *talk apart.*

CASSIUS.

Messala.

MESSALA.

What says my General?

CASSIUS.

Messala,
This is my birth-day; as this very day
Was Cassius born. Give me thy hand, Messala:
Be thou my witness that against my will
As Pompey was, am I compell'd to set
Upon one battle all our liberties.
You know that I held Epicurus strong,
And his opinion. Now I change my mind,
And partly credit things that do presage.
Coming from Sardis, on our former ensign
Two mighty eagles fell, and there they perch'd,
Gorging and feeding from our soldiers' hands,
Who to Philippi here consorted us.
This morning are they fled away and gone,
And in their steads do ravens, crows, and kites
Fly o'er our heads, and downward look on us,
As we were sickly prey: their shadows seem
A canopy most fatal, under which
Our army lies, ready to give up the ghost.

MESSALA.

Believe not so.

CASSIUS.

I but believe it partly,
For I am fresh of spirit, and resolv'd
To meet all perils very constantly.

BRUTUS.

Even so, Lucilius.

CASSIUS.

Now, most noble Brutus,
The gods today stand friendly, that we may,
Lovers in peace, lead on our days to age!
But, since the affairs of men rest still incertain,
Let's reason with the worst that may befall.
If we do lose this battle, then is this
The very last time we shall speak together:
What are you then determined to do?

BRUTUS.

Even by the rule of that philosophy
By which I did blame Cato for the death
Which he did give himself, I know not how,
But I do find it cowardly and vile,
For fear of what might fall, so to prevent
The time of life, arming myself with patience
To stay the providence of some high powers
That govern us below.

CASSIUS.

Then, if we lose this battle,
You are contented to be led in triumph
Thorough the streets of Rome?

BRUTUS.

No, Cassius, no: think not, thou noble Roman,
That ever Brutus will go bound to Rome;
He bears too great a mind. But this same day
Must end that work the Ides of March begun;
And whether we shall meet again I know not.
Therefore our everlasting farewell take.
For ever, and for ever, farewell, Cassius.
If we do meet again, why, we shall smile;
If not, why then this parting was well made.

CASSIUS.

For ever and for ever farewell, Brutus.
If we do meet again, we'll smile indeed;
If not, 'tis true this parting was well made.

BRUTUS.

Why then, lead on. O, that a man might know
The end of this day's business ere it come!
But it sufficeth that the day will end,
And then the end is known. Come, ho! away!

Exeunt.

SCENE II. *The same. The field of battle.*

Alarum. Enter BRUTUS *and* MESSALA.

BRUTUS.

Ride, ride, Messala, ride, and give these bills
Unto the legions on the other side.

Loud alarum.

Let them set on at once; for I perceive
But cold demeanor in Octavius' wing,
And sudden push gives them the overthrow.
Ride, ride, Messala; let them all come down.

Exeunt.

SCENE III. *Another part of the field.*

Alarum. Enter CASSIUS *and* TITINIUS.

CASSIUS.

O, look, Titinius, look, the villains fly!
Myself have to mine own turn'd enemy:
This ensign here of mine was turning back;
I slew the coward, and did take it from him.

TITINIUS.

O Cassius, Brutus gave the word too early,
Who, having some advantage on Octavius,
Took it too eagerly: his soldiers fell to spoil,
Whilst we by Antony are all enclos'd.

Enter Pindarus.

PINDARUS.

Fly further off, my lord, fly further off;
Mark Antony is in your tents, my lord.
Fly, therefore, noble Cassius, fly far off.

CASSIUS.

This hill is far enough. Look, look, Titinius;
Are those my tents where I perceive the fire?

TITINIUS.

They are, my lord.

CASSIUS.

Titinius, if thou lovest me,
Mount thou my horse and hide thy spurs in him,
Till he have brought thee up to yonder troops
And here again, that I may rest assur'd
Whether yond troops are friend or enemy.

TITINIUS.

I will be here again, even with a thought.

Exit.

CASSIUS.

Go, Pindarus, get higher on that hill,
My sight was ever thick. Regard Titinius,
And tell me what thou notest about the field.

PINDARUS *goes up.*

This day I breathed first. Time is come round,
And where I did begin, there shall I end.
My life is run his compass. Sirrah, what news?

PINDARUS.

Above. O my lord!

CASSIUS.

What news?

PINDARUS.

Above. Titinius is enclosed round about
With horsemen, that make to him on the spur,
Yet he spurs on. Now they are almost on him.
Now, Titinius! Now some light. O, he lights too.
He's ta'en!

Shout.

And, hark! they shout for joy.

CASSIUS.

Come down; behold no more.
O, coward that I am, to live so long,

To see my best friend ta'en before my face!

PINDARUS *descends.*

Come hither, sirrah.
In Parthia did I take thee prisoner;
And then I swore thee, saving of thy life,
That whatsoever I did bid thee do,
Thou shouldst attempt it. Come now, keep thine oath.
Now be a freeman; and with this good sword,
That ran through Caesar's bowels, search this bosom.
Stand not to answer. Here, take thou the hilts;
And when my face is cover'd, as 'tis now,
Guide thou the sword.—Caesar, thou art reveng'd,
Even with the sword that kill'd thee.

Dies.

PINDARUS.

So, I am free, yet would not so have been,
Durst I have done my will. O Cassius!
Far from this country Pindarus shall run,
Where never Roman shall take note of him.

Exit.

Enter TITINIUS *with* MESSALA.

MESSALA.

It is but change, Titinius; for Octavius
Is overthrown by noble Brutus' power,
As Cassius' legions are by Antony.

TITINIUS.

These tidings would well comfort Cassius.

MESSALA.

Where did you leave him?

TITINIUS.

All disconsolate,
With Pindarus his bondman, on this hill.

MESSALA.

Is not that he that lies upon the ground?

TITINIUS.

He lies not like the living. O my heart!

MESSALA.

Is not that he?

TITINIUS.

No, this was he, Messala,
But Cassius is no more. O setting sun,
As in thy red rays thou dost sink to night,
So in his red blood Cassius' day is set.
The sun of Rome is set. Our day is gone;
Clouds, dews, and dangers come; our deeds are done.
Mistrust of my success hath done this deed.

MESSALA.

Mistrust of good success hath done this deed.
O hateful Error, Melancholy's child!
Why dost thou show to the apt thoughts of men
The things that are not? O Error, soon conceiv'd,
Thou never com'st unto a happy birth,
But kill'st the mother that engender'd thee!

TITINIUS.

What, Pindarus! where art thou, Pindarus?

MESSALA.

Seek him, Titinius, whilst I go to meet
The noble Brutus, thrusting this report
Into his ears. I may say thrusting it;
For piercing steel and darts envenomed
Shall be as welcome to the ears of Brutus
As tidings of this sight.

TITINIUS.

Hie you, Messala,
And I will seek for Pindarus the while.

Exit MESSALA.

Why didst thou send me forth, brave Cassius?
Did I not meet thy friends? And did not they
Put on my brows this wreath of victory,
And bid me give it thee? Didst thou not hear their shouts?
Alas, thou hast misconstrued everything!
But, hold thee, take this garland on thy brow;
Thy Brutus bid me give it thee, and I
Will do his bidding. Brutus, come apace,
And see how I regarded Caius Cassius.

By your leave, gods. This is a Roman's part.
Come, Cassius' sword, and find Titinius' heart.

Dies.

Alarum. Enter BRUTUS, MESSALA, *young* CATO, STRATO, VOLUMNIUS *and* LUCILIUS.

BRUTUS.

Where, where, Messala, doth his body lie?

MESSALA.

Lo, yonder, and Titinius mourning it.

BRUTUS.

Titinius' face is upward.

CATO.

He is slain.

BRUTUS.

O Julius Caesar, thou art mighty yet!
Thy spirit walks abroad, and turns our swords
In our own proper entrails.

Low alarums.

CATO.

Brave Titinius!
Look whether he have not crown'd dead Cassius!

BRUTUS.

Are yet two Romans living such as these?
The last of all the Romans, fare thee well!
It is impossible that ever Rome
Should breed thy fellow. Friends, I owe more tears
To this dead man than you shall see me pay.
I shall find time, Cassius, I shall find time.
Come therefore, and to Thassos send his body.
His funerals shall not be in our camp,
Lest it discomfort us. Lucilius, come;
And come, young Cato; let us to the field.
Labeo and Flavius, set our battles on.
'Tis three o'clock; and Romans, yet ere night
We shall try fortune in a second fight.

Exeunt.

SCENE IV. *Another part of the field.*

Alarum. Enter fighting soldiers of both armies; then BRUTUS, MESSALA, *young* CATO, LUCILIUS, FLAVIUS *and others.*

BRUTUS.

Yet, countrymen, O, yet hold up your heads!

CATO.

What bastard doth not? Who will go with me?
I will proclaim my name about the field.
I am the son of Marcus Cato, ho!
A foe to tyrants, and my country's friend.
I am the son of Marcus Cato, ho!

Charges the enemy.

BRUTUS.

And I am Brutus, Marcus Brutus, I;
Brutus, my country's friend; know me for Brutus!

Exit, charging the enemy. CATO *is overpowered, and falls.*

LUCILIUS.

O young and noble Cato, art thou down?
Why, now thou diest as bravely as Titinius,
And mayst be honor'd, being Cato's son.

FIRST SOLDIER.

Yield, or thou diest.

LUCILIUS.

Only I yield to die:
There is so much that thou wilt kill me straight;

Offering money

Kill Brutus, and be honor'd in his death.

FIRST SOLDIER.

We must not. A noble prisoner!

SECOND SOLDIER.

Room, ho! Tell Antony, Brutus is ta'en.

FIRST SOLDIER.

I'll tell the news. Here comes the General.

Enter ANTONY.

Brutus is ta'en, Brutus is ta'en, my lord.

ANTONY.

Where is he?

LUCILIUS.

Safe, Antony; Brutus is safe enough.
I dare assure thee that no enemy
Shall ever take alive the noble Brutus.
The gods defend him from so great a shame!
When you do find him, or alive or dead,
He will be found like Brutus, like himself.

ANTONY.

This is not Brutus, friend; but, I assure you,
A prize no less in worth. Keep this man safe,
Give him all kindness. I had rather have
Such men my friends than enemies. Go on,
And see whether Brutus be alive or dead;
And bring us word unto Octavius' tent
How everything is chanc'd.

Exeunt.

SCENE V. *Another part of the field.*

Enter BRUTUS, DARDANIUS, CLITUS, STRATO *and* VOLUMNIUS.

BRUTUS.

Come, poor remains of friends, rest on this rock.

CLITUS.

Statilius show'd the torch-light; but, my lord,
He came not back: he is or ta'en or slain.

BRUTUS.

Sit thee down, Clitus. Slaying is the word;
It is a deed in fashion. Hark thee, Clitus.

Whispering.

CLITUS.

What, I, my lord? No, not for all the world.

BRUTUS.

Peace then, no words

CLITUS.

I'll rather kill myself.

BRUTUS.

Hark thee, Dardanius.

Whispers to him.

DARDANIUS.

Shall I do such a deed?

CLITUS.

O Dardanius!

DARDANIUS.

O Clitus!

CLITUS.

What ill request did Brutus make to thee?

DARDANIUS.

To kill him, Clitus. Look, he meditates.

CLITUS.

Now is that noble vessel full of grief,
That it runs over even at his eyes.

BRUTUS.

Come hither, good Volumnius; list a word.

VOLUMNIUS.

What says my lord?

BRUTUS.

Why, this, Volumnius:
The ghost of Caesar hath appear'd to me
Two several times by night; at Sardis once,
And this last night here in Philippi fields.
I know my hour is come.

VOLUMNIUS.

Not so, my lord.

BRUTUS.

Nay I am sure it is, Volumnius.
Thou seest the world, Volumnius, how it goes;
Our enemies have beat us to the pit.

Low alarums.

It is more worthy to leap in ourselves
Than tarry till they push us. Good Volumnius,
Thou know'st that we two went to school together;

Even for that our love of old, I pr'ythee
Hold thou my sword-hilts, whilst I run on it.

VOLUMNIUS.

That's not an office for a friend, my lord.

Alarums still.

CLITUS.

Fly, fly, my lord! there is no tarrying here.

BRUTUS.

Farewell to you; and you; and you, Volumnius.
Strato, thou hast been all this while asleep;
Farewell to thee too, Strato.—Countrymen,
My heart doth joy, that yet in all my life
I found no man but he was true to me.
I shall have glory by this losing day
More than Octavius and Mark Antony
By this vile conquest shall attain unto.
So fare you well at once; for Brutus' tongue
Hath almost ended his life's history.
Night hangs upon mine eyes; my bones would rest,
That have but labour'd to attain this hour.

Alarums. Cry within, "Fly, fly, fly!".

CLITUS.

Fly, my lord, fly!

BRUTUS.

Hence! I will follow.

Exeunt CLITUS, DARDANIUS *and* VOLUMNIUS.

I pr'ythee, Strato, stay thou by thy lord.
Thou art a fellow of a good respect;
Thy life hath had some smatch of honor in it.
Hold then my sword, and turn away thy face,
While I do run upon it. Wilt thou, Strato?

STRATO.

Give me your hand first. Fare you well, my lord.

BRUTUS.

Farewell, good Strato.—Caesar, now be still:
I kill'd not thee with half so good a will.

He runs on his sword, and dies.

Alarum. Retreat. Enter ANTONY, OCTAVIUS, MESSALA, LUCILIUS *and the Army.*

OCTAVIUS.

What man is that?

MESSALA.

My master's man. Strato, where is thy master?

STRATO.

Free from the bondage you are in, Messala.
The conquerors can but make a fire of him;
For Brutus only overcame himself,
And no man else hath honor by his death.

LUCILIUS.

So Brutus should be found. I thank thee, Brutus,
That thou hast prov'd Lucilius' saying true.

OCTAVIUS.

All that serv'd Brutus, I will entertain them.
Fellow, wilt thou bestow thy time with me?

STRATO.

Ay, if Messala will prefer me to you.

OCTAVIUS.

Do so, good Messala.

MESSALA.

How died my master, Strato?

STRATO.

I held the sword, and he did run on it.

MESSALA.

Octavius, then take him to follow thee,
That did the latest service to my master.

ANTONY.

This was the noblest Roman of them all.
All the conspirators save only he,
Did that they did in envy of great Caesar;
He only, in a general honest thought
And common good to all, made one of them.
His life was gentle, and the elements
So mix'd in him that Nature might stand up
And say to all the world, "This was a man!"

Antony. This was the noblest Roman of them all. *Act V. Scene V.*

OCTAVIUS.

According to his virtue let us use him
With all respect and rites of burial.
Within my tent his bones tonight shall lie,
Most like a soldier, order'd honorably.
So call the field to rest, and let's away,
To part the glories of this happy day.

Exeunt.

SEAWOLF
PRESS

Made in the USA
Middletown, DE
17 November 2022